THE TRUTH

or something

—— *a novel* ——

jeanne willis

HENRY HOLT AND COMPANY | NEW YORK

Henry Holt and Company, LLC
Publishers since 1866
115 West 18th Street
New York, New York 10011
www.henryholt.com

Henry Holt is a registered trademark of Henry Holt and Company, LLC
Copyright © 2000 by Jeanne Willis
First published in the United States in 2002 by Henry Holt and Company.
Originally published in England in 2000 by Faber and Faber Limited
under the title *The Hard Man of the Swings.*

Library of Congress Cataloging-in-Publication Data
Willis, Jeanne.
The truth or something / Jeanne Willis.
p.   cm.
Originally published under the title: The hard man of the swings.
Summary: Growing up poor and neglected in post–World War II England,
young Mick, longing to be part of a loving family as he is shuttled from home
to home, must harden himself against disappointment and cruelty—and,
finally, against the abusive father he only recently met.
[1. Child abuse—Fiction. 2. Abandoned children—Fiction.
3. Poverty—Fiction. 4. England—Fiction.]   I. Title.
PZ7.W68313 Tr 2002   [Fic]—dc21   2001051897

ISBN 0-8050-7079-6
First American Edition—2002
Printed in the United States of America on acid-free paper. ∞
1   3   5   7   9   10   8   6   4   2

For Mick the Builder

The Truth or Something is based on true events. If you need to talk to someone about any of the issues raised in this book, Childhelp USA® is a free national helpline for children and young people. It provides a confidential phone counseling service for any child with any problem twenty-four hours a day, every day.

You can contact Childhelp USA® at 1-800-4-A-CHILD® (1-800-422-4435).

Web site: www.childhelpusa.org

THE TRUTH

or something

o n e

I don't know if I've killed my dad or not. I'm not sure a .22 bullet can kill a man. All I know is, it only takes one to kill a squirrel and I used the whole tin. He was making enough noise when I left.

I got my ticket alright and there's hardly anyone on the train. Just someone's granny in a fur coat and she's nodded off. It's so cold, the snow hasn't melted on her hat. Any minute now, a big lump of it is going to plop onto her lap like an ice cream. I'm expecting the police to turn up, but there's no sign of them so far. I keep checking out of the window in case they ride up alongside, like the Cherokees in *Wagon Train*. I'm firing at them with my imaginary gun. Two fingers . . . Piaow! Piaow!

I was on this same train with my mum a few years ago. She was doing a runner too, only I never knew it at the time. I never knew nothing. She made sure of that.

I remember falling asleep sitting next to her. I can even remember the dream I had, because I still have it. Over and over again. I thought once I'd found out what really happened to my sister, it would go away, but it never has. It's like my head's the Odeon and when the lights go down, the operator can only show this one film, and the worst of it is, I never get to see the ending.

In this dream, I'm four. Maybe three. And I've got these new wellingtons. Bright red wellington boots. They're the business. I love these boots to bits and I'm marching up and down in the gutter, showing them off. I want the little girls over the way to notice them, only they're too busy skipping.

The rain stops. The sun comes out. It's too bright to look at. It's making little mirrors everywhere. If I stand still, the wellingtons steam up. I'm wondering whose wellingtons they were before I had them, because they ain't brand new. Almost new though. Newer than anything I've ever had, anyhow.

"Look at these!"

I hold my foot up under my chin, but the girls are too busy turning their rope and every time it slaps the road, it sounds like a stinging thing. They're singing:

I know a boy who's double-jointed,
He kissed you and made you disappointed,
Alright, Kath, I'm telling your mother
For kissing Harry round the corner.

I'm listening to them and thinking, that's my dad's name, Harry. Not that I'd ever seen my dad, far as I know. I'm thinking, maybe those girls have seen him. Maybe he's come back to live with us. I'm about to go and ask them when, suddenly, my wellingtons start trembling. At first it's quite nice, but then I realise it ain't just the wellingtons trembling, it's the whole street. Now the girls can feel it too. They stop skipping and look scared. One of them, the smallest, turns to her sister: "What's that, Shirley?"

"I don't know. Thunder?"

They listen, but it's a different sound to thunder. Lower, like it's coming from under the ground.

"Probably an earthquake."

"Not in England."

"What then? A doodlebug?"

"I dunno, do I?"

Then the one who's the littlest puts her fists in her eyes and starts crying. She runs off down the road away from us. Then she stops. She starts running backwards really slowly, like something's winding her back. Her mouth is wide open but there's no sound coming out, then this dirty, skinny horse comes hurtling round the corner, steaming towards her, like a machine.

A string of spit swings off its top lip and lands across my wellingtons. I can't move my legs. Where are the girls? Out the corner of my glasses I can see colours of girls being thrown to either side, and through the middle of their rainbow of colours this screaming metal carriage skids and scrapes along behind the horse, piled high with skeleton chairs and mouldy beds.

It shudders to a stop outside a house. Our house. Number 39. And that's my mum coming out, pushing the pram.

"Mum?"

But she doesn't hear and she pushes the pram up the path, right past me.

I can see eyes staring at her from behind curtains, but it's like she's asleep. She's wearing her dress with the yellow roses and gloves and lipstick, like she's going somewhere. No apron or nothing.

A man with a yellow beard and yellow fingers climbs out of the cart and he's arguing with my mum. She's saying, "I want five bob," and he looks under the pram hood and snorts, "What, for that? I'll give you three-and-six."

"Three-and-six, you tight beggar? You're joking, aren't you?"

But he's not joking, so she pulls a face and shrugs and the man grabs the pram and throws it onto the cart, and Mum takes his money and puts it in her purse.

I can hear a baby crying. The cart starts to move off. My sister is in that pram.

"Eileen!"

I try to chase after the cart, but I've been standing in soft tar and my wellington bottoms are covered in black glue. When I grab the back of the cart, they come off my feet with a suck and my mum is shouting, "Those are *new* wellingtons, Mick. Don't you dare lose them wellingtons. Can't you look after anything?"

She grabs hold of my feet. I'm clinging to the cart and the horse is pulling one way and Mum's pulling the other. My arms are about to pop out and my fingers are tearing off one by one . . .

"Ei-leen!"

I always wake up when I get to that bit. First thing I do is check to see if I've wet myself, because that's what usually happens. I was alright that time. I had a quick feel and my hand was dry. My neck was stiff and I couldn't work out where I was, being half-asleep still.

Trees and houses were whizzing past and for a while I thought I was still dreaming. Then I realised it was me that was moving, not the trees.

Me and Mum are on a train. There's this spivvy-looking bloke picking chips up off the floor, giving me a look.

"You done that," he says, "waving your arms in your sleep."

I ain't got a clue what he's going on about.

"You knocked them chips out of my hand while you was asleep. You went like that . . . whoerr!" He flicks his hand in the air to show me what I done. Mum wakes up and jumps out of her seat, panicking.

"Oh, no! Don't say we've gone past our stop."

She notices me eating. "Where d'you get that? Off the floor?"

"Found it."

She tries to hook the chip out of my mouth with her finger. "Spit it out! Spit!"

The bloke whose chips they are comes to my rescue. "It's alright. He never got it off the floor. I gave it to him. Want another one, mate?" He shakes the bag at me. I look at Mum.

"Oh, go on then," she says, and smiles. She ain't done that for a while. She takes a packet of fags out of her handbag and rattles about for some matches. He's all ready with his flashy lighter, clicks it and leans across with his legs wide open. She nods at him and sucks on the fag with her orange lipstick.

"Ta."

"Where you going, doll? Southend?"

She nods again.

"Me an' all."

"Good."

He grins. Mum fiddles with her wedding ring.

"I just meant if you're going, we haven't missed our stop. That's all."

She flicks her fag into the ashtray and a little bit lands on her stocking and she flinches, because it's hot. There's a hole in them now. She's been saving and saving those stockings for today. They cost a pound. She looks like she's going to cry but then her face goes hard. She crosses the leg with the hole in behind the good one.

He's watching her all the time, looking her up and down.

"I know you," he says. "Live down the Cally Road, don't cha?"

Mum won't even look at him.

"Seen you up the club, dancing. It's Connie, innit?"

"No." She gets a hanky out of her bag and scrubs my face with fag-and-spit soap.

"Yeah. You're Harry's missus. What's a nice sort like you shacked up with him for?"

I put my head in the chip bag. Right in, so all my face is covered, ears and all, and I breathe the smell. I breathe so hard the newspaper gets sucked into my nostrils and makes a little farting sound.

"I can smell the sea!"

She snatches the bag off my head. "Pack it in, Mick."

That spiv's got his hand on her knee. She never moves it away, she just stares out of the window with frozen eyes. He seems a bit annoyed with her.

"What's up? You queer or something? Only I heard your old man was."

The train starts pulling into the station.

"Why don't you ask him?" she says. "That's him, over there!"

The train shudders on the rails. She points to this huge man in a uniform, waiting on the station. She pulls down the window, all excited, and shouts to him.

"Harry! Over here! There's a lad wants to ask you something."

The man in the uniform sees her and he grins. "You what?" He puts his hand to his ear to try and catch what she's saying over the racket of the train. He comes over to our carriage, great big strides. The train stops.

The spiv takes one look at him and legs it in the other direction. Only in his hurry, he skids on a chip and cracks his head on the ashtray. I'm laughing so hard I fall out through the carriage door and stick my foot down the gap.

"Mum!"

"Get up, you twit . . . Harry!"

He seems huge, this Harry man. But maybe he only looks huge because I'm sitting on my suitcase and I'm a short-arse.

Whatever, he's a lot bigger than my mum and she's got high heels. She has to stand right up on her toes to kiss him. Then she shows him the hole in her nylons.

"Look. I've gone and done my stockings. A pound, these cost me."

"Never mind. Soon have them off," he says, and kisses her again.

When he kisses her, she comes right up off the floor, he's so strong, and she says, "Oh, Harry, I missed you," and he says, "Have ya?" and she starts crying like a seagull. She's always crying. I dunno why. I'm wondering if it was because of the cat, because we had a cat, but it went missing.

I liked that cat. Never got round to giving it a name, but I liked it all the same. I had a popgun at home. A little rifle, it was. I forgot to bring it, but it had a cork on a piece of string, only I took the string off. When the cat was asleep, I used to fire the cork at it and it would jump up in the air and do a somersault. I never hurt it. I'd never hurt an animal. To this day, I don't know why it ran off.

Anyway, I'm thinking about the cat and picking my nose because there's a chip up it, when Harry comes over and ruffles my hair. I can see my face in his shoes, they're so shiny.

"Hello, Mick. Alright, son?"

"Are you my dad?"

My mum laughs. Harry don't. He just smiles and looks a bit awkward.

"Whadda you think?" he says.

"Can I have a bucket and spade?"

All the other kids have got buckets and spades and if he's my dad, he'd get me one, wouldn't he?

He grins, puts his arm round my mum's waist and makes a noise at me with his mouth, a clicking noise, like they make to horses to gee them up.

"Come on, little Mick."

I'm having to run to keep up with them. "Why can't I have a bucket and spade?"

Mum has a go at me. "People who ask don't get."

"Can I have a pie then?"

"No. You've already had chips."

We must have walked a hundred miles. It's getting dark and a bit shivery and I haven't got a coat or nothing. Or a backside in my trousers.

"Is he alright?" Harry says.

"Yeah, he's alright."

I'm not. I'm freezing. I thought it would have been warm at the seaside.

"Can I have a bucket and spade?"

Mum shakes her head. "Shut up about buckets and spades, will you? Your dad's found us somewhere to live."

So he is my dad. Only I wasn't sure, I'd never met him before.

"How come he didn't live with us before, Mum?" She don't answer straight away.

"He was in the army, weren't you, Harry?"

Harry stands to attention. "Royal Engineers," he says. "These hands are deadly weapons."

They look like it an' all. They look more like those metal things on the end of diggers than hands. I put my palm on his. His skin is dry and warm. He folds his fingers round my hand and shakes it, like a man.

"How d'ya do?" he says. We walk some more, then he stops.

"We're here. This do you, Connie?"

It's a tall house. Much taller than our one in London. By the time I'm halfway up the steps, I'm gasping for air. I'm so tired I start snivelling. Mum's not having it.

"Come on, Mick. Come on, you big baby."

"I can't."

I sit down on the step with my head between my knees. I can't go another step.

Harry gives me a fireman's lift. Mum tells him he's too soft by half but he says, "Give over, he's only little." I melt into his shoulder and it's nice, even though his buttons are digging into my face, and he smells of fags and Brylcreem and salt.

I've never smelt a dad up close before, so I keep breathing him in, breathing him in like he's a warm meat pie and I'm starving. I'm feeling a bit dizzy in the head with the sea air, but I'm not shivering no more. Not shivering. Just going up those steps, feeling heavy. Feeling like Harry and me are one person.

Next thing I know, I'm standing in my red wellingtons in the gutter again.

t w o

I think I'm still in Hornsey when I wake up, only my bed's round the wrong way. I'm just lying there, trying to figure out what's what, when I realise my feet are cold but my arse is steaming. Wet myself again.

I can hear a swooshing noise. Then it all comes flooding back. This isn't London. I don't live in the Hornsey house no more. We're in Southend, me and my dad and mum. My dad, Harry. Or did I just dream I had a dad?

"Dad! Da-a-ad!"

Footsteps. But not his. They're Mum's. I know her even in the dark.

"What's up?"

"Where's my dad?"

"Asleep. Least he was asleep till you started shouting."

"Is it time to get up?"

"No." She wrinkles her nose up. "Have you done what I think you have?" She feels under me and sighs.

"Get up, Mick."

I climb out of bed and stick my head under the corner of the curtain. It's starting to get light outside. The sun looks like it's bleeding.

"Look at the bleeding sun, Mum."

"Don't swear."

"I'm not. Look! It looks like blood, doesn't it?"

She looks up quickly. "Yeah . . . I s'pose."

She's wearing a shiny nightie with thin straps and her hair's all messed up. Pretty hair, she's got. Sort of red. Only she says it's not red, it's chestnut. That's what it says on the bottle, anyway. She bends over and strips off the sheet.

"What did you have to go and do that for?"

"Couldn't help it."

"Well try and help it next time, will you? I'm sick of doing sheets. Look at my hands. They're raw with sheets."

My dad comes over in his pyjama trousers. He never had the jacket on, just his bare chest. There was a tattoo on his arm with a name on it, only the name's crossed out. He takes the wet sheet off my mum.

"Doesn't matter," he says. "I'll do that. Go back to bed, Con."

He never told me off. Just flipped the mattress over so it's wet side down. I ask him if we can have a cat.

"Thought you wanted a bucket and spade."

My mum's still standing there, watching. "Stop asking your dad for stuff."

"Go back to bed, Mrs."

She smiles at him, opens the window and goes over to their bed, on the other side of the room.

"Can I go out, Mum?"

She sits down and flicks her slippers off. "Mick, it's a quarter to six in the morning."

My dad says to let me go. I can't come to no harm.

"Oh no? What do you know about kids?"

Odd she should say that when he's a dad. She says I'll fall in the sea and drown. My dad looks behind the curtain and laughs.

"He'll have a job. The tide's out. Out you go, son."

The air's so sharp outside I can feel the salt scraping the inside of my throat, all the way down. I'm gasping, like something's gone down the wrong hole. My belly hurts. Maybe it's because I've had no breakfast. Haven't had no tea, come to that.

There's a man sweeping litter up on the front. A black man. I never saw one before. Knew of them, but never saw one. My mum told me if I saw a black man, it was lucky. I think, maybe this is my lucky day.

There are steps down to the beach and a shingle slope. I reckon if I slide down the slope on my bum it'll be the quickest way down.

A bit painful, some of the stones. Ow! The sand's dry and gritty at the top. Then there's a thick, wavy line of brown, smelly seaweed with little things trapped in it and further down, in the damp sand, there's a seagull throwing something about. It's a crab.

I run at the bird and it waits until the last minute then flies up, swearing its head off because I made it drop the crab. The crab's only got three legs, poor thing. No wonder it never got away. I pick it up, but it ain't moving. It's stiff and it stinks.

It's got a nice shell though. I could keep it if I give it a wash. I could wash it in the sink. If we've got a sink. I never bothered to look round the new place. Just went straight out.

There's a man putting deckchairs out. He's got a big pile of them and it looks like he wishes he hadn't. He's really skinny, this bloke, and the hairs stick out of his nose like little copper wires. Every time he picks up a deckchair, all these purple tubes pop out in his wrists. I stand there watching him for eight deckchairs. Every time he puts one up, he puffs out his cheeks and puts his hands on his hips. Then he walks all the way back to the big pile.

I go with him each time, there and back. Puffing out my cheeks. Hands on my hips. Like it's a game. He never says a word until the ninth deckchair, which he sits down in. I sit next to him. Then he explodes. "Will you piss off, there's a good man." He never looks at me, just folds his arms and stares out to sea. I'm not even sure it's me he's talking to.

"What, me?"

"Of course you. Who else is there?"

I look around. There is no one about.

"Can't I help?"

He looks me up and down.

"No, you can't. The putting up of deckchairs takes years of experience. Now piss off and build a sandcastle, why don't you?"

Except I ain't got a bucket and spade.

"With what?"

He looks like he's going to strangle me.

"With sand, eejut! With sa-a-a-and!" Then he waves at the beach with a long swoop of his hand and whispers in my ear.

"Do you know the best place for to build sandcastles?"

"No."

"As far away from me as possible." He points to the line where the sea meets the sky and walks back to the pile of deckchairs. I wave ta-ta and run off in search of the right sort of sand.

I dig holes and make things out of other people's old lolly sticks all morning. There are loads of lolly sticks, so I make a warship by sticking some of them upright in the sand and balancing the others on top to make the deck. I'm the captain of course.

I'm just about to sink another German U-boat, which is really a seashell in disguise, when this poodle comes barking up the beach and cocks its leg on my destroyer. So that's the end of that war. Being as I've got nothing else to do, I decide to go down the pier.

You're supposed to pay to get in but I just keep my head down and pretend I'm some mother's kid. No one notices.

The tide's in under the pier. I can see it, dizzy and black through the gaps in the planks. What if one of the planks rotted and a kid fell through? Would it drown? If so, how long did it take and would it hurt? Only I can't swim.

People are fishing over the side. I've never been fishing but that's because my dad's in the Royal Engineers. If he'd been around, he'd have taken me fishing most likely, only not in the sea, because there isn't one in Hornsey. Lots of fish and chips though.

I'm desperate for a go on the penny machines. There are rows and rows of them. There's one with a knob on the end like a tomato and if you put a penny in the slot and pull the handle, it rolls round and rows of fruit come up.

Some bloke gets a row of lemons and the machine coughs up all these pennies and he's going "Yeah!" and scrabbling in the little metal dish for his winnings.

When he's gone, I try the handle. It isn't half stiff. I swing on it but I still can't get it to come down. I check the tray to see if he's missed a penny but he hasn't.

Still, it's nice just to look at the machines with their lights flashing and I get to thinking, maybe if you were lucky, you wouldn't have to get a job delivering coke to the gasworks. You could just get a row of lemons and you'd be rich.

You could buy Mars bars. Anything.

I'm wondering if my dad would give us a penny if I went home and asked. It's worth a try. I start walking home. I'm going past Pier Hill when I see all these lads sitting on a rail up above me. The rail must have been put there to stop people on the pavement from falling into the ornamental gardens. It's quite a big drop.

Just then, one of the lads pulls a handkerchief out of his pocket to wipe his nose and when he does that, money falls out of his pocket into the flowerbeds below. He never notices nothing, but I know exactly where it went.

There must be twenty or thirty lads on that rail. One of them pulls his lighter out and it happens again. Another coin, straight into the dahlias. I'm thinking to myself, that flowerbed must be a gold mine.

I know what I'm going to do, but I don't want to make it obvious, so I just potter about in the gardens until just before dark.

When nobody's looking, I creep round in the flowerbeds. The earth is sparkling with coins. I'm so excited, I can't cram them all into my pockets and I'm dropping threepennies and sixpences everywhere and giggling to myself, backing into the plants and snapping the stalks.

"Oi!"

I freeze. I've been caught by somebody. My heart's banging away, I've got my face shoved so far into a flower I can see the earwigs and something's tickling the back of my knees. I'm crapping myself in case it's a spider but I daren't flick it away in case I get spotted.

I stay like that for hours, I reckon. I don't know which bastard shouted "Oi!" but they can't have been yelling at me or they'd have done something about it by now, surely? So, thinking I've got the all-clear, I try and make a grab for the spider and go "Ugh!" and fling it away. Only I've been crunched up so long, my legs have gone to sleep and buckle under me.

Suddenly I'm on my back with my feet in the air looking up at the stars, laughing and laughing and laughing, because it ain't even a spider. It's just a little bit of cotton dangling where the hem's coming down on my shorts.

I roll onto my knees and I'm stuffing coins down my socks, in my shoes, everywhere. I'm staggering bow-legged across the lawn into the shadows and the coins are so heavy they're pulling what's left of my trousers down. I'm having to clutch the waistband with both hands and I'm roaring! Roaring out loud at how funny I must look and how rich I am.

On the way back, I see the black man and thank him.

"What for?" he frowns.

"Because you're lucky!"

He looks at his pile of rubbish and leans on his broom. "Ain't I jus'," he sighs.

three

I run the rest of the way home in the moonlight, money jangling in my pockets like music. I can hear a wireless on inside our house. It's *Dick Barton*. My dad's listening to it with Mum sitting on his lap.

"You're early," she says. "Couldn't you find nothing to do?" She never minds what time I come back in, which is a good thing except when it's cold.

"I found this." I show them my crab.

"Get it out of the house. It stinks."

"I'm going to wash it, then it won't."

"Wash it in the garden tomorrow. And keep it in the garden. I'll know if you've brought it in."

Her shins are starting to go red and puffy in front of the fire. It's a bit early in the year to have a fire but it's damp in here. She says she wants the fire going to dry the walls out a bit. There's a pot in the fire with spuds in. When *Dick Barton*'s finished, she asks if I want one.

"No thanks, I've had something."

"How come? You ain't got any money. Did you give him some, Harry?"

"No. I would have done, but he'd gone. I was going to give you something for a pie, Mick."

"I got my own pie. Look. I'm loaded." And I show them my treasure.

Mum hits the roof. She thinks I've nicked it.

"No I never. I found it!"

She folds her arms. "I suppose it grows on trees, does it?"

"Flowerbeds. It was in the flowerbeds."

I tell her about the lads on the railings and then she knows I ain't lying because how could I make up a thing like that? I never lie. I can't.

"Don't do it again though, Mick. Alright?"

"Why not?"

"What if one of them had seen you? You'd have got a right pasting."

She's not cross though. She pulls the potatoes off the fire and my dad eats them with a bit of salt. Mum pokes the fire.

"We haven't got much coke left, Harry."

"I'll drop a couple of bags off tomorrow."

He's got a job on the lorries, delivering coke to the gasworks. I look at my dad in the candlelight. He's not bad-looking for a dad. Not fat or bald or nothing. His hair's the same colour as mine, only it's really short, almost like bristles at the back, and he's got a thick, muscly neck and muscly ears.

"What are you looking at, son?"

"Nothing." I'm a bit scared of him to be honest.

"Come here." He pulls me towards him.

"Why? What have I done?"

"Nothin'."

He turns to my mum and laughs softly. "He thinks I'm going to belt him one." Then he sits me on his knee. I feel a bit embarrassed and hold my breath. I'm watching Mum all the time to see what her face is saying, but she seems to think everything's alright. This must be what dads do. They sit their sons on their knee. Quite nice really. I breathe out again.

"Pass me that candle," he says.

He takes the candle and drips the hot wax onto a fag packet until it makes a shiny puddle. Then he waits till the puddle gets a wrinkly skin and rolls it into a ball between his finger and thumb.

"What are you making?"

He holds one finger up.

"Watch." And he rolls the wax between his fingers and pinches it and stretches it and stands it in my palm.

"It's a cat!"

"Yep. You said you wanted a cat, didn't ya?"

"It's great. Can you make me a shark?"

Mum takes the dish away.

"What happened to 'please'? Make me a shark, please," she says.

"Please, Dad?"

He drips more wax onto the fag packet. "It's going to be a Great White, Mick. A man-eater, like yer mum." He winks at her. Then he rolls and squeezes the wax and with the edge of his fingernail he levers open the jaws of the shark and pulls on the wax to make its teeth.

"Can I have it, Dad? Can I keep it?"

He nods. "Hold on a minute. I ain't finished yet." He takes the candle again. I can't take my eyes off his hands. It's so exciting trying to guess what animal it's going to be.

"Is it a pig?"

"No."

"A dog?"

"Nope."

Mum comes back in her dressing gown.

"Mick, there's a lady called Mrs. Pearce who's going to look after you mornings."

"Why?"

"Because I'm working. She only lives down the road. It'll be nice. She's got a boy your age. What did you say his name was, Harry?"

"Stephen, wasn't it?"

"That's it. Stephen."

The candle is down to a stub.

"Got any more candles, Connie?"

"One. And I'm saving that in case there aren't any at the shops."

It's really dark. The little animals glow like ghosts.

"Put the lights on, Mum."

"Don't be daft. There's no electric."

I wish I didn't have to be looked after by Mrs. Pearce. I bet she's a right old cow. I tell Mum I'll be alright on my own.

"No, you won't."

"I been out all day on my own. And all evening nearly."

"And look where you ended up. In the flowerbeds."

My dad taps his fingers on his tobacco tin.

"'Bout time you went to bed, innit?"

"But it's early."

"Go on . . . get!"

I daren't argue with him. My bed's in the corner against the wall. Theirs is on the other side of the room. They've moved the wardrobe to make a wall between me and them. It wasn't like that the night before.

Apart from the wardrobe, there's the fire and two chairs. No bath. No bog. If you want to go for a leak, you have to go all the way down the corridor in the dark. It's a shared bog. Everyone in the house uses it, because it's flats here. Six flats, and ours is on the top floor.

"Goodnight. There's a bucket under your bed if you need it."

"'Night, Mum. You're not going out, are you?"

"No."

I ask, because sometimes I've woken up in the night and called for her and she ain't been there. But that was when we were in Hornsey. Things are different now, probably. She'll stop in because of my dad.

The mattress is still a bit damp from before, but it's not too bad. I arrange the little animals on the window sill, then I look for my dummy under the bed. There it is, right at the back, covered in dust.

I know I'm far too old for it but I can't give it up. It's just one of those things. It's a bit worrying because I think, what if I get married and my wife finds out?

I'll have to wait until she's asleep and then suck it. But what if she wakes up before me and sees me with the dummy in? I decide I'll have to wake up first every day of my married life so she never knows. Better not to get married in the first place maybe. It's so cold, I go to bed with all my clothes on, stinking of crab.

Next thing I know, it's daylight and Mum's dragging me out of bed.

"But I've only just got in!"

"No, you haven't. Up! Come on, Mrs. Pearce is having you, remember?"

She sees the state of my trousers. The hole in the back seems to have got a lot worse overnight. That's because I was running in my dreams.

"What have you been doing to them?" she moans. "I patched those before we left."

"I dunno. They tore."

"Take them off. I can't have Mrs. Pearce seeing you like that. What will she think, eh?"

Then she sees what the time is. "No . . . it's no good. I'll be late. I'll have to sew them on you." She licks a piece of cotton and stabs it through the eye of her needle.

"Hold still!" She crouches down. She's got a scarf over her curlers.

"Where's Dad?"

"Work. Hold still, will you?"

"Ouch!" She jabs the needle in my bum.

"Oh, be quiet. There." She snaps the cotton off with her teeth. Nice teeth, with orange lipstick on them. She whirls me round and puts her hands on my shoulders to examine me.

"Look at your hair. It's all sticking up!" She attacks it with a brush and water.

"Ouch!"

"I'll give you ouch in a minute."

Then I'm frogmarched downstairs and across the street to Mrs. Pearce's.

"But I haven't had my bread and milk."

"Well, you should have got up a bit earlier. I'll see you later and don't be cheeky to Mrs. Pearce."

She knocks on the door.

Mrs. Pearce has a face like two bricks banged together. She looks me up and down and waves me into their front room. I can hear my mum apologising for my trousers. Stephen is sitting on the settee looking at a comic. I sit next to him.

"Alright, Stephen, what you reading?"

He scowls and swings himself away from me so I can't see the comic. Mrs. Pearce shuts the door on my mum and folds her arms.

"I'm doing this out of the goodness of my heart," she says, "so behave. Got it?"

I nod.

"Got it?"

I scratch my head, not sure what to say, because I've already nodded.

"Say, 'Yes, Mrs. Pearce' . . . Why are you scratching? Have

you got nits? You better not have." She grabs me in a headlock and rakes through my hair with one eye shut.

"Alright. You'll do. I can't see anything. Stephen, play nicely with Mick."

Stephen closes his comic. "Where's my apple? You said I could have an apple."

He's got a really whiny voice and he never said please or nothing. She asks him if he wants it peeled, like he's a little prince or something.

"Yes. You know I don't like the skin."

He's a rude little git. If I spoke to my mum like that, I'd have got what for. Anyway, she brings him the apple, all peeled, and he never even says thank you.

He looks at me and takes a tiny bite out of it. He knows I want some but there's no way he's going to give me any. I can tell. He's only eating it to wind me up. He's sitting there, chewing this tiny bit for ages, like a chipmunk, then he throws the apple on the floor and runs out into the garden, where his mum is hanging out the washing.

It seems stupid to waste it, so I pick the apple up and eat exactly half. I want all of it, but I only have half, because otherwise it ain't fair on Stephen, even though I hate his guts.

A minute later, he comes back in and when he sees I've eaten some of his apple he goes mental. He runs back out to his mum with the apple, screaming and bawling.

She comes running up the garden with a mouthful of pegs, so I hide under the table. I know it's a waste of time. I know what's going to happen, like a dog does, but I still hide.

She drags me out by the ear and yells and slaps me.

"You" —*slap*— "naughty" —*slap*— "horrible" —*slap*— "boy" — "how" —*slap*— "dare you?"

She's throwing me round like a rag and old Stephen's standing there, blinking. He doesn't even want the rest of the apple.

I don't cry, because I expected her to be like this. I know I shouldn't have done what I done, but I wouldn't have done it if she'd given me an apple too. Only she never.

She could have cut it in half and given us a piece each, couldn't she? That's what I'd have done if I was a mother.

"Right," she says. She looks a bit surprised that I'm not crying. "To make up for it, you can go up the chemist's for me. Can I trust you?"

I shrug. She looks a bit scared somehow.

"That didn't hurt, did it? Only I can't have you mucking about. It's enough looking after Stephen."

It was like she wanted to apologise. She puts a note in my hand and gives me five bob.

"And I want every bit of change back," she says.

"OK."

She straightens my clothes for me and examines the slap marks. The backs of my legs are bright red and swelling.

"It's nothing. It'll soon go down," she says. She makes me put on a pair of Stephen's trousers with longer legs — just long enough to cover the slap marks.

"Well," she says, "at least you're not a cry-baby. I'll say that for you."

Stephen doesn't like her praising me, I can tell by his face. She opens the front door.

"You know where the chemist is? Right. When he gives you what's written on the note you're not to look in the bag. It's women's things."

I nod and walk slowly down the path.

"Not like that," she calls.

"What?"

"Swing your arms! When you walk, swing your arms. It's good for circulation."

I whirl my arms round like a monkey and she almost smiles.

"Not like that! Like a soldier," she says.

I keep swinging until I hear her front door close. Then I stop. My hands are tingling and my legs sting, but it's nice to get out of the house and away from Stephen. I don't mind being on my own. When I go into the chemist's, a little bell rings. *Ding!* It's such a pretty noise I go out and come in again. *Ding!* Go out and come in again. *Ding!*

The chemist stops serving and gives me a look.

"Do come in if you're coming," he says and he's just about to serve an old lady when — *boom!* there's this almighty explosion and he dives onto the floor behind his counter. The old lady stands there. She drops her bottle of medicine and starts going, "Oh . . . Oh . . . OH!"

Something terrible has happened but I can't figure out what. The glass has blown out of the chemist's door and the cardboard lady in the window has fallen over and taken the rest of the display with her. Suddenly there are all these people running around with confused faces and they're saying, "It's over there!" and pointing to where I just came from.

I run out of the shop. There's a choking smell of smoke and over there, on the other side of the street, a streak of fire is boiling up into the sky.

That's when I get frightened and start to panic.

Then Mum comes running round the corner with a wet mop in her hand and I can see she's scared like everyone else. She's pointing to the flames and screaming, "My boy's in there! My boy's in there!"

She doesn't see me standing nearby. She thinks I'm in the fire.

"Mum!"

At first she doesn't hear.

"Mum!"

I grab her hand and shake it and push my face in her apron. She pushes me away, like she can't believe it's me, then realising it is, she slaps my face.

"I thought you were dead! What are you doing here? Why are you here?"

"I was sent out to do some shopping."

She pats my cheek gently where she slapped it, pulls me into her chest and starts sobbing, "I'm sorry, I'm sorry, I'm sorry."

Fire, police, ambulance. It's pandemonium. It turns out a plane has crashed a few yards down from our place and it's taken three houses with it.

Including Mrs. Pearce's.

four

Seems like we've only just got here and we're on the move again.

The landlord's been banging on the door and me and Mum had to pretend we wasn't in. We wasn't in last week either. The week before that she said she'd had her purse nicked.

Now she's packing all her clothes into a suitcase. She stuffs her knickers in her shoes and throws them in the bottom. It seems a funny place to put your pants.

"Why are you doing that?"

"It saves space, putting little things in your shoes."

I hold a lacy pair up, stretched between my thumb and fingers. "Mum . . . these ain't little!"

She snatches them off me, flicks me round the earhole and grins. Maybe we're not moving after all. Maybe we're going on holiday.

"Why are you packing? Are we going to Butlin's?"

I never got much for my birthday, so for a few stupid seconds I got it into my head that we might be going on a surprise holiday. I knew what the answer was going to be as soon as I opened my mouth.

"What do we want to go to Butlin's for? We live by the sea. Lots of kids would love to live here," she says.

I do love living here and I say so. So why is she packing? Where are we going now?

"I'm not paying nineteen bob for this dump. Stuff it. Go on, get your things."

But I haven't got any things.

"Clothes and that," she says, "get your clothes."

I fetch my shoes. They're falling to bits underneath. I put the dummy in one of them and the wax animals and the crab shell in the other. She watches.

"What are you doing, Mick?"

"Saving space."

"Not with that crab shell, you're not. Leave it in the garden."

"Why? It's only a little thing."

"It'll make the clothes stink."

My clothes already stink. I had the Eileen dream again last night. At least, it started as the Eileen dream but then it changed. In it, I was trying to make a world. I don't know what out of, but whatever it was, I was making it wrong.

I was making this world wrong. Then it was like someone grabbed hold of my head and started squeezing and squeezing it until I could feel the bones in my skull sliding over one another and my face going pointy.

Then I started screaming and screaming but no noise came out, just little puffs of air, and I couldn't catch my breath and I was choking, like I was going to die. Then just before I died, I decided that being dead might be quite interesting and I relaxed and went all floppy and warm.

My mum was standing over me and for a split second I thought, maybe it's her. Maybe it was her all along trying to suffocate me and there wasn't a dream but I was still half asleep. My mattress was soaked.

"You've done it again, haven't you?" she says. "Well, you're going to have to lie in it. Sorry."

She never said it nastily or nothing. She was just so tired. She couldn't have got it dry anyhow because we had no coke left. And, because she couldn't make a fire, a whole week of washing was still damp. She never had a clean shirt to put me in but she would have if she could. I know that.

It's coming up late afternoon and the street lights have come on. The shirt I slept in is almost dry now, except for the tails. I won't tuck them in because of it. Mum's writing a letter to somebody.

"Where's Dad?"

They keep having rows. The last one was a right ding-dong. I'm thinking, maybe he's run off or something.

"He's gone over Canvey Island. There's been a flood. He's helping to rebuild the sea wall."

"Is he coming with us?"

"He'll meet us later. He's on lates."

"Mum . . ."

"What? I'm trying to write."

"How can he drive the tipper in the dark?"

"I expect there's lights."

She folds the letter and bungs it in an envelope.

"Who's that to?"

"No one. Got everything?"

We're going now. She has one last look around the place and puts her hat on.

"Where are we going?"

"To our new place. Tuck your shirt in." She shoves the damp tails down my trousers. It feels like a frog's gone down them. They're Stephen's trousers. I'm wearing a dead boy's trousers.

"I hate these trousers."

"I'll get you some new ones when we win the pools, Mick. You haven't done your hair, have you?"

She tries to push a quiff into the front but it won't stay. She gets cross with it.

"Oh, Mum! Who's going to see us in the dark?"

She puts her hand over my mouth. "No one I hope. Now shh!"

She puts her fingers to her lips. Orange lips. The last scrapings from the lipstick tube. She had to dig it out with the end of a spoon. She opens the front door very carefully, steers me out and peers down the stairwell. Then she closes the front door with the softest click and tiptoes down the stairs with her shoes in her hand.

It's like a game. I want to shout, "Boo!" I nearly do it, but I don't quite dare. I mouth it silently all the way down the stairs, behind her back.

"Boo! Boo! Boo!"

She turns round and catches me doing it. Her mouth moves. I can see what she's saying.

"You silly little sod!"

She's shouting it silently with her orange-peel lips. Somewhere above, someone opens a door. Mum presses herself into the shadow of the stairwell, looking scared. I decide to ask her something.

"Mum, when it's my next birthday, right, can I have a — "

She rolls her eyes and hisses at me. "You won't have another birthday if you don't shut it!"

We run the last few stairs. She grabs my hand and I come up off the ground and the next thing she's shoving her shoes back on. We clatter all the way down the outside steps, the suitcase rattling and thumping against her legs. Along the road we go, across another one to the seafront. Then down more steps. *Ker-*

chunk, kerchunk, kerchunk. On the last step, she goes over on one heel and swears.

"What did you say?"

"I said flip."

"No, you never."

"No, I know I never."

She flops down onto the step and I sit next to her. She pulls her shoe off. The broken one. The heel is hanging on by a thread.

"Look at that! My best sho-o-o-es."

She shows me the shoe. Then she stands up and throws it as far as she can across the beach. It spins through the air and smacks onto the sand. She's a good shot.

"Can I throw the other one?"

"If you want."

"Give us it then."

She takes the other shoe off and wriggles her toes.

"Mum, I bet mine goes further."

"How do you work that one out?"

"Women can't throw."

"Is that so?"

"Yeah. Dad said. Watch. I'm gonna get it in the sea."

I throw the shoe as hard as I can and for a minute, it's like she's not my mum. She's my girl. I'm going to show her how strong I am. The shoe don't spin. It goes up in a straight line and then crashes back down a few feet away, kicking up dry sand.

"Goes to show how much your dad knows about girls," she says.

She gets up, takes her stockings off and starts walking down the beach in her bare feet. It's a cold night but we're not cold because of all that running. The stars are floating in the sea like little chunks of ice.

"Mum, what are stars made of?"

"How should I know? Rocks, I think."

"What, sparkly rocks?"

"Yeah. Something like that."

"Are the stars in heaven?"

"Probably."

She walks fast, not really listening.

"Mum, if the stars are in heaven and I can see them, how comes I can't see dead people?"

The vicar said dead people go to heaven at the funeral after the plane crash, so how comes you can't see them? It don't make any sense. By rights, I should be able to look up and see Stephen, Mrs. Pearce and King George at the very least, because he's dead an' all.

"So why can't I, Mum?"

"I don't know. Stop going on," she says.

"You must know. You're a grown-up. You must know."

"Grown-ups don't know everything," she says.

I never knew that. I thought grown-ups did know everything. If they don't, that's very worrying because when I'm grown up, I thought I'd know all there was to know and I wouldn't be scared no more. I thought I'd have all the answers by then. I was banking on it. I can't help crying about it. I try not to let her see, but she can tell.

"Don't, Mick. I'm tired an' all you know. We're nearly there."

I'm not crying because I'm tired. I'm crying because suddenly my mum don't know everything and I thought she did. I know even less than she does and we're trapped between the beach and the sky like ants in a jar. And I swear she gave Eileen to the rag-and-bone man and he boiled her down for glue.

"Mum."

"What?"

"Where's Eileen?"

Her eyes change, like someone's snapped a light off. They go dark and still and far away, like she's blind. She turns away.

"Where's Eileen? Mum, where's Eileen?"

See, she doesn't know or she won't say. Her face is all screwed up and twisted and she drops her head backwards so that her chin points to the stars and her hat falls off and her hair falls back over her shoulders.

She falls onto her knees like she's been shot, making a low growling noise. It don't sound like her at all. It doesn't even sound human.

"Mum, don't."

I watch her for a while, not sure what to do. She can't hear me. "Mum. Stop it."

She's like a statue in the sand, except for that ugly noise. It's embarrassing me now. I walk away from her towards the sea with my fingers in my ears. There's a stick lying in some seaweed. I pick it up and push it in the sand where I think the next wave is going to reach and I start yelling at the sea.

"Come on! I dare ya! Wet the stick!"

A wave creeps forward . . . forward . . . forward, then it rolls back like it doesn't trust me. I chase after it and crouch down in the foam.

"Come on, lick my hand!" It gives me a little lick and runs away again. I move the stick a bit further up the beach.

"Chicken! Chicken! Get the stick."

I turn my back on the tide, crouch down and shut my eyes. "I ain't looking. Come and get it!"

I'm curled into a ball, my face pressed in the sugariness of sand. The sand is breathing. I can hear it. *Thump, thump, thump*, like it's got a heart. It smells a bit like Mrs. Pearce.

Mrs. Pearce is dead. Stephen is dead. That pilot is dead. He was supposed to land in Rochford in the airfield, but he never.

He landed on top of Mrs. Pearce and Stephen. I bet Stephen never finished that apple either.

A kid called Adrian Roberts found the dead pilot on top of the air-raid shelter. He didn't have any eyes when they found him. Just holes. No wonder he crashed the plane.

I'm wondering why he didn't have no eyes, when suddenly it's like someone's chucked a bucket of freezing water over me. It's up my nose, in my ears, in my mouth. The tide has crept up and slapped me on the arse. I scrabble to my feet and whisk round, swearing at it and throwing stones.

"You sneaky bastard!"

I'm soaking wet. Jumper, trousers, shoes — everything. I wouldn't mind, but my shirt had almost dried. Now look at it.

"Mick . . . what are you playing at?"

Mum's come back to life. She's shaking her head and opening the suitcase for dry clothes and saying this is all she needs.

She pulls my wet jumper over my head and a strip of seaweed slides over my face like a wet slug. She pulls my trousers down but we can't get them over my shoes. The shoes are jammed up the trouser legs. So, I'm lying on the sand with my legs in the air while she grabs hold of the hems and tries to pull them over the shoes. She pulls so hard I'm sliding across the beach on my bare bum and we're both shrieking our heads off. In the end, the trousers tear over the shoes. The seams just split.

"Here! Put this on!" She's still laughing. I think that I must have dreamed that thing when she was a statue on the rock. I like her like this. This is my real mum.

She makes me wear one of my dad's shirts rolled up about a hundred times in the sleeves and a pair of her old slacks. I look a right idiot, but at least I'm dry.

Mum digs out another pair of shoes for her and we walk down the beach and up the steps, carrying our suitcase like nothing's happened. Mum posts her letter.

Our new house is right on the sea front, 38 Shaftesbury Avenue. It's a corner house. Mum says there's a cricket pitch over the way, and a park and a pond.

This time, we're on the ground floor. We've never been on the ground floor before and it's massive. There's a front room, where I'm supposed to sleep. All it's got is a bed in it, but it's not as lumpy as the last one. I put my wax animals on the sill, all in a row.

I'm looking at them and thinking about my dad when there's a knock at the door. It's him.

"Thought you were on lates," says Mum, and he says he knocked off early to give her a hand, like.

"Oh," she says, "you're not checking up on me, then?"

"No. Look, if you say you ain't seeing no one, you ain't. Sorry for even thinking it."

Next thing, they're all over each other. They go into the next room and close the door in my face.

Next morning, I have a good look round and suss the place out. Down the hall is where Mum and Dad sleep. They've got a double bed and a wardrobe. There's even a mirror hanging on the wall.

Then there's a scullery with a table and a couple of chairs and an old sofa. There's a stove too. That's for the water. And we've got a bath on the left and a toilet to the right.

Imagine that. A bath *and* a toilet. We've never had that before, so this must be one of those posh places. Probably costs a lot because Mum's off to look for another job.

I'm going up Canvey Island today with my dad. He hasn't finished mending the sea wall yet, so that's what we're going to do.

We start walking towards the bus stop and I sit down and wait.

"What are you sitting there for?"

"I thought we was going on the bus."

"No, we're not. We're walking."

"Oh, Da-a-ad! It's miles to Canvey Island, walking. I can't walk that far."

"Yes, you can. I've only got enough for something to eat and I need some tobacco, so you'll have to."

So we walk. And walk and walk and walk. Then we get to a field and he says we have to go through it to get to his lorry.

We're halfway across when these big brown shapes start appearing from under the trees. I grab his hand.

"Dad . . ."

"What?"

I point to them, terrified. He looks and laughs.

"It's alright, Mick. They're only cows. Haven'ya seen a cow before?"

I have, but only in a picture. I never knew they were that big. One of them's looking at me. It starts galloping towards us.

"Dad! Run!" My legs are pedalling in the air.

"It's alright, it won't hurt you."

He says that, but it's got these sharp curly horns and all these teeth and steam coming out of both ends. It's going to eat me. I know it is.

"They eat grass, Mick."

Yeah. And I eat cabbage but I eat meat and all.

"Dad!" I'm climbing up him. Scaling my dad. I've got both feet on his belly. He scoops me up, puts me on his shoulders and runs towards the cow.

"No, don't! Dad! It's coming for us!"

The cow stands there and jerks its head up. Then it starts munching grass and flicking its tail. Dad charges at it. "Moooo!"

"Dad, don't! You'll make it mad!"

"Moo!"

I'm hysterical by now. Screaming. The cow steps backwards, gives my dad a look and trots back under the trees with its mates.

Phew. I thought I was a goner. That would have been Mrs. Pearce, Stephen, all the people in the war, the pilot, King George and me. All gone to heaven. There won't be room to move up there at this rate.

There's a little kiosk nearby. Dad buys half an ounce of Golden Virginia and a cake. Then we pick the lorry up, fill it with muck and drive down to the sea wall to tip our load.

I'm sitting on my dad's lap, doing all the steering. It's the most fun I've had in ages. I've even had some of that cake and a sip of tea out of his flask. I'll be smoking his roll-ups next.

He twists the top off one he's just made and it dangles out of his lips, unlit.

"I'm going for a fag," he says. "Take over for a bit, will you, son?"

He shuffles out from under me and before I really know what's happening, he climbs out, slams the door and stands on the running board, grinning at me.

"Go on, son. Drive it on your own."

My belly tightens up and I almost do one in my trousers. My feet don't reach the pedals. It's not going all that fast though. It's on tickover. My dad's smiling and smoking, so it can't be all that dangerous. That's OK, then. I'm OK. I loosen my grip on the steering wheel and the pink comes back into my hands.

It's great, this. I'm loving it. I can hear the other men shouting to my dad.

"That your boy, Harry?"

"Yer!"

"Nice one."

It's good having a dad. Especially one what lets you do this.

"Alright, Mick. That's enough."

"No, it ain't." I've got a taste for it now. I don't want to let go of the wheel.

"Come on, shove over."

"No."

He flicks his fag away, lifts me up with one hand and sits me back on his lap like a baby.

"I was doing it, Dad."

"I've got to get on now. Don't moan. And don't tell your mum what you done."

We knock off early. Mum's not there. When she comes in, she looks a bit surprised to see us. First thing I do is forget not to tell her about driving the lorry.

"You'll never guess what I done today, Mum."

"What's that, then?"

She looks really pretty. Got a nice dress on and stockings. You can't see the mend. I tell her about steering the tipper and she calls my dad all the silly sods under the sun and tells him he can't be trusted. He just stands there, grinning.

"Anyway," he says, "where've you been, looking like that?"

"Looking for a job, remember?" she says. Only she says it too quickly. "I'm going for a bath."

My dad stops smiling. "Oh, yeah?" And he follows her out of the room.

five

I'm starting school today. I should have started September, but I never got round to it for some reason. Moving, perhaps.

I had my bath last night and even a hairwash. And Mum cut out some new cardboard from a cornflakes packet to put in my shoes so I don't wear the socks out. The socks need garters, but we ain't got none, so Mum has this brilliant idea of using a couple of rubber seals off the inside of two jam-jar lids. They're a bit tight, but she says they'll ease up after a bit.

"See you then, Mick. Be good."

She can't take me because she's on the mops. She's arranged for me to go with some other kids. I can't turn to wave because I don't want her to see I'm crying and I don't want the boy I'm walking with to see neither.

But it's alright, because he's crying too and doesn't want me to see him. So there I am with this kid called John Sculley being pushed through the school gates by his big sister Joan. She's having a right go at us.

"What are you both skriking for? You don't even know what you're crying for, you big babies."

He's blubbing out loud now. "I don't wanna go. I wanna go home."

She pulls a face at him. "God, John! It's not that bad. You're in Miss Hudson's class. She's got big bosoms." Joan pulls at her blouse to make bosoms, giggles and runs off.

John looks at me. I look at John and he rolls his eyes round and round at the thought of bosoms large, small or medium. He looks so funny I start laughing and soon we're kicking a ball about in the playground with some other lads.

A bell rings and all these kids, millions of kids, stop playing and stand in lines.

John Sculley doesn't know where to stand so me and him make our own line, just the two of us, John in front, me behind. Some big kid starts laughing.

"Ya! Look at those soppy gits." All his mates start laughing too.

"Johnson! Face the front!"

Who said that? It's the fierce little geezer in glasses. He's only little but you can tell he's hard because the Johnson kid steps back in line straight away.

"You two boys over there!"

Now who's he yelling at?

"Us," says John Sculley.

"Move it!"

I run one way, he runs the other.

"This way!"

The whole school collapses laughing at us. My National Health glasses bang up and down on my nose as I run. I'm trying to look over the top of them to see where John's gone. The headmaster is still shouting his head off.

"Here, lad! No, no . . . to the LEFT!"

I've gone blind. It's just a sea of kids and I don't know where I'm supposed to go. Then someone grabs my collar and pushes me into a line between two other boys. They're much taller than me, so I can't see over. All I can see is a grey gaberdine.

We start moving. I don't know where we're going, so I just follow the lad in front. If we'd been walking over the edge of a cliff I wouldn't have known until I smashed to the ground.

Perhaps we're going to the gas chambers, like the Jews and the gypsies. Our old draper, Mr. Liebowitz, his dad was put in a gas chamber and never come out. I know because my mum went to Liebowitz's to get some cheap curtains off him and the shop was closed due to mourning. Mum wasn't half fed up with the wasted bus fare and we had to make do with a couple of sheets pinned up at the window instead.

We're in the big hall now. It's got a wooden floor. There's a piano playing. Suddenly, everyone sits down on the floor and crosses their legs.

I do whatever everyone else is doing, but when I cross my legs my trousers split underneath. Mum only sewed them up again last night but they still split and I'm hanging out of the hole because I've got no pants on. I scoop myself back in but the hole's too big. The only thing I can do is to kneel up and squeeze my thighs together to try and trap my nuts. Course, by now, the jam-jar seals are cutting into my legs and I'm all pins and needles.

"You at the front! Sit down! Cross your legs!"

"I can't."

"I can't, *sir*. There is no such word as can't."

A woman marches over to me, sits me down on my bum, grabs both feet and crosses them. Then she sees the problem.

"Ah," she says, "come with me."

She takes my hand and marches me out of the hall. She walks into a huge cupboard and roots through a cardboard box, looking me up and down.

"Trousers off, dear."

I'm standing there in my shirt and willy. I can hear them singing in the hall, "Stand up, stand up for Jesus."

"Try these, dear." She gives me a pair of thick, blue pants. Holds the legs out for me to step into. They're far too big in the waist and they hang off like a nappy.

"I'll pin them for now," she says, grabbing the elastic. Then she finds a pair of PE shorts. Quite smart ones, actually, even though they nearly reach my ankles.

"That's better. What's your name, dear?"

"Mick. I'm Mick Spicer."

"Well, I'll put these old ones in a bag for you. Mother can see to those."

I didn't like to tell her they're my new ones. She fetches a list and looks my name up on it.

"Spicer . . . Spicer . . . ah!"

She takes me along to an empty classroom and leaves me there. I'm all alone in a wooden chair, facing a blackboard covered with scribbles.

Then an angel walks in. At least, she looks the closest to an angel I've ever seen. Blonde hair tumbled up and down. A blue dress covered in flowers which goes into a deep V-shape at the front, with a fluffy cardigan draped over her shoulders. The arms dangle like snowy wings. And she's got dimply legs which she crosses high up, sitting on her desk.

"You must be Michael Spicer."

I'm speechless. I just stare at her. Maybe she's not real. Maybe someone's just drawn her on my glasses. I take them off and rub my eyes.

"Are you Michael?"

I nod.

"I'm Miss Hudson. Your teacher. The others will all be back from assembly in a minute. Would you like to sit next to John Sculley? He's a new boy too."

I just stare and stare.

"Is there something wrong with your glasses, Michael?"

"Yes, miss. I can't believe what I'm seeing."

I just blurted it out. Never meant to. Couldn't hold it in. She never laughed outright but she did this lovely thing with her lips where she bit the bottom one with her top teeth and flickered her eyelashes, turning her head to one side. Then she straightened up.

"Do you have any brothers or sisters?"

"Yes. No. I don't think so."

I think she thought I was stupid, but I don't know about Eileen, do I? Not for sure. That's all I was trying to say.

"I see. And where do you live?"

"In . . . In an 'ouse."

I forgot my address for a minute. Well, we hadn't been there long had we?

"In a what, sorry?"

I don't think I could have said it very clearly, only she didn't seem to understand at first.

"In an 'ouse on the seafront, miss."

"Oh, a *house!* Were you born in Hornsey, by any chance?"

"I was as it happens, miss."

She claps her hands together.

"I thought so! I've got an uncle who lives there and his accent is just like yours."

She's got this beautiful posh voice, dead soft, like her cardigan. I don't feel a bit shy now. I ask her where her uncle lives.

"Is he anywhere near the Cally Road, miss?"

"He's near the Nag's Head. Do you know it?"

"You can walk it from my old house."

It's lovely just nattering to her like this. Nattering and looking up her dress. Then all the others come in and ruin it. My heart sinks. She stands up.

"Good morning, class!"

They stand behind their desks. I stand too.

"Good morning, Miss Hudson."

I say it the loudest. In fact, I shout it, but I've lost her. She's talking to us all but she never looks me in the eye like she done before.

We've all got to write what we done at the weekend and if we're stuck and don't know what to do we're to go up to her desk one at a time and she'll explain.

I go up fourteen times. I can't write, full stop, but even if I could, I'd have pretended I couldn't, just so I could talk to her.

She never mentions the uncle in Hornsey again or nothing. No more chit-chat. Sit down, please, Michael. She's taken her cardigan off now. Joan was right about the bosoms.

I'm up like a shot again.

"What is it this time?"

I point to the blackboard where she's written some helpful words.

"Is that a B or a D, miss?"

"It's a B. The same as it was the last time you asked me."

"Oh."

"Try and work by yourself. There are other children in the class besides you."

"So, it's a B, then?"

"Yes, Michael, it's a B."

B is for "Bosoms." If you turn a big B upside down, that's what bosoms look like. I'll never forget B ever again.

On the way home from school, Johnny sees this tipper coming down the road from some wasteland.

"Grab it," he says.

"Do what?"

"Grab the bar running along the back. I seen some older kids doing it the other day."

We both run after the tipper and jump on the back of it. My legs are swinging.

"Mick. Put your feet up, like I'm doing."

So I copy Johnny and put my feet up on the spare wheel.

"Good to get a lift, innit?" he yells.

"Yeah!"

The lorry's coming up to turn left round my street so I jump off. Johnny waves his cap at me.

"See ya, Mick!"

"John."

He's been scratching all day. I think he must have nits. I expect I've got 'em now.

When I get in my mum's in a really good mood.

"Did you have a nice day?" She never usually bothers to ask.

"It was alright."

"What happened to your trousers? Those ain't yours."

"They split. The teacher put them in a bag but I forgot it."

She grabs her handbag. It looks like we're off somewhere. I hope we're not moving house again.

"Where are we going?"

"To the pictures. My treat. We didn't do much for your birthday, did we?"

"What, both of us going, like?"

I've never been anywhere out-out before with her. Nowhere special.

"What's up? Don't you want to come?"

Of course I do, only it's a bit of a funny time to go, isn't it? Be better if Dad could come. He'll be home soon wanting his tea anyway.

"Your dad's stopping over Canvey Island tonight," she says. "He's on earlies tomorrow."

She sprays some perfume behind her knees. I've got an itch.

"Are you scratching, Mick? It's not nits, is it? Oh, it blimmin' well would be now, wouldn't it?" She looks at her watch like we're late for something.

"'S not nits. It's just an itch."

She goes to look for her comb, then puts it away again. "Remind me to look later or we'll miss the start."

When we get to the picture house, she tells me to sit right at the end of a row, away from her. I thought we'd be sitting together. Still, we're in the one-and-nines. You can see quite well from there.

"Why can't I sit next to you?"

"You'll see better there."

"No I won't."

"Also, if you sit there, a lady will come and give you a free gift. Eat your popcorn."

Lots of other people want to sit in the same row and I keep having to fold my chair back up and sit on top of it to let them past. I'm spilling popcorn everywhere and they're all treading in it.

The lights go down. Every time I try and chew what's left of the popcorn the woman in front turns round and glares at me. When she's not looking, I balance a few blobs of it in the back rim of her hat. It doesn't half look funny.

I don't think much of the film. There are no cowboys and no Indians, just this geezer and his girlfriend who keep saying goodbye to each other.

There's no sign of the woman with the free gift, but when the lights go up for the interval, I see my mum sitting next to a man with dark hair having a right old chat. I don't know who he is. I've never seen him before. It's odd, because there's plenty of other seats. I don't see why he has to sit next to her. I lean forward and try to catch her attention.

"Mum . . . Mum! Who's he?"

"Who?"

"Him. Sitting next to you."

She shrugs. "Here, keep an eye out for that lady I told you about."

When the lights go down, I'm sure I see them holding hands, but when I look again, they aren't. Maybe I just imagined it.

"Mum!"

"What?"

"Tell that man if he sits at the end, he'll get a free gift. Then you'll have more room."

"Watch the film."

It's so boring, I fall asleep. Mum wakes me up, tapping my shoulder. The cinema's empty.

"Come on, Mick. We're going now. Did you enjoy yourself?"

"Eh? Oh . . . Yeah, it was alright. What about my free gift? I haven't got it."

"Haven't you? Oh, she must have been when you was asleep."

He's still there, the man with the dark hair, standing near my mum.

"Mum, he's still there. Who is he?"

"Who's who?"

I point to him.

"I dunno," she says, "just a man."

We walk to the bus stop in the dark. The same man sits behind us on the bus. He never speaks or nothing. Just sits behind us. The bus conductor comes up.

"One and a half to the Kurzaal, thanks."

Then I heard the bloke behind us. "Kurzaal, mate. Cheers."

He's going our way too. I reckon he's following us. The bus stops. We get out and he gets out and stands around, not looking at anything in particular. Mum fiddles in her bag and gets her purse out.

"Did you enjoy that?" she says again.

"Yeah. It was great. What's for tea?"

She gives me a handful of change. "Here y'are. Go and play on the pier. Buy yourself some chips. I'm going round to a friend's, so don't come back before ten, alright?"

She's smiling. I think she's going to cuddle me, but she don't. Almost, but not quite.

I can't believe my luck with all this cash. I run off. Then I realise I never waved, so I turn round to wave to her. But she's gone. And so's he, funnily enough.

After the chips, I have a go on the machines. I put most of the money in but I never get a row of lemons. I'm a bit bored so I decide to go down to the beach. There's a concrete pipe that runs out to sea about a hundred yards. It's mostly covered in seaweed. I've climbed along it before, but only a little way. Tonight, I'll try to get all the way along to the railings at the other end. Just for a laugh. Just to see if I can.

The front bit's easy because the pipe's quite dry. I can just walk along it, like walking along a wall.

In the middle I have to sit on it and pull myself along because it's too slippery to stand. Then I go belly down and pull with my arms. There's no one about much. Everyone's on the pier.

I look back along the pipe. It looks a lot longer from this end than it did when I started out. I don't really fancy crawling all the way back up it. I'm knackered now.

Maybe when I get to the end I'll just slide off it somehow onto the sand. Then I'll walk back. Only a few more feet to go and I'm there. If I grab hold of the rail I can pull myself up to standing. I wonder how deep under the water this pipe goes when the tide comes in. Which it is doing, I notice.

Quite quickly.

Suddenly, I feel a bit scared. I'm just about to turn round and crawl back when my foot slips on some seaweed and gets jammed between the railings.

I try to wriggle it out but I can't move it. I try pulling, but it's agony. I'm standing there, hopping on one leg, pulling until my ankle starts bleeding. I look round, but there's nobody about.

"Help!"

I'm roaring now. I'm roaring my lungs out. "Help!"

The tide's under the end of the pipe now. My foot's gone numb and my knee's starting to swell.

"Help me-e-e-e!"

It's really windy and the words get blown away. No one can hear me. I'm going to drown. Mum's going to kill me if I get these shorts wet.

"Save me-e-e-e!"

"I'm coming, you bloody eejut!"

It's the deckchair man. He's panting from running all the way down the beach. He comes as near as he can, wading into the water.

"Aghhh. The water's bloody wet! I've called the fire brigade now."

"But I'm not on fire. My foot's stuck," I scream.

"They'll cut it off, son."

"My foot?"

"Not your foot, the pipe, eejut! Of all the eejut things to do!" He shakes his head.

"I'm bleeding."

"Yo're a bleeding eejut. Have you no sense at all, climbing on a slippery thing like that?"

"I done it before."

"And I suppose you'll do it again, will ye?"

"I'm cold."

I start swaying. Fainting maybe. This panics him.

"Ah, now . . ." he says. "No you don't. Keep a hold! You'll soon be home and . . . hold on! Jesus, you nearly gave me a heart attack there."

I start to sob I'm so scared and cold. The deckchair man starts humming a jig and doing a dance in the sea.

"Ah, come on, now, I'll sing you a little song to cheer you up." The sea is up to his waist, splashing his face. He spits as he hums and dances.

"Oh, dee, diddly, diddly, diddly . . . are you watching me, eejut? Good! That's good! Dee diddly, diddly . . . keep watching . . . diddly, diddly . . ."

Suddenly I hear the sirens and he stops dancing.

"Ah, that'll be the fire brigade," he says, "come to cut you out."

"G-g-good." I'm shivering with cold and fright. The deckchair man don't look too hot either.

"I'll say it's good. I can't bloody swim."

Three firemen run down the beach with a ladder. One stands there holding a blanket and the other two wade into the sea in their rubber boots. I think of my red wellingtons. Wherever did they go?

The sea is up to the firemen's thighs. They wedge the ends of the ladder into some rocks under the sea and lean the other end up against the pipe.

"To you, Jim . . . steady . . . to me . . . that's it! Hold it . . . hold it."

The biggest man climbs up and puts his hand on my back to steady me.

"What's your name, son?"

"John."

I say that so my mum won't find out. He has a look at my foot.

"Does it hurt at all, mate?"

"Can't feel it."

"Alright. You'll be alright."

He feels round my ankle with his fingers and frowns. Then he pulls a metal wrench thing and some cutters off his belt.

"Don't cut my leg off! Don't cut my leg off!"

"Easy, John. Easy, son. Keep still, there's a good lad."

He tucks the end of the wrench between my skin and the rail and puts all his weight against it.

"Owwww!"

The rail bends just enough for me to slip my foot out.

Nee na! Nee na! Nee na! Ambulance. Police. All the 999s.

The fireman carries me down the ladder and through the sea on his shoulders. The waves are hitting his chest. When we reach dry land, the other fireman wraps me in a blanket and helps me over to the ambulance. The deckchair man is talking to the police. The ambulance man is talking to the firemen.

"He's alright. Just shaken, I think."

"Right you are. Now then, young John, let the dog see the rabbit." I'm taken into the ambulance to be examined.

"How old are you?"

"Eight," I lie.

"Eight? Are you sure about that? When were you born?"

"On my birthday."

He laughs and looks up from my wound.

"Not much wrong with you," he says. "Just a bit of a cut ankle."

He cleans it up and puts a dressing on it.

"Don't get it wet and get your mother to change it every day. You're lucky someone saw you. It's high tide tonight. Another ten minutes and you might have drowned."

The policeman comes up. "Come on, son. Let's get you home."

"No one's in. Mum's out. Dad's up Canvey Island."

"Whereabouts?"

"Dunno."

"Got any older brothers and sisters?"

"Not that I know of."

He turns to the ambulance man. "We've got a right one here," he says. "What are we going to do with you?"

"Send me to prison?"

I'd rather go to prison than face my mum. She'll do her nut if she finds out I crawled along the pipe. The deckchair man taps the policeman on the shoulder.

"Well now, constable, why don't I keep an eye on him and take him home when his mammy gets in?"

"And who are you, sir?"

"The name is Finbarr Quinn. I do the deckchairs. Shall I get you one? Take the weight off your new shoes."

The deckchair man marches the policeman over to one of his chairs and talks to him. I can't hear a word he's saying. The firemen pack their ladders and the ambulance drives off. Then the policeman finally escapes from Finbarr Quinn and pedals off on his bicycle.

Finbarr walks over to me, beaming. He steers me up the beach to his wooden hut and tells me to go inside. There's an oilburner going. He takes his wet shoes off. Then he takes his wet trousers off and sits down in his grey string underpants. He pulls a bottle out from the side of a chair and waves it at me.

"Now, John. Would you like a little drop of brandy for the shock?" He takes a swig and wipes the top and hands it to me. I take a big glug. My eyeballs nearly pop out of my face.

"It's good stuff," he says. "It's medicinal."

The heat from the brandy spreads right inside my ears and into the corners of my soggy shoes.

"And now," he says, "now that you've got your strength back, you can help me with those bastard deckchairs. I'd do it myself but I'm in my pants."

One at a time, I gather deckchairs from the front. After a while, I lose count of how many. When I'm too tired to carry on, I go back to the hut to ask if it's alright to do the rest tomorrow. He's asleep. I don't like to wake him.

I'll have to walk home on my own. It don't matter. I've done it plenty of times before. I'm warm now, at least. And I'm alive and it's a starry night. It takes a lot longer to get home than usual for some reason. Could be because I can't seem to walk in a straight line.

I arrive at our house just as the man with the black hair is leaving.

s i x

Nine months later, my brother Terry is born.

It's "Terry" this and "Terry" that. They all love Terry. But I don't mind. I love him too. I've never had no one look at me the way he does and I love the way he moves his hands. He does a thing like he's playing an invisible piano when he's happy, which is most of the time.

When he does cry, I can make him stop. What I do is hold him with one hand under his bum, and the other under his head, and I pretend to be a Red Indian. Singing and dancing like that in made-up Red Indian language.

When I do that he goes dead quiet, like he understands what I'm saying. Which is odd, because I don't.

I sing, "Way, yay, wah wah, way yay, wahh, wahh," in a really low voice. Perhaps it means "Shut up, Terry" in Cherokee. I found all this out late one night when he started bawling in his cot. I called out for Mum but she weren't there and nor was Dad.

"Mu-u-um!"

Nuffing.

"Da-a-ad!"

Nuffing. Must have gone up the pub again. Anyway, Terry's screaming his head off and all the covers are kicked off, so I pick him up. He snotters all over my shirt, but it don't matter. Anybody else's I would have minded, but not his. I try and find some milk for him. There's a bottle in his cot, but he's had all that. I try him with some cold tea but he's not having any of it and he's going purple.

I don't know why it came into my head to be a Red Indian for him. It just happened. "Wey, yey, yoi yu," up and down the scullery.

All the time, I'm looking deep into his eyes. The little tears have stopped coming now. His eyelashes are all wet and the little black dots in his eyes are getting bigger and bigger.

All the purple puffiness melts away and his face is round and bright like the moon. I make a little den by folding my mattress in half.

"This is our wigwam," I tell him. "I'm the Indian chief and you're my papoose, alright? Your name's Laughing Wax Cat."

He doesn't mind being the papoose.

"Wait there, Tel. Don't roll off."

I go and get a Mars bar and cut it into slices with my penknife.

"White man food. You eat. Make brave Terry warrior."

He sucks the chocolate off but he's got no teeth so he gets in a right mess with the caramel. It's all round his face and in his hair.

"Terry, you're meant to swallow it, you messy git."

I clean him up as best I can. He's quite happy in our mattress wigwam.

I tell him about all sorts. About cowboys and Miss Hudson. I show him the wax animals.

"This one's a cat and this one's a pig. It don't look like a pig because someone trod on it, but it was one once. Dad made it. I expect he'll make you a pig one day, if you ask."

He can't say nothing yet. He just nods.

I look round to see if Mum's left any fags in the drawer, but she ain't. I find some old Rizla papers but no bacca. But there is tea leaves. I can use the tea leaves. I tip them into the little fold in the fag paper and roll it up with my thumbs, packing the leaves in tight like I've seen my dad do. Lick it up one side. Then twist the end so it don't all fall out.

Matches. Matches. Where are the matches?

By the time I find some, Terry's gone to kip in the wigwam. His hands have rolled into loose fists over his head and his knees are spread open like a puppy.

The fag unravels a bit. It looks more like an ice-cream cornet than a fag. I must have licked it too much. As we haven't got any sticky tape, it'll have to do.

I love the smell of match-heads when you strike them. I put the fag in my mouth. Light it with a wobbly hand. *Whoosh!*

"Flippin' 'ell!" It's a tea-leaf bonfire. There's a big, blue flare on the end, creeping towards my nose. I'm sucking and blowing at the same time, choking on gobfuls of smoky tea. Bits of hot PG Tips are dropping on my knees.

"Ow! Bollocks! Ow!"

I throw the fag on the floor and stamp on it once, twice. Then I go all dizzy, open the window and puke. I think my lungs have stuck together. Puke again. Cor, that's better. Wow.

I sink into the bed, getting my breath back.

Every day Mum takes Terry down the seafront and every day after school I have to go up there and find them. She'll be lying there in her swimming costume, smoking Weights and Terry will be sitting up with his blue spade, eating sand. He's so suntanned he looks like a little black boy without the frizzy hair.

My hair's brown, like Dad's. The man who came to the pictures with us, he had very dark hair, I seem to remember. I tell John Sculley this on the way to school.

"So what?" he says.

"So how come Terry don't look like me?"

"I dunno, Mick. Perhaps he's got a different dad."

"No, he ain't."

"Well, perhaps you have then."

That got me wondering and confused. Then cross.

"No, I haven't. Harry's my dad."

"How do you know?"

"I just do, alright?"

"Ever asked your mum?"

"Yeah."

I never asked her straight out, but I wasn't telling him that.

"I bet you never."

He's really winding me up about this. I'm about to have a go at him when we see these older kids playing with fireworks. Penny bangers.

We stand and watch them for a bit. They're quite a bit older than us and they're standing by the grass bank behind the amusement arcades. What they do is light the bangers, then throw them. *BANG!*

"Where do you think they got them from, Mick?"

"Dunno. Not Bonfire Night for ages, is it? Not for months."

"Let's arst."

They've spotted us screwing them.

"What you looking at?"

That's the leader. He must be about ten, eleven?

"Where d'you get the bangers?"

"Found them in a shed."

"Got any more?"

He had pocketfuls of them. Not just bangers either. He had all sorts of fireworks, squibs, rockets, Roman candles. He reckons they were left over from the Coronation. There was a street party near us, only we wasn't invited.

"Go on, give us a banger, mate."

The leader waves one in my face.

"What's it worth, four-eyes? Got any money?"

I'm skint and so's Johnny, so we just shrug.

"Na."

"Piss off out of it, then."

We're just about to go when they start whispering to each other. Then they call us back.

"Oi!"

"What?"

"Go on then. Herey'a." He holds out a handful of bangers and points to a hole in the bank.

"Bet you can't get one down there." The hole's about twelve foot away.

"Easy."

"Go on then. Let's see you do it."

Johnny has a go and misses. In fact, his doesn't even go bang.

"Ya! You ponce. My sister could do better than that."

"It was a dud!" Johnny looks really fed up. It's my turn.

"Right. Watch this!" I fling my banger and it drops straight down the hole. I can't believe it.

"Yes!" squeals Johnny.

There's a muffled boom. Next minute, a big clump of bees come swarming out. All the big kids scatter in all directions. I throw myself on the ground, but the bees are all looking at Johnny and he's standing there like a lemon, not believing what's happening. Then, one stings him on top of the head.

"Aghhhh! Arghhhh!"

He falls over, like he's been tripped up by a wire, and he slides down the bank on his backside, right over a piece of broken glass.

"Arghhhhh!"

Last I see of him, he's running off into the distance clutching his head and his bum, blood pouring down his legs.

He never come to school the next day. We don't have Miss Hudson no more, we've gone up into Mrs. Willet's class. She said Johnny had to go up the hospital for stitches and perhaps his friends ought to make him a get-well card as he wouldn't be back for a while.

I done a cracking one, but she told me to rub all the bees off of it. Thing was, there was so many bees, by the time I'd rubbed them out there was no card left.

Course, now there's no Johnny to walk home with, so I've got to walk home on my own. Joan's got choir practice, or so she says. I don't think she likes me much to tell the truth. Either it's because I'm a boy, or it's because I smell. Could be both.

No big deal. Quite looking forward to it as it happens. On the way to school there was a little boat floating upturned in the pond. It was lying on one side, like it needed fixing. It must have belonged to some kid, but he'd left it there. I never had time to wade in and get it because Joan was worrying about being late for school. I don't think she knew I'd been throwing penny bangers with John. If she did know, she never said nothing.

All day I've been wondering if the boat's still there, floating in the reeds. I've got plans for it. I'm going to fix it up and paint it. Miss Hudson borrowed me her own paintbrush out of her pencil case. I asked Mrs. Willet, but she wouldn't let me take a school paintbrush home in case I forgot to bring it back.

Miss Hudson had a peach petticoat on with lace round the bottom. I'm thinking about the petticoat and the boat on the way home. I'm thinking, maybe I'll paint the boat peach, when I hear footsteps behind me. When I turn round, I see this kid from the juniors called Robert Paisley. I know it's Robert Paisley because I heard one of the dinner ladies yell at him for pulling a girl's skirt up in the playground.

"Did you see the bees?" he says. "Did you see them sting Johnny?"

"Might have."

"Are you going home or staying out playing?"

"Home."

I said that because I don't want him to see the boat. If he sees it he might want to keep it, or he might know whose it is and tell. He wants to know where I live.

"On the front. Shaftesbury Avenue."

"Did you know there's a stream down by the trees?" he says.

"Where?"

"I'll show you. It's got a minnow."

"What's a minnow?"

He looks at me funny, like I'm stupid or something.

"You know. A fish."

What? A big fish? A small fish? I don't know, so I follow him over to the trees.

"In there," he says.

I kneel down and look in the water, poking it with a twig. I can see something wriggling, but it ain't a fish. It's his reflection.

"I can see something. What's that?"

He kneels down next to me. He ain't got nothing on! He's starkers. He's taken everything off, even his shoes. It's cold and all the little hairs are standing up on his arms.

"You can take yours off if you want," he says.

"What are you doing? Going for a swim?"

"No. I like taking my clothes off and playing in the nude."

He goes in a crouch and hugs his knees.

"You do it," he says. "Go on."

"No, thanks."

I'm a bit scared to walk off in case he follows me, but I can't stop here. Not with him like that. It's not right. I get up like there's nothing wrong and brush my knees. I pretend to look for more minnows while I plan my escape. He's a lot bigger than me.

"Can't see any minnows. I've got to go now, Robert."

"Why?"

"My mum."

"What about her?"

"She'll have my tea ready."

He stares at me. He's breathing too hard, like he's got asthma or something. He picks up a stone and starts playing with it. Then he throws it at my leg, really hard. It don't half sting.

"Ouch. What was that for?"

"I'm only playing!" He throws back his head and laughs like a donkey. I start walking away from him, really slowly. My knees are shaking. Any minute I'm expecting a rock on the back of my head. Nothing so far.

If I turn round quickly, he'll be right behind my shoulder. I think I can hear him breathing but it might just be my own breath. My heart's thumping so hard, it's making my ears echo. Then I start thinking, perhaps I'm being stupid. Maybe he was only playing. It was only a little stone.

What's he doing? I daren't look. I can only imagine and what I'm imagining is probably far worse than what he's doing in real life. I don't turn round, I just start to walk faster, then a bit faster, so he don't notice I'm getting away. Suddenly, everything tells me to run full pelt and I go tearing down the hill.

I run all the way across the golf course and down to the pond without stopping. I've got this evil stitch in my side and my glasses are all steamed up. I throw myself down the bank and hide.

Has he gone? I peer through the reeds, looking for him, but there's no sign. I'm worrying about how I'm going to get home on my own from school tomorrow when, suddenly, I spot the boat. There it is, right in the middle of the pond.

I take off my socks and shoes and wade in. The mud at the bottom feels horrible. It sucks my toes, so I try and get it over with quickly. I grab the boat and turn back towards dry land.

"Hello, Mick!"

It's Robert Paisley. He's got my shoes. He's holding them next to his belly and pointing at them. He still hasn't put his clothes back on. If I run to the other bank and leg it home, he's not going to follow me, is he? Not with nothing on, surely?

"See you, Robert."

I wave. I can't believe I waved at him but something in me is so scared I want him to think I'm his friend. Keep him sweet. He's waving and calling out to me: "Mick, you forgot your shoes!"

I pretend I can't hear him. I skip and hop as fast as I can in the other direction, trying to look normal. Somehow, I get home in one piece with the boat. Only I've got no shoes and socks. Mum has a go at me and I try to explain, but it comes out sounding like a lie.

"This lad took them. He had no clothes on."

"What lad? What was he, a beggar or a tramp?"

"No. He goes to our school."

"Get them back off him or else. Where'd you get the boat from?"

"Found it."

"You didn't swop your shoes for it by any chance?"

"No."

"Oh, yeah?" She doesn't believe me.

"I never. Honest!"

She clips me round the head. She's been in a right funny mood lately. They both have. I think it's because she's skint. She's not on the mops no more and she doesn't like arsting Dad for money I don't think.

"What are you going to do for shoes, then? You're not having a new pair."

I've never had a new pair so I wasn't expecting any.

"I don't know what your dad's going to say when he gets in."

Not a lot, I don't expect. He doesn't say a lot these days. Things have changed. They don't sit together in the same chair no more, not like they used. I'm wondering if it's because I keep wetting the bed.

Maybe Johnny was right. Maybe my dad ain't the same as Terry's. It makes sense. Mum never liked me like she loves Terry. Not that I mind. Terry likes me a lot. He's walking now. In fact he's been walking quite a while. I learned him to walk. I put slices of Mars bars round the room and every time he stepped near a slice, I moved it away a bit. He soon cottoned on.

The only sad thing is, he don't play his invisible piano any more. Perhaps that's a sign of growing up. Anyway, he likes watching me fix my boat. I've given it a wash and dried it off on the boiler and now I'm trying to fix it up. I've even found some old paint in the shed. It ain't ours, but I don't suppose the landlord will miss it. It's green, not peach, I'm afraid.

The door bangs. It's my dad. I can hear my mum having a go at him.

"Don't say hello then. What's the matter with you?"

"Something's wrong with my eye."

"Like what? There's always something with you, isn't there?"

"How should I know? I'm not a bloody doctor, am I?"

"Alright. No need to bite my head off."

I can hear her slamming pans about. I'm having a bit of trouble getting the lid off my paint tin. It's all stuck round the edges. I can hear my dad shouting.

"Stop crashing about with those pans? Put them down! I've got a flaming headache right over this eye."

"Pardon me for getting your tea ready."

Right, I've got the paint lid off. Now, where's Miss Hudson's paintbrush? Terry's got it. He's chewing the end.

"Give us the brush will you, Tel?"

"No!"

"Go on, mate. I want to paint the boat."

He shakes his head. I grab the end of the brush. I don't snatch it or anything, just try and take it off him.

"Give it, Terry."

He goes nuts. Starts screaming because he don't want me to have it.

My dad bellows from the other room: "Will you two leave it out!"

I shut the door so he can't hear us. Terry's sucking the brush again. He's gonna ruin it.

"Come on, Tel, give us the brush."

I'm being really patient with him, but he's not giving in. He's stamping his feet now.

"No! NO! NO!"

So I take it. His eyes open wide and he does this really monkey-like screech. Suddenly, the door flies open and my dad marches over and *BANG!* smacks me right in the face. I never saw it coming. I thought he was going for Terry because it was him making all the noise but he never. He just kept coming towards me, then *BLAM!* Right on the button. Knocked me straight over the bed.

I stay where I fall, my legs and arms in the air and my arse on the floor. Folded in half, blood pouring out of my nose. My face don't hurt but something else hurts like it's killing me. I can't get my head round this. He decked me when it wasn't my fault. No warning. Nothin'.

Now where's he gone?

seven

I'm sure I've got a broken nose.

"No, you haven't. It's just bruised." Mum's looking at it by the window.

"Mum . . . it wasn't me making a noise."

"It was the both of you, but Terry's only little."

Her eyes are all red. Overnight, the bruise has spread right into both my cheeks. Dad's gone. I don't know where.

"He's working."

He ain't. How can he drive a lorry with an eye like that? It must have been really hurting him for him to have done what he done to me.

"Look . . . about what happened. It's got nothing to do with you, Mick."

"How come it was my nose that got hit then?"

She hasn't got an answer to that.

"Oh, you'll live," she says. "You're alright, aren't you?"

I nod. But I'm not alright. I've got an ache in my stomach, which is odd, because he never hit me there. It's a really deep punch of an ache. She can see I'm gutted. I wish she'd hold me, but she's holding Terry, so she can't. She opens a tin box and takes something out.

"Herey'a. Want a Wagon Wheel?"

I don't really. I only want one because I want her to give me something nice. To make up for being hit.

"Thanks." But I can't eat it. It wouldn't go down, even if I poked it with a stick.

"What's up? Don't you want it?"

"Can I save it?"

"You can eat it on the bus."

Mum and Dad have got friends in Rochford. Thelma and Ted. They've just bought a new house there. It's still a big building site with all new homes going up. I'm going to stay with them for a bit. She never said for how long. She gives me the bus fare.

"Mind you don't lose it, Mick. Put it in your pocket with the Wagon Wheel, yeah?"

"When am I coming home?"

"You haven't even got there yet. They've got a son called Peter about your age. You'll like him."

That's what she said about Stephen.

"Will you come and get me or Dad?"

"We'll see, shall we?"

She walks me to the bus stop in her slippers. It's not far but my bag's heavy. I remembered to put the boat in. I can show it to Peter when I get to Rochford.

Terry starts crying when I get on the bus. He's holding out his arms. He wants to come with me. I can see him mouthing my name.

"See you, Terry."

I tap on the window. "Terry . . . see you!" But he's going into one, kicking and yelling. Last I see him, Mum's put him under one arm, his little legs kicking the air like mad. Poor thing.

Mum's given me a note for Thelma. When I get there, I give it to her. She reads it quickly, breathes hard and gives it to Ted.

"Alright, duck. Go through," she says. "Peter's in the kitchen." I can hear her whispering to Ted in the hall.

"That must have been some whack Harry gave him. I don't think that's on, do you?"

"Must have really wound him up to have done that. Harry's not that way, is he?"

"There's no knowing, is there, Ted?"

Peter's playing with Meccano on the kitchen table and eating a jam sandwich.

"Wotcha, Peter. What you making?"

"It's a Spitfire."

He looks up. "Blimey. Who done that to your nose?"

"My dad."

"Why? What did you do?"

"Nothing."

"You must have done something."

I'm beginning to think he had a point. He wouldn't just have hit me for nothing, would he? I'm racking my brains to think of a reason as to why he done it so I could explain it to myself.

"I was painting a boat. I'll show you if you like." I get the boat out.

"Ah, that's good. Where did you get it?"

"Found it in the pond near my house."

He turns it over in his hands, admiring it. "I've got some other paints. Airfix paints! Will that work on wood, do you think?"

"I reckon."

I ask him if he's got any peach colour and tell him why. He wants me to tell him more about Miss Hudson. His teacher is an old dog, he says.

"So's Mrs. Willet. Wouldn't even lend me a paintbrush."

He goes to a different school than me. I'm telling him about seeing Miss Hudson's stocking tops and he's giggling like anything, then his mum comes in. He goes bright red.

"I see you two are getting on," she says and starts doing me some jam sandwiches.

I've never seen so many jam sandwiches in all my life. And they've got butter in. Not marg. I reckon my mum still thinks there's a war on.

"There you are, duck."

"What . . . all of them?"

"Well, only eat what you can manage."

My appetite's come back. I ask Peter if she always makes that many sandwiches and he says, yeah, like it happens every day. I show him my Wagon Wheel.

"I like them," he says. So I break it in half. I measure to make sure they are exactly the same size or it wouldn't be right. Like, if there's one apple and two kids, they should get half each. If they don't, your house gets smashed in by an aeroplane.

"There. That's your bit, Pete."

"Oh, thanks!"

I'm stuffed after the Wagon Wheel. I can't believe this house. It's brand new. Really clean and it's got loads of furniture, telephone, the lot. Peter's mum puts her hand on my shoulder.

"Come upstairs, Mick. I'll get you something for your nose."

The house has even got an upstairs.

"Coming, Thelma."

She don't want me to call her Thelma, only I wasn't sure of her last name.

"It's Mrs. Bracey."

She never said it nastily though. She sits me on the side of the bath and gets some ointment out of the cabinet and some cotton wool. She takes my glasses off.

"Ouch."

"Oh, you poor old soldier."

The ointment stinks.

"It's a bit smelly," she says, "but it'll do the trick. It'll take the bruising down."

She strokes my nose with the cotton wool. Good, firm strokes right across my cheeks. She shakes her head sadly and tuts. Not at me but at my wounds. The cotton wool comes away black.

"I don't know," she sighs. "What a business!" She starts running a bath.

"It's not bedtime yet is it, Mrs. Bracey?"

"No, but you'll feel better after a bath. It will help the ointment sink in."

"But I had a bath."

"When?"

"Er . . . can't remember. But I did have one."

She laughs quietly. "We have a bath every night in this house. I'll get you some of Peter's old clothes. I can always take them in a bit."

She leaves me to get undressed, which is good, because I'm feeling a bit shy.

"I'll be back in a minute to wash your hair," she says. "There's plenty of soap."

I lie back and close my eyes. The ointment is making my nose throb but it's a numb sort of throbbing. Quite nice, in fact. The water's not very deep but it's hot and the heat is making me sleepy. That and the sandwiches.

I think about Terry and wonder what he's doing and if he's stopped crying. Then I start crying. Not because my nose hurts but because of Mrs. Bracey being so kind. Why is she being so kind? Maybe that's what was in the note. My mum has asked her to be nice to me because she's sorry for what my dad done. That'll be it. Oh, well, she'll soon get fed up with me. Mrs. Bracey, I mean. Then she'll start behaving like a normal mother.

I make a little island for the soap with the sponge, biffing it up and down the bath. It's posh soap with writing on it, and it's pink. Our soap at home is yellow and hard.

"How are you getting on, Mick?" Mrs. Bracey comes back in and examines my neck.

"This bit's still dry," she says.

She soaps the sponge and scrubs my neck, under my chin, all over. She scrubs places that have never been scrubbed before, all the time giving me orders.

"Lift your foot. Arms up. Bend over."

Little bits of skin are floating round the edge of the bath. The water looks like someone's been peeling spuds in it.

"I think I'd better do your hair over the sink," she says, pulling the plug out. "Up you come!"

I hold my hands over my nuts so she can't see.

"Oh, give over," she says. "I've seen it all before. I used to be a nurse."

She wraps me up in a big, thick towel.

"Warm enough? How's your nose?"

"Throbbing."

"That's a good sign. That's the cream working."

She picks my clothes up, puts them in the bag and drops them out of the window. Then she guides me to a stool, sits me backwards with my neck against the sink and says, "Hairwash."

She checks my hair all over first with a nit comb, parting it and peering at my head.

"That's . . . fine," she says and starts lathering me up. She rubs so hard I think my head's going to come off. I'm going dizzy with it and I can't see too well without my glasses. She even whirls her fingers into my ears. When she pulls them out, they pop. She's so close I can smell the talcum powder under her arms.

She throws a jug of water over my hair. It's boiling.

"Sorry . . . is it too hot? Sorry, duck."

Then she throws a jug of cold over. I gasp.

"Too cold! Too cold!"

"That makes it nice and shiny," she says. "I read it in a magazine."

She puts another towel over my head and rubs hard. My lips are going all rubbery. I can't see a thing. She whisks the towel off.

"Boo! . . . Right, let's cut your nails."

By the time she's finished with me, I don't feel like me any more and I don't look like me. She's parted my hair differently to how I do it. I look a right twerp but she looks so pleased with me I don't say nothing. I don't want to hurt her feelings. I go downstairs in a pair of Peter's pyjamas. He grins at me.

"Didn't recognise you. Not going to bed are you?"

"Na. Your mum says I'm not to go out with me hair wet."

"Your hair's a different colour," he says. "I thought it was brown."

"So did I."

It's not though. Now she's washed it, it's gone almost blonde. Nothing like my dad's, unless his needs a good wash an' all. She must have washed all the colour out.

"See that building over there?" Peter points out of the window at a half-built house.

"Yeah."

"That's where we all meet."

"Who?"

"Well," he says, "there's me, Brian Seaward, Tony Crowley, Kenny, Cottie and Barry Lucas. Only we don't like Barry Lucas."

"Why not?"

"He's mental."

I tell him about Robert Paisley taking his clothes off.

"Ugh," he says. "Is he a faggot?"

"What's a faggot?"

"You know." He flaps his wrist.

"Oh yeah, I think he was. Definitely one of those." I haven't got a clue what he's talking about, but I don't let on in case he thinks I'm an idiot.

"Barry Lucas isn't that way," he says, "he's just a headcase. I saw him trying to hang a dog once."

"What? By its neck?"

"Yeah."

"Did he kill it?"

"Na. The branch broke. It was a big dog."

I don't like the sound of that.

"If I saw someone trying to kill a dog, do you know what I'd do?"

Peter can't guess.

"I'd kill him." I wouldn't really. I couldn't kill anyone, but what I wanted him to know was how sorry I was for the dog. Pete looks thoughtful.

"Hmm . . . I don't think anyone could kill Barry Lucas."

"What? Not even Hitler?"

"Hitler couldn't, could he? He's dead isn't he?"

"Yeah, but if he was alive he could kill Barry Lucas, couldn't he?"

Peter shakes his head seriously. "I doubt it."

"Peter . . . this Barry Lucas . . . is he big or what?"

Peter shakes his head. "He just thinks he is."

Far away, I can hear the sound of windows being smashed.

"That'll be him," says Pete.

eight

I think the best way of dealing with this Barry Lucas is to just be friendly and not wind him up. So I look up at him, smiling all the while, craning my neck.

"Alright, Barry?"

"Who are you? A monkey's arse?"

He's sitting on top of the main beam of an unfinished house, having a fag. I reckon he must be what? Thirteen?

"He's nine," says Pete.

"But he's got a moustache."

"I know. And he's got hairs under his arms."

Barry is swinging off the main beam by his knees now.

"Look, monkey arse. No hands."

"Where'd you learn to do that then, Barry?"

He takes a drag of his fag, still swinging by his knees, and ignores me. If he falls, he'll be dead.

"Leave him," says Pete. "If he don't want to talk it's best to just ignore him."

"I don't like him calling me monkey arse. Why's he calling me that?"

"Maybe it's your trousers."

"They ain't *my* trousers, they're yours."

I'm wearing Pete's old ones. He's a lot bigger than me and where his mum's taken the waist in it's made the arse stick out like a baboon's. Pete apologises.

"She's not very good at sewing."

"I thought she was a nurse. Nurses have to stitch people up, don't they?"

"Yeah. And, Mick . . . say someone had his hand cut off, she'd probably sew it to his foot, wouldn't you think!"

We're chortling with laughter.

"And, Pete . . . listen to this one . . . if someone had his head cut off she'd sew it to his bum."

Pete doubles up.

"And, Mick . . ."

"What?"

"Look what she's done to your hair!"

The tears are rolling down his face now. My hair's meant to flop over at the front but she didn't like it doing that. No. What she done is rub it with soap and comb it up and over, in a high quiff on top. Like a wave. It feels like a lump of cardboard. You could sit a marble in it and it would stay there.

"Want to play marbles?"

Another kid comes over. Brian Seaward. He's got really white hair and no eyelashes. Big for his age. He takes a little leather pouch out of his pocket and rattles it at us, then nudges Pete.

"Who's he?"

"Mick. He's Mick. He's staying with us."

Brian puts his hand out for me to shake which I think is a funny thing to do, but I shake it anyway.

"Alright, Brian?"

"Who done that to your nose?" he says. "Barry Lucas?"

Pete answers for me. "No. He was in a fight."

I don't know why he lied like that for me. Maybe he thought if people knew my dad done it, I'd be embarrassed. I changed the subject.

"I ain't got any marbles. I want to play, like, but I ain't got any."

Brian shrugs. "Doesn't matter. As long as you give them back after. You playing, Pete?"

Peter nods and we both follow Brian. He wants to choose the spot where we're going to play. Which is fair enough, what with them being his marbles. Suddenly there's a shout from the rafters.

"Oi! Seaward! Where are you going?"

Brian sighs deeply and tuts. But Lucas wants an answer.

"Seaward! Where are you going, I said!"

"To play marbles."

"Wait."

We look up. Barry Lucas is scuttling along the main beam of the house like a crow. I swear he's going to fall. Deep down, we're all hoping he does. Not because we wish him any harm, but we don't want him to play and it would be a good way of avoiding it. And it would be exciting to see a dead body with real blood.

"Hey, monkey arse!"

I really hate him calling me that, especially in front of the others. I look up. He's standing on a beam, right above my head.

"What?"

"Catch."

He jumps. There must be a thirty-foot drop at least. I think he's going to land on top of me. If he does, that's it. I'm dead. And if he doesn't? I'm still dead, because he'll probably kill me for stepping out of the way.

As it is, he lands on his feet, skids on his haunches and kicks one leg out from underneath me. I'm completely winded. Pete grabs me under the arms and pulls me back up.

"You OK?"

"I dunno."

Brian reckons I've gone a bit pale. Barry Lucas is lying there, pretending to be dead with his eyes rolled up and his mouth hanging open. He's dribbling. We all ignore him and eventually he rolls over until he's right up against Brian. Then he puts his hand out and begs for marbles.

Brian dishes them out. They're really lovely, some of them. My favourites are the clear ones with the twists of green in the middle and the really small, sparkly ones. I don't like the solid ones though. Brian's given me a dirty white one with yellow streaks on.

"Can I swop it, Bri?"

"Why? It's a good'n."

"It looks like a blind man's eye."

"Yeah, but it's nice and heavy. It's a good striker, Mick."

I don't like the look of it at all. I've seen this eye in my Eileen dreams. In the end, Barry Lucas swops it for a twisty one for which I am very grateful.

"Cheers, Barry."

"That's alright, monkey."

He never said "arse" that time. Just "monkey," which I don't mind. Maybe he's not so bad after all. We start to play. It's a bit windy and the marbles keep cheating. Running away from wherever we put them. I'm doing OK as it happens. I've won three off Pete and one off Barry and now I'm after Brian's big one. He calls it his Kingy.

"Go on, Kingy him!" says Pete. "You can do it easy!"

I line my twisty one up and close one eye. I'm about to flick it when Barry looms right into my face with the blind man's marble screwed into one eye.

"Agh!"

I miss.

"Ah, that's not fair. See what he did? What'd ya do that for, Lucas?"

I can feel all the anger steaming through my body. I'm surprised at how narked I am, because I don't usually get like that. Pete looks a bit scared.

"It doesn't matter, Mick. Take it again. He can take it again, can't he, Bri?"

But that's not the point. I've really got the hump with Lucas now, or maybe it's all been building up and Lucas has tipped me over the edge.

"Lucas, you stupid git!"

I shouldn't have said that to him, because now Lucas has pulled a steel comb out of his jacket. He's sharpened the end of the comb to a point, like a dagger. Pete pulls me away.

"Run, Mick! Quick! Before he combs you!"

Brian's scrabbling for his marbles and me and Pete are skidding and sliding across the wet grass.

"Is he following?"

"I dunno . . . just run!"

Me and Pete dive inside a workman's hut and catch our breath. Pete grabs my sleeve and panics.

"Mick, where's Bri?"

"I thought he was behind us."

We're thinking the worst when Brian strolls into the hut looking really hacked off.

"What's up, Bri? Did he comb you?"

"No. Worse."

"What?"

"He ate my Kingy."

We peer out of the doorway one by one and there's Lucas squatting in the dirt, eating marbles like they was boiled sweets. We sit there in silence, feeling trapped. Pete's the first to speak.

"What shall we do now?"

Brian says he's got to go and have the brace tightened on his teeth. His mum will tell him off if he's late. He seems quite scared of her but surprisingly not all that scared of Lucas.

"By the way," he says, "you shouldn't have run off like that. If you run, he'll chase you like a lion. The only reason he never came after you two is because I stood my ground."

Pete pulls a face. "You're joking, aren't you?"

He shakes his head.

"What you want to do is give him a piece of string or something."

I ask him what the hell for.

Brian shrugs. "He likes string."

Brian feels sorry for Lucas and says it ain't surprising he's the way he is. I'm dying to know what's up with him, in case it's catching.

"His old man knocks him about," says Brian. "Brain-damaged him when he was little. That's right, isn't it, Pete?"

Pete takes one look at me and tells Brian to shut his face.

"Why? It's true. What's up? What are you going 'shh' for?"

"Shut up, OK?"

"No! What for, anyway?"

Brian doesn't understand what he's done wrong, because Pete won't tell him in front of me. He goes off in a huff. Pete's a bit worried for his safety.

"Just forget it, Brian. I didn't mean anything by it. Shall we come with you?"

"No need."

"Yeah, but what about Lucas? It'll be safer with three of us."

Brian screws his nose up.

"I can handle him. Anyway, it's you he wants to kill, Mick. You're the one who called him a git."

We watch him go. Lucas doesn't even look up at him.

Pete says he could understand in a way why Brian respects Barry Lucas. Barry's like a dog you don't know. If a dog gets vicious, it ain't its fault, not if someone's been horrible to it. You just have to be on your guard.

"Yeah, but aren't you scared of him, Pete?"

"Are you?"

"Only if you are."

It's an exciting sort of scared though. I loved it when he jumped off the beam even though I hated him calling me monkey arse and knocking me over. But he never knocked me over on purpose. I thought he was brave, jumping off that beam. Deep down, I think in a way he was doing it to make us laugh, so we'd like him more.

I even loved it when he pulled that comb out, even though I was crapping myself he'd stick it in me. I was even a bit disappointed when he didn't chase us. I think if he'd of hurt me, he wouldn't have meant it. It was just the way he played. So what's my dad's excuse?

"Pete."

"What?"

"Why did Barry's dad knock him about?"

"He was an alky."

My dad doesn't drink much. He goes to the pub but he never gets legless or nothing. He hit me sober. I could have understood if he'd had a few.

Barry's dad is dead now. We wondered what Barry would have been like if he hadn't had his head battered from an early age.

"Probably really boring," Pete reckons.

"Yeah."

It's been raining for days now, so we're stuck indoors mostly. I've been doing a bit more to the boat, varnishing it and that.

Pete's dad, Ted, otherwise known as Mr. Bracey, seems quite interested in it.

"That's looking nice," he says.

"Thanks."

"You've got a bit of a flair for that sort of thing, I think. What do you want to be when you leave school?"

"I dunno. Deckchair man, maybe."

Pete's dad rubs his chin. "Deckchair man? Hmmm. Can't be much fun in bad weather. What you need is a trade. A proper skill."

Pete's rolling his eyes. His dad works for British Road Services. He starts telling me all about it while I touch up my ship's hull. Peter's drumming his fingers and pulling bored faces behind his old man's back.

"It's stopped raining," he says. "We can go out on the skate board. Coming, Mick?"

"I want to finish this bit."

"Finish it later," he begs.

Peter lives on top of a hill, so what we do is get a piece of board, put it on a roller skate, sit on it and come flying all the way down.

"Steer it, Mick!"

"How?"

"From side to side."

I soon get the hang of it. It's a good crack. Mind you, it doesn't half make a noise because of the metal wheels.

After about an hour we've managed to get ourselves shouted at by all the neighbours.

"Clear off, you boys."

"Peter Bracey, I know where your mother lives!"

In the end, there's no one left to annoy, so we decide to go back up to the building site to make a camp.

Mr. Bracey says Harold Macmillan is building a new Britain after the war. I don't know who he is. A builder, I suppose.

Funny thing is, as fast as he puts his houses up, kids like us are pulling them down again.

It's something to do, innit?

There's a load of kids already there when we arrive. Tony, Brian, Brian's brother Kenny, Tony's sister Vivian and a lad called Adrian Cottington, Cottie for short. Barry Lucas is nowhere to be seen, but that don't mean he ain't there.

Over the way, in one of the finished houses, there's a cripple sitting in his garden in a wheelchair. I say garden, but really it's just mud at the moment. Mud and a path and a fence.

Cottie is saying, "Go on, it's your turn," to Kenny, but Kenny don't want to do whatever it is Cottie's telling him. Cottie puts his foot down.

"Go on! Otherwise you can't be in our camp."

"Go on, Kenny," says Vivian.

I ask Pete what Kenny's got to do.

"Watch," says Pete. "It's really funny. You'll crease up."

So Cottie pushes Kenny out of the doorway of our camp into the muddy wasteland in between the half-built houses and everyone else urges him on.

"Go on, Kenn-eeee!"

Kenny slopes away from us, grinning. I'm not quite sure what he's going to do and by the looks of him, nor's he. Then he runs up to the man in the wheelchair, stops, and does a silly dance, sticking two fingers up at him all the while. The bloke in the wheelchair ignores him.

"GO on, Kenny! GO on, Kenny!"

So Kenny grabs a handful of mud and throws it at the wheelchair wheels. Now the man turns round, waves his stick at Kenny, waves his stick at us and all the kids are wheezing and laughing. Little Vivian's got her hands stuffed up her dress going, "Don't! I'll pee! I'll pee!"

"Told you it was funny!" roars Pete. "It's funny, isn't it?"

"Yeah." And I start laughing. But I'm not laughing at the bloke in the wheelchair. I'm laughing because they're laughing, that's all.

"Your turn," says Cottie.

I'm still laughing my socks off. "Your turn, Mick," says Pete, tears rolling down his face.

"What?"

I stop laughing. What does he mean, my turn? I don't want to do it. It don't feel right doing that to the bloke somehow. But it can't be all that bad if Pete's doing it because he's a good sort. He's my mate.

"How come it's my turn?"

"Everyone else has had a go," says Vivian.

"No, they ain't."

"Yeah. Earlier. You wasn't here then, Mick. It was a right laugh," says Tony. "Vivian showed him her drawers, didn't you, Viv?"

I turn to Pete. "You go first."

"No. It's alright. You can." He smiles cheerfully, like he's doing me a favour. There's no getting out of this, not that I can see.

"Go on, Mick."

I saunter out of our door and across the wasteland, like I'm going the shops for my mum. The man in the wheelchair has got his back to the fence. What I could do is run up and give the wheelchair a shove. Not to hurt him. Just to show the others I'm not chicken.

I keep telling myself, "The cripple in the wheelchair is a stupid git . . . the cripple in the wheelchair is a stupid git," to force myself to do it. Any minute now, he'll turn round. I'm starting to hate him now for sitting there and being part of the game. For putting me through this.

Any second now he'll turn round and wave his stick at me. Maybe even before I get there, so then I won't even have to touch the wheelchair. That's all he's got to do . . . wave the stick and I'll leave him alone. It's a bit like "What's the time, Mr. Wolf?" Just a game.

I creep forward a few more yards. A few more . . . a few more. I'm just about to yank the wheelchair handles down when two enormous hands grab me round the waist and lift me right off the ground.

"Got you, you little sod."

Whoever's got me tucks me under his arm and runs off round the back of the house. My glasses are banging up and down on my nose and all the blood is rushing to my head.

I can hear someone yelling. And then I realise it's me. Argggggh! Where are we going?

Round and round the wasteland, past our camp. I can't hear or see the others. Everything's whizzing past upside down. I can hardly breathe and Peter's trousers are riding down on me. I try to hoist them up with one hand and hold onto my specs with the other. It's like the nastiest fairground ride ever.

We're slowing down. The man carrying me boots open the cloth door of a workman's hut and throws me into a chair. We are not alone. There's the bloke in the wheelchair and two other men. They look like him, only younger, without the beard. He's got what looks like a stick-on beard.

Perhaps they're his sons. Funny. I never thought of him belonging to anybody before, having a wife and sons. I just thought he was a cripple.

They're all staring at me, saying nothing. I think they're going to murder me. I don't know where to look except away.

Then one of them, the one who grabbed me, starts kicking my chairleg. Kick. Kick. Kick. I'm sweating like a pig. I clench my bum cheeks together in case I do one. Kick. Kick. Kick. This bloke's fists are the size of my head, I reckon. Big, horny, yellow thumbnails. Any minute now, he's going to kick the chair away. I know he is.

"Why are you kids taking the micky out of this man?" He says it ever so quietly.

"What?"

"Why are you taking the micky out of this man?" He puts his hand on the old man's shoulder.

"I don't know. Wasn't me. It was the others."

"You what?"

"It was the others."

I think that is the worst thing I could have said because now I look like a double coward. I'm a bully and a grass.

The man in the wheelchair puts his head in his hand and looks at me thoughtfully, head on one side, like he's trying to work out what sort of animal I am. He don't look angry. He just looks like he's deciding what he's going to do to me. Or have done to me. The man with cabbages for fists kicks my chair again. This time it moves slightly.

"Are you sorry?"

"Yeah."

"Well, tell him that." Kick. Kick. Kick.

"I'm sorry! I'm sorry! I'm sorry!"

The man in the wheelchair looks at me like I'm a maggot in his meat. I revolt him.

"Get rid of him. He stinks."

His voice sounds bored and empty and it's the emptiness of it that puts the wind up me. He's past caring what happens to him. He's going to have me murdered. Two of them grab me by the shoulders and pull me out of the chair. They drag me to the door. I've probably only got a few minutes to live.

"Please don't strangle me I don't want to be strangled anything but strangled."

I'm not sure if I'm saying it out loud or just thinking it. They drop me onto the mud outside, onto my knees. I roll into a ball and cover my head. Expecting what? To be beaten to death with a cripple's stick? To have my ribs kicked in by three pairs of boots bigger than my dad's? Why me? Why not Cottie or Brian or Tony?

I wait. And while I wait I step right out of my body and have a look round. I'm calm now. I'm thinking what a lovely day it is, with the weather. Cold but bright. I see this little slug of a kid curled up in the damp grass with his mate's trousers half-off and I think how funny he looks.

I can see the three men laughing at him and one of them says, "And if any of his mates give our dad any grief, they'll be sorry."

It's like film running in slow motion. It's not for real. I close my eyes. Fade to black. Interval.

Next thing I know, Barry Lucas is shaking me like a rat. "Are you dead, monkey? Or what?"

I'm not sure, to be honest.

n i n e

I never took the mick out of anyone after that. Pete said all the others thought I'd been murdered. They knew they should have come and got me but they were too scared, in case the same happened to them. Thanks, lads. The only one who came to my rescue was Barry Lucas and that was only because he liked dead things, I reckon.

He was a bit disappointed when he realised I was still breathing.

Mrs. Bracey is calling me up the garden. She's pegging my bedsheet on the line.

"Are you upset about something, Mick? Only this is the second time this week and you've been fine for ages."

The sheet flaps about, telling the whole street what I've done.

"I'm fine."

She don't believe me but she doesn't press charges. Just looks at me with her kind face, pegs sticking out of her mouth. I give her a hand with the clothes prop.

"Sorry about it, Mrs. Bracey. I can't seem to help it. I have these dreams."

"What dreams?"

I tell her about the head-squashing dream. She listens very carefully.

"I wonder what that's all about?" she says. "It sounds horrid."

"It is."

It's been getting worse ever since the man in the wheelchair business. The more I think about it, the more I wonder why it was me that got caught. I never started it and I never actually done nothing. And if I had done, it would only have been because they'd have done me if I'd chickened.

It was like my dad hitting me all over again. It wasn't me making the noise. It was Terry.

And Mrs. Pearce should never have given Stephen an apple and not me. It's like, I've been put on this earth to be given a good hiding. I never said that to Mrs. Bracey though. I didn't want her to think I was a whiner.

"Maybe it's to do with the plane crash," she said. "Your mum told me about that. She was in a right state about it. Especially about Stephen, poor little soul."

Quite a lot of people turned up at the funeral. Most of the street, in fact, because it wasn't just Mrs. Pearce and Stephen who got killed.

There were two other little girls. Sisters, they were. Sandra and Susan Carter. Their mum had gone up the hairdresser's and left them on their own in the house. They both had measles at the time. The firemen had to dig them out of their beds with spades. It was in all the papers.

One of my jobs at home was to cut the newspaper pages into six squares and thread them on a bit of string to hang on a nail by the toilet. The day after the crash, there was a photo of Sandra and Susan sitting back to back on a stool, smiling in white dresses and shoes.

I was just about to cut the page when Mum snatched the scissors off me.

"Don't!"

"What? What've I done?"

Her face was really pale. "Don't . . . cut them. Just don't."

She turned her back on me and looked at the page she'd grabbed. Then she dropped her arm to her side and sobbed into her empty hand.

"Mum . . . but you said I was to cut the paper and I was just . . ."

"I'll be alright in a minute," she said. "Go out, please. Go on . . . Go ON!"

She wiped her eyes and the newspaper print made a big black streak under them. I tried not to laugh, but I ended up making this noise like a donkey. She looked so funny and so sad with her wet, streaky face.

"Don't you bloody laugh. You think this is funny, do you?" She waved Sandra and Susan at me.

"No."

"Two little dead girls. Is that funny?"

She threw a cup at me. It didn't break.

"Mum!"

She stood there for a few seconds. Then she walked over, picked the cup up, put it back on the table and went out of the room.

"Where are you going? Don't go, Mum." Because she did walk out once, after a ruck with my dad. I thought she wasn't ever coming back.

"I'm going to wash my face."

Her voice broke at the end of it. I heard her running the tap and over the top of it I could hear her sobbing in great big gulps. I never meant to make her cry like that.

I walk with Mrs. Bracey back up the garden path.

"Stephen was your pal, wasn't he?" she says. "You must miss him."

I didn't. I didn't ever really get to know him, did I? What I did know of him, I didn't like. I couldn't feel sorry for him. I really tried. I tried to cry at the funeral like everyone else, but nothing came. I don't think he was so horrible he deserved to be killed, but he might have been. Him being dead didn't make him any nicer.

"Your mum said it could have been you." Mrs. Bracey snaps a dead rose off a bush. Could have or should have? I've been here nearly five weeks now. No letters, nothing. It's like they've forgotten all about me. Maybe they've moved.

I'm still wondering what's happened to them weeks later when the summer holidays are over and I've gone back to school. I'm still living at Pete's, but I'm at my old school, only in the juniors.

I've got a man teacher called Mr. Arnell. Johnny reckons he's a faggot but his sister says he isn't, he's just French. No one can believe how I've grown. I'm still one of the smallest in the class but at least I've grown into Pete's trousers. And I've gone up a shoe size. Mrs. Bracey says she's fattening me up for Christmas.

Anyway, I'm sitting in the school dining hall in my new shoes (Pete's old ones) mashing jam into my semolina when all the little bristles start tingling on the back of my neck. They used to be hairs, those bristles, only Mrs. Bracey shaved them off with Mr. Bracey's razor to make me smart for the new term.

My stomach's gone into a knot. I can hear footsteps coming across the wooden floor and they sound like Mum's. I'm sure it's her, but I daren't trust my feelings, just in case I've got it wrong. I keep staring at my pudding with my spoon in the air, listening but not daring to look. The footsteps come nearer and nearer and then they stop. I can't move.

"Hello, Mick."

"Alright, son? What's for pudden?"

It's Mum and Dad. I stare at my plate.

"I dunno. Semolina." I still can't look at them.

"Terry's here."

I can look at him. Terry! Ah, Terry! At least, I think it's him. He's got so big. He don't look like a baby no more. He's a proper little kid.

"Say hello to Mick then, Terry."

Terry's not sure what to do. For an awful minute, I think he's forgotten who I am, then he says, "Give us some dam, Mick, yeah?" He couldn't say jam yet.

I can hear the other kids whispering in the background. Why are his mum and dad here? What happened? What's he done now?

I scrape some jam up on my spoon and give it to Terry to lick. I want to give him such a cuddle but I can't in front of everyone.

"Well," says Mum, "pleased to see us?"

"What are you doing here?"

I wasn't being funny, I just didn't know why they'd come. It had been so long. Maybe someone had died. Soon as I said it, all these thoughts went through my head and I wished I'd never asked her the question. I didn't want to know the answer.

"Something's happened." Mum is smiling.

"What?" I feel really dizzy now. *Thump, thump, thump.*

"You'll never guess."

I don't even bother to try. I couldn't bear the disappointment.

"I've only won the pools." She said it so loud the whole hall went silent. I just shook my head and kept shaking it.

"She has, son. She's won the pools. We've come to take you home."

He puts both hands on my shoulders and gives them a squeeze. I'm too choked to speak. I think it's because deep

{91}

down I thought she was going to say she'd got Eileen back. Winning the pools just seems like another smack in the face.

"Are you pleased?"

"Course he's pleased, Connie. Look at him! He can't speak, can you, son?"

If I did, I'd crack up. I'm happy about the money. Course I am. But I'm used to living with Peter and I'd put Mum and Tel and Dad at the back of my mind where I wouldn't miss them so much and where Dad couldn't hurt me no more.

"Seventy-five grand, Mick," he says. "Seventy-five grand."

I try and concentrate on the money. I try and imagine what seventy-five grand looks like but I can't. I can't even imagine one grand or half a grand. I get up from the chair and push it under the table noisily.

"Oi, Spicer! Where do you think you're going?"

It's some clever git from the next table. Really lippy, he is. Top juniors. Dinner monitor. And I'm not meant to stand up until he tells me. I stare at him. Usually I'd be scared but my dad's standing behind me and I know he can hit.

"I said, where d'you think you're going, Spicer?"

"Out . . . I'm going out. We've won the pools and I ain't coming back."

The room goes quiet again. Then, as I turn to leave, I can hear them all murmuring, "What did he say?"

"He said he'd won the pools."

"He never has, has he?"

I can feel them all watching me as I walk out. Johnny runs after me.

"Is it true what they're saying?"

"Yer. It is, Johnny."

"Aren't you coming back, Mick?"

"No."

"Oh."

He says it really sulkily, like I've let him down. I don't know why I thought I wasn't coming back. I just felt that now I was a rich kid, I could do whatever I liked. There wasn't a lot of point in learning nothing, because I wouldn't need a job now. I was made.

There's a car outside. Dad goes over to it and starts fiddling with the door.

"Mum . . . someone will see him!"

She laughs. "So? It's our car."

Our car. Just like that. We've got a car . . . a Ford Anglia. The Spicers have got a car. Spicers don't have cars. But there it is. I'm getting into it. My Spicer arse is sitting in the Spicer car.

"How much did it cost, Mum?"

"What?"

"The car. How much?"

She looks at my dad.

"Oh, ten shillings, thereabouts," he says.

That seems a bit cheap for such a lovely motor. I mean, it's brand new by the looks of it.

"It's good for that, isn't it, Mum?"

"Oh no, we didn't buy it." She laughs. "It's hired. Your dad hired it."

He laughs too now. "That's what it cost to hire. We ain't keeping it."

"Oh."

I really want to keep this car.

"Why not? Why can't we keep it, Mum?" I'm talking to her but he keeps answering.

"What for?" he says. "What do we want a heap of junk like this for? No, we're gonna get a decent motor. We're gonna get a Lanchester Drop-head Coupé." He pats my mum's knee.

"That's a real sporty car."

"Get off," she squeals. "You only want me for my money." And he says yes.

We're going all the way to London.

"Why are we, Mum?"

He never lets her speak. "Your mum's got to go to the bank."

She's got to go to a special bank. You can't just go to one in Southend, not when you've won the pools.

When we get to London, Dad parks the car in the Holloway Road and Mum gets out.

"Ta-ta. Won't be long."

"Ta-ta."

She's got a new coat and new shoes. Real new, I mean. Maybe she hired those and all. Who knows? I watch her as she walks away. She still hasn't asked me how I am, but I suppose it doesn't matter now. We're rich and when you're rich, you're happy.

"We're rich, Terry," I tell him.

I'm glad he's sitting in the back with me. I don't want to be on my own with my dad right yet because I haven't got the measure of him. I don't want to catch his eye in the mirror, so I just look out of the window all the time, praying Terry don't start kicking up because if he does, it might rile my dad and he'll think it's my fault all over again.

"Did you enjoy your holiday?" he says.

"It was alright."

So that's where I've been. On my holidays. Having a little holiday round at Pete's. Like it was the truth or something. Well, maybe it is.

"You've shot up."

"Thanks."

"You're much taller."

How he can tell, I don't know, because I'm sitting down. Then Terry starts.

"Dad, I'm hungry."

"Alright, Terry. Terry, get your feet off the seat."

"Why?"

"You'll get them all dirty."

I give Terry a warning look but he doesn't take any notice. He's not scared of my dad one bit, I can tell.

"I won't, Dad," he shouts. "Dad! I won't!"

"Be a good boy or you won't get no sweeties."

Terry takes one foot away and leaves the other one on the chair in front, just to be bloody awkward. Dad just shakes his head and grins.

"You little sod."

I'm beginning to think I must have dreamed my battered nose. This is my dad. My real dad. He ain't scary, he's nice. He wouldn't hit me.

"Dad."

"Yes, Mick."

"You know that boat I got out of the pond?"

"What boat?"

He's forgotten all about it. Maybe he's forgotten all about hitting me too.

"I finished painting it. I'll show you if you like. I'll get it off of Pete when I next go there for me holidays, shall I?"

"Alright. What'd you paint it with? Gloss?"

"Airfix paints. Pete's got loads of them."

"Yeah. They're good those. Hard to get off the brush though."

"Yeah. You have to use turps, Dad."

I can't wait to show him the boat. Mr. Bracey thought I done it nicely, so Dad will probably think it's smashing. I might even let him keep it as a present. To say sorry for making Terry yell like that when his eye hurt.

"There's your mum, look."

She's walking so lightly and she looks so happy. She waves her purse at us and gets back in the car, all breathless.

"Did you get it, Mum?"

It must be folded up really small, I'm thinking, to fit in her purse. Or maybe she's stashed the rest in her handbag. Even so. Seventy-five grand? It must be a bit of a squeeze.

"Have you got it, Mum?"

"Not all of it, silly. Just a hundred for now."

"Just!" says my dad.

She opens her purse and shows us.

"Blimey."

She takes a pound note out and gives it to me. I've never held one before. It feels lovely and crisp.

"There y'are, Mick."

"What? Is it to keep, like?"

"Course it's to keep."

She can't believe my face.

"Look at him, Harry!"

My dad laughs. "What are you going to buy, son?"

I don't know. I don't know what I'm going to buy. I've only ever had pennies and sixpences and threepences before, except for the stuff I found in the bushes and even they were mostly coppers.

"Is it enough for a cap-gun?"

Dad says it's enough for three cap-guns. I only want one, but I want one desperately.

When we get back to Southend I ask him to drop me off at the shop. The shopkeeper's just about to close, but I wave my pound note at him and he nods his head. Money opens doors.

I buy a cap-gun, loads of caps and a holster for seven-and-sixpence and he still gives me a load of change.

I sit on the wall and put my new holster on. I load the caps and crouch down behind a wall. When the shopkeeper comes out to lock up, I shoot him.

"Pee-ow! Pee-ow!"

"And a very good evening to you too, sonny," he says.

Me? I'm the fastest draw in Shaftesbury Road.

ten

It didn't take long to spend the quid. Bought a load of caps for my gun and ate the rest in Mars bars. It's strange. I thought we'd have moved to a posh house by now, but we haven't. And the car's gone back.

Mum's got more new clothes. Had to, really, she's getting so fat. Even my dad's noticed.

"Oi . . . fatty!" and he'd slap her on the arse. Not hard or nothing. Just enough to make her tell him off a bit. She was laughing though.

Even I'm fatter now we're buying proper food. We had bacon the other day. It took Mum a while to get used to eating good stuff. It made her sick at first, but she seems alright now.

It seems like a million years ago since I was living at Pete's. I ask Mum, why don't we go and live near him, in Rochford? On Pete's estate. It's all new houses. All with toilets indoors and proper kitchens and baths you can fill just by turning the taps on and empty just by pulling the plug out. That's gotta be better than doing it all with a jug.

If we bought one of them houses, I could have my own room, instead of sharing with Terry. Not that I mind sharing with Terry, it's just that he fiddles with the little wooden models I've been making. He doesn't mean to break them, but he does and it isn't half annoying.

"It's want, want, want with you," Mum says.

"It ain't just for me though, is it? It's for all of us. And now you've won the money . . ." She rolls her eyes.

"Money, money, money. Stop going on about the money," she says, "and put that cricket bat down before you knock something over."

"Give us a game. Go on."

"Ask your dad."

"He's reading the paper. He won't. Just give us a few overs."

"I'm too tired."

"Just a few . . . please?"

"Oh, for God's sake." She throws the tea towel down. She wobbles slowly downstairs like she's sulking and kicks her shoes off onto the grass.

"They're killing me. Where am I supposed to stand?"

"Bowling or batting?"

"How should I know?"

"Go that end."

She takes ages. I can tell she don't want to play. I make a little crease in the lawn with the bat.

"Don't do that. You'll spoil the grass."

"I've got to. It's a crease. That's what you have to do in cricket."

"What? Spoil the grass? Can't you mark it with a stick or something?"

Mothers. What do they know about cricket?

"Bowl, then, Mum."

She tuts. She throws the ball underarm and it goes up in the air and lands in a rosebush.

"Mu-u-um!"

"What? You said to bowl."

"That's not bowling. You're meant to throw it overarm, like this."

I demonstrate, doing a run-up and throwing an imaginary ball. "You're meant to aim it at the wicket!"

"I'm not running about like that," she says. "I'll throw it but I'm not running about."

I try to get the ball out of the rosebush and a thorn gets stuck in my jumper.

"Mum . . . I'm stuck."

"Don't pull. You'll make a hole in the wool."

"Don't worry. You can buy a new jumper. We're rich aren't we, Mum?"

Dad sticks his head out of the window. "Telephone," he calls.

It ain't our telephone. It's in the hall. Everyone uses it. You have to put money in it, like the fruit machines. Mum frowns, then she hurries indoors, like she can't wait to get away from me.

"Mum! You said you'd play!"

"The phone," she says.

I try to unhook myself from the thorn, but I can't. So I try to wriggle out of the jumper while it's still hooked to the bush. My head's pulled inside it, like a tortoise. The world looks ever so funny through knitted wool. I manage to pull one arm out of my sleeve, still with my head inside, but then the other sleeve gets trapped on another thorn and I can't back out. I'm trapped. It's quite scary, because I can't see properly and my face is roasting.

Suddenly, someone kicks me up the bum. It's Terry.

"Dad says come quick. Mum's got to go up the hospickle. What you doing?"

"Looking for my cricket ball."

"Oh. Can I play, Mick?"

"Unhook me."

"Only if you let me play."

"Yeah, alright, Terry. Who was that on the phone?"

"Nan somebody."

"Nan who?"

He don't know.

"Nanoo, Nanooo."

He's good with his fingers for his age. He unhooks the thorn and I wriggle out of my jumper, leaving part of it stuck to the bush. Dad shouts at us to come in. Terry sulks.

"But we're playing cricket! Mick said I could."

Dad don't look best pleased, so we go inside.

"Come on, Tel."

"It's not fair."

"No, I know it ain't. Why's Mum going up the hospital, do you know?"

"She's getting a baby."

Nobody tells me nothing. Dad never says much on the bus on the way to the hospital. All Mum says is, "Why did we give the car back?" over and over again. She's been crying.

"Mum. How come you never told us about the baby?"

"I thought you knew."

"I never. How come you never said?"

She shrugs and bites her lip. She keeps clutching her back.

"Who's Nan, Mum?"

My dad whips round and shouts at me. "Go and sit with Terry. Go on!"

Tel's up the front of the bus. He likes to pretend he's the driver. He's sitting there, using the metal backrest like a steering wheel and making bus noises.

"Ask me where I'm going, Mick."

"No . . . I'm thinking."

I'm thinking, what if Mum gives this baby to the rag-and-bone man, like she done to Eileen.

"Go on, Mick! Say, 'Are you going up the pier?' Because I'm the driver."

"Are you going up the pier?"

"No, I ain't."

Mind you, I reckon she had to give Eileen away because she needed the money. She had me to feed. She'd never have got rid otherwise because she must have loved her. How could she not love her own baby?

"I said I ain't going up the pier, Mick. You've got to guess somewhere else."

"What?"

"Say, 'Are you going up the hospickle?' Go on, say it!"

"I know you're going up the hospital. And it's hospital, not hospickle. Talk properly."

"It isn't. It's hospickle. Mum, it is hos*pickle*, innit? Mick says it ain't."

Dad glares at us. "Shut up the pair of you or I'll bash your heads together!"

Everybody on the bus stares at my dad. He stares back.

"What are you looking at?"

Everyone looks away. I wonder if Eileen looked like Dad. She'd be five now, if she was alive. If she was alive? If? Suddenly I have a wonderful thought. Maybe she ain't dead after all. All this time, I'd thought she was turned into glue by the rag-and-bone man, but he could have just bought her off Mum because his wife couldn't have no kids or something.

She's somewhere out there. A little rag-and-bone man's girl. I'm going to try and find her and bring her back home to Mum. Because we're rich now. We could afford her. Ahh . . . My own little sister, eh?

I'm so excited thinking about this I never said 'bye to Mum and Dad at the hospital. They went off with the nurse and left us in the waiting room. It's a nice place. It's all done up for little kids with a rocking horse and old jigsaw puzzles. Terry's giving it plenty on the horse.

"Look at me, Mick! I'm Roy Rodders."

"Watch it. You'll fall off."

Still, if he's gonna fall off, this is as good a place as any, I s'pose. I pretend to be an Indian for him, sneaking up behind and whooping in his ear. I try to jump on the back to wrestle him off, but the horse is too slippery.

After a bit, we get bored of the horse, so we take it in turns jamming the waste-paper basket on our bums, pretending to be snails. The one who's turn it is not to have the basket has to be the slug. We have slithering races like that, round and round the chairs.

I've done three jigsaws by now, all with bits missing. It's gone three o'clock and we're getting hungry. We've been here ages and it's way past our dinnertime for a Sunday.

"Mick, when are we going home?"

"I dunno. When Mum's had the baby."

"I'm starving. I want a Mars bar."

"You'll have to wait. I ain't got a Mars bar."

I try to take his mind off it. "What do you want, a baby brother or a sister?"

"I want a Mars bar."

Terry's no good when he gets hungry. Usually he's a good kid, but when he's hungry, he starts going on a bit.

"Watch out, Terry. There's a policeman!"

There is too. And a policewoman. Maybe they've come to visit a thief. Terry shrinks down behind a chair until they've gone. Then he starts again.

"When are we going home, Mick?"

We really have been here ages. Everyone's going home from visiting now.

"Won't be much longer, Tel."

An hour later, we're still sitting here like a couple of char-lies. Then a nurse comes over and tells us to stop playing with the curtains.

"What are you doing here, children?"

"Waiting for our mum."

"Which ward? Leave the curtains alone!"

"I dunno. She's having a baby."

"And your name is?"

"I'm Mick. He's Terry."

"Your surname?"

"Spicer."

She frowns. "Spicer? Are you sure?"

She walks off in the other direction, leaving me a bit confused. Terry's pulling at my arm.

"Mick, has she gone to get the baby?"

"Dunno, mate."

"Will she let me hold it? I won't drop it or nothing. I'm strong."

"If you sit on a chair they might let you. Long as you don't fidget."

"I won't fidget."

God knows where the nurse has gone. Terry's winding himself up in the curtain.

"Mick, what will we call the baby?"

"Janice or something. Carol, p'raps."

"What if it's a boy?"

"Probably call it after Dad."

He thinks about this and looks at me as if I'm stupid.

"You can't call it 'Dad.'"

"No, dopey. We'll call it the same as Dad's name, Harry."

The nurse creeps up behind us.

"Curtains!"

Terry unravels himself. To my amazement, she laughs.

"That made you jump, didn't it? Now then, what's all this nonsense about mothers having babies? There isn't a Mrs. Spicer here."

I thought she was still joking. "Yes there is. She went in with my dad. He's Mr. Spicer."

"I should hope he was," she said. "OK. Off you go."

"What?"

"Off you go. Go home. This isn't a playground."

I'm getting a really horrible feeling about this. She's practically pushing us out of the waiting room. Not angry or nothing. Just not believing a word I say.

"I want to see my mum."

"She's not here."

"I want to see my dad."

I step out of her way, try to get past her.

"Not here . . . Where are you going?"

"Need the toilet."

She pushes the toilet door open for me and I duck under her arm, pulling Terry with me.

"I don't need one, Mick. I been before I went, yeah?"

I think that nurse is never going to let go of the door.

"Straight out once you've been, please," she says.

I go into one of the cubicles and sit on the bog. Terry's in there with me.

"You haven't taken your trousers off, Mick. You've got to."

"Shhh."

"Why?"

"I'm only pretending to go until that nurse goes. Then I'm going to find Mum."

"Oh. What if the nurse doesn't go?"

"She will if she thinks I'm going for real."

"Fart then."

"Alright."

Only I couldn't for the life of me. Terry's creased up laughing.

"Shut up. . . she'll hear you! If you're so clever, you do one, Terry."

"Long one or short one?"

"Anything as long as it's loud, OK?"

Terry braces himself. At first, he's giggling with the effort. Then he realises the importance of what he's got to do and his face straightens.

"Remember, you're doing this for Mum, Tel."

He salutes me like a little soldier, holds his nose, bends his knees and lets rip. It starts off with a few little claps, like it's building up to something, and then there's a sort of sliding whistle followed by a World War Two bomb. The nurse shuts the door. It's worked! I flush the toilet and ruffle his hair. He looks exhausted but happy.

"Nice one, Terry. It sounded just like a real crap!"

"It was."

He's standing there with his legs bent, pulling a face.

"You got pants on?"

"Yeah."

"Well, take 'em off and flush them down the toilet, OK?"

I leave him by the sink while I go and look for Mum. This is ridiculous. The nurse must have got it wrong. Probably got Spicer muddled up with Spencer or something. I ask a porter the way to the baby ward and he sends me down a long corridor with pictures of teddies on the wall. I keep an eye out for the nurse, but she's nowhere to be seen. I have a squint through the glass window. There are loads of women in bed wearing nighties, but I can't see Mum.

"You're not supposed to be here, dear. Can I help you?"

It's a different nurse.

"I'm looking for my mum, Connie Spicer?"

"Spicer . . . Spicer? . . . She didn't come in today, did she?"

"Yeah, she did. With my dad."

"Hmmm . . . if she'd have come in today, it would be on the chart. And there are no fathers in the waiting room, to the best of my knowledge."

Another nurse walks past and my nurse calls out. "Sister, there's a young man here, looking for his mum . . . Connie Spicer. We haven't got a Connie Spicer, am I right?"

The little nurse shakes her head. "Spicer? No. No Spicers."

"Sorry, love. You sure you've got the right hospital?"

Someone calls her and she leaves. "Stay there," she says. "Won't be a minute."

But I know in my bones what's happened. We've been tricked. Mum and Dad have run off with the money. They've walked out on us.

eleven

I'm trying to stay in control here, but Terry's lost it. He's crying his eyes out. We haven't had no dinner and we've got no money to get home. Home? What if we get home and there's no one there? Where are we gonna sleep? Where are we gonna live?

"Mick, I want Mum. Where's Mum, Mick?"

I hold Terry's hand across the road. I know the way back to our house roughly, but we're going to have to walk.

"I wanna go on the bus, Mick."

"We got no money."

Then he sits down on a wall and won't get up.

"Come on, Terry. It's not that far."

"My legs hurt. I want a carry."

There's no way I'm going to be able to carry him all the way back to Southend. It's miles away.

"Alright. Just for a bit."

He climbs up on a wall and I give him a piggyback. He's quite heavy and he keeps grabbing me round the neck, trying to strangle me.

"Don't, Tel."

"I know . . . you be Trigger and I'm the Alone Ranger."

"Alright."

"You've got to make horsey noises, yeah?"

I'm not in the mood. Where the hell have Mum and Dad gone anyway? Where would they go? They haven't got a place to go unless they secretly bought a house with the winnings. I could have almost understood it if they'd left me because I'm just a nuisance but they really love Terry. Why would they leave him? He's only a baby himself.

"You're not doing the noises. You've got to say 'hee haw.'"

"Hee haw."

"Not like that!"

He starts blubbing again. "That's not how it goes."

He's got snot running down the little grooves under his nose. Number elevens, Dad calls it.

"Sorry, Tel. I'm trying. It's just a bit difficult 'cos I can't breathe. Get down a minute."

He slides off, drops to the pavement and snorts his number elevens back up.

"Where's Dad, Mick?"

"He had to go off and do something."

I keep thinking maybe Mum was there at the hospital all along. Maybe she'd forgot to tell people what her name was, or used a different name because she wasn't thinking straight. Sometimes she does use a different surname when she signs the rent book. Dad had probably just gone out to get some more fags.

Then I start thinking, they're going to be furious if they come and look for us in the waiting room and we're not there. Thing is, we're nearer home than we are to the hospital now.

"Are we nearly home, Mick?"

"Yeah. Will you walk a bit?"

"No."

"Oh, go on. Walk for Mick. My back's killing me, Terry."

He takes little steps. He's trying to be good for me, poor little thing. We're never going to get home at this rate.

"I'll race you, Tel. OK? Want to play races? I'll let you win."

"Alright."

"Ready . . . steady . . ."

I run really slow, but then he belts past me, knees going so high he kicks his bum. I catch him up and try and grab him, but he's so excited, he don't look where he's going and he trips over a low wall and smashes his knee on the pavement. For a moment, he don't make a noise. Then he stands up with his hands spread out and he's roaring. There's gravel stuck to his hands and some's gone under his skin and there's a thin line of blood trickling down his sock.

I pick him up and he sobs into my neck. "I want Mum. I want Mum. Want Mum."

I carry him up the hill like that, all the way with him sobbing and sobbing.

"Shh, Terry. Come on, shhh. It'll be alright. Mick's got ya."

I carry him like that all the way to the main road, then we turn left and head towards Southend Pier. The sobbing's getting quieter and quieter until all he's got left is little shudders and sniffs. Then just as we get to the station, I see Dad.

He's just walking along normally, like nothing's happened. You'd think the first thing I'd do is call his name, but I never. I want to see how he'll react. Testing him, like.

I stand there till he spots us. His eyes say it all. He looks surprised to see us, like he couldn't figure out how we got here.

"I was just coming to find you," he says. Smiling.

I know he's lying. He knows I know he's lying. I tip my head back so no tears fall out.

"It's alright," he says, "I'll take you up the tea shop for a cake. Wanna cake, Terry?"

We follow him to the tea shop. Terry's all over him, letting himself be tickled, dipping his cake in his tea and everything. I'm too choked to eat.

"That cake alright for you, Mick?"

"Yeah."

"Want another cup of tea?"

"No, ta. It's a bit strong."

He calls the waitress over. I don't want him to. I don't want her to see I'm upset and ask why.

"His tea's too strong. Can you put a bit of milk in it, love?"

"It's alright, Dad."

"No, it ain't. It's too strong."

The waitress pours milk in my cup. "Sorry about that," she says. "I keep telling Betty it's three level spoons of tea but she heaps them up."

Dad winks at her. "Never mind, eh? Cheers, love. Get that down you, son."

I ask him where Mum is.

"They've taken her up London."

He gets a fag paper out and starts rolling one. He never looks at me.

"Why?"

He twists the paper neatly and gets his lighter out and clicks it twice. It won't light.

"The baby was coming too early. She had a bit of a shock, like, and it set everything off."

"Can we go and see it?"

He clicks the lighter again, but there's still no flame.

"Run out of petrol. Do what?"

"When can we see the baby?"

"The baby ain't been born yet. That's why she's had to go up London."

He calls the waitress over again. "Got a light, love?"

She pulls a box of matches out of her apron pocket and lights his fag for him. He takes a deep puff and eases himself back in his chair.

"Everybody had enough?"

And that's it. That's the end of the conversation. The waitress clears our plates, Dad pays and we follow him out onto the streets. Dad picks Terry up and we walk off down the road. Only instead of going the normal way home, he suddenly turns right.

"Where are we going?"

"Home."

"But our house is that way."

"This is a different home. We're going to stay in a new one."

So, he has bought us a new house. Maybe that's what all this is about. It's all meant to be a surprise. We're going to a big posh new house. Mum probably went on ahead to get it nice for us. I thought it would be something like that. What else could it be? Suddenly, I don't feel so tired no more. Stupid thing, I am. Getting the wrong end of the stick.

"We're going to a new house, Terry. Good, innit?"

Then I remember all my old stuff back at the old place.

"What about my models and things? My boat and that? Can I go and get them and put them in the new place? . . . Can I, Dad?"

"We'll get all new stuff," he says.

We turn a corner and he stops and peers at the door number. Then he takes a key out of his pocket.

"That's it. Number 127. Be alright, won't it?"

It don't look much from the outside. It's quite big though. I expect Dad will make it nice. All it needs is some paint.

"Can I help you paint it?"

"What for?" he laughs. "We ain't going to be here long, I hope. It's only one room."

"What?"

"It's only digs. You'll have to share a bed with Terry for a bit, that's all."

"I thought . . ."

"What?"

"Nothing."

He can see my eyes are filling up, but I ain't going to cry again. In fact, it's all so mad, I want to laugh. It's like, every time I get my hopes up, it's bad luck. I've got to stop having these happy dreams.

He opens the door and we go in. The place stinks of damp. We're on the top floor again. There are no carpets on the stairs, nothing. He opens our flat door with another key. It's cold inside. There are two single beds, a sink, a fireplace, a stinking old settee and an ugly old wardrobe. I recognise our suitcases on one of the beds. Mum's ain't there. He's been here earlier.

"Mick. Come over here, I've bought you something."

He sits down on the other bed and feels in his pocket.

"What?"

"It's a ring. It's solid gold."

He gives me the ring. Puts it in my hand. It feels quite heavy.

"It's too big for me."

"No it ain't. Try it on. It's twenty-two carat. I bought it for your birthday present."

"It ain't my birthday yet."

"Don't matter. It was a bargain. It still cost me a lot though."

"Really?"

I don't like the ring all that much, but I'm pleased it's worth something, because it means he must like me a little bit to have spent all that.

"Thanks, Dad."

"It's twenty-two carat."

"Yeah, you said."

It'll be alright at this place. I can put up with it for a little while. Dad says it's only for a little while. I'm not sure where Mum's going to sleep though. I start looking through my case. Dirty shirt. My old shoes. Two pairs of trousers. Socks. Pants.

Then right at the bottom, there's a tobacco tin. And in it, my wax animals.

twelve

We're going to London on a steam train, to visit Dad's sister, Lena. I've never seen her before. Nor's Terry. She's got three kids, that's all I know. Two boys and a girl. I wonder what the girl's like and that gets me thinking about Eileen again. I want to ask Dad about Eileen but I daren't. Nobody speaks her name. It's like she never happened.

All I can remember for sure is sitting on a seat on the front of her pram when I was really little, and it was a sunny day and she was propped up on a pillow behind me. It was a big blue pram and there was a string of little animals threaded on elastic across the front, stretched between two metal knobs. Every now and then she would bash them and they would spin on the elastic and that would make her happy.

People used to come up and push their heads under the pram hood and say how lovely she was, but I can't remember her face. I've invented how she looked. A bit like Terry, only a girl. I think she'd have had blue eyes though. I like blue eyes.

Of course, she won't look like that now. When we get to London and if I can find where the rag-and-bone man lives, I need to look out for a five-year-old girl. I wonder what she'll think when she knows she's got a big brother? Especially a rich one. She won't want to live with the rag-and-bone family then, because they're poor. She'll want to come away with us, to our palace. When we get it, that is.

I hope Mum's alright. I haven't told her about my plan for finding Eileen because it's going to be a surprise. Can't wait to see her face. Hope she's alright.

"Oi . . . Dolly Day-dream. Anything you want to take with you?"

Dad's packed a big bag. It looks like we're stopping over Lena's the night.

"Dad . . ."

"What?"

I slip off the ring he gave me and show him my finger. "Look . . . my finger's gone green."

"You're joking, aren't you? It's just dirt."

I rub the dark ring. It looks like a bruise.

"No, it ain't. The ring done that. If it's gold, it shouldn't do that, should it, Dad?"

Dad holds it up to the light. Then he rolls his eyes and makes a disgusted face.

"I paid good money for that," he says. "I've been conned. It's rubbish."

He gives the ring back to me. I'm not sure whether to put it on or not. Which would upset him most? I dunno. I just pretend to look at it until he goes over the other side of the room to have a shave.

It's quite insulting, having a rubbish birthday present like that. I know it weren't his fault, but I'm cross with him for letting himself be conned like that. Makes him look a right prat somehow, whereas before I thought he was pretty sharp.

I'm not going to wear it. Just before we leave for the station, I stuff it down the back of the sofa with all the other rubbish. If he asks, I'll pretend I've lost it. I've got my pride.

The best thing about being on a steam train is when we go through a tunnel. If you open a window, the carriage fills up with smoke and everyone starts choking and spluttering. No one can see until the smoke's cleared. Least of all who opened the window. I thought Dad was going to kill hisself coughing. Tel slapped him on the back really hard, like Mum done when he choked on a boiled sweet.

"Ow! Which silly so-and-so opened that window? I could have choked to death."

"Wasn't me, Dad."

"Wasn't me neither."

I never used to tell lies, did I? But I'm learning.

It takes ages getting to London. Terry's gone to sleep with his head on some bloke's shoulder. The man looks really awkward and keeps trying to shift him off, but there's no room to move away because there's a big, fat woman sitting next to him. Her arms look like they've been blown up with a pump, the skin's so tight and shiny.

Reminds me of the time I was on the pier back home and I saw a man making poodles out of twisted balloons. He'd stretch a balloon, blow a bit of air in and the balloon would get all fat and curly and then he'd twist it in the middle with a snap. I was amazed it never burst. I was waiting for the bang, but it never happened, no matter how many times he twisted it. Then he blew up more balloons and twisted them into poodle legs and soon he had a whole poodle, all bulgy and wobbly, just like the woman on the train. I keep looking at her, waiting for the bang. She catches me staring at her and she stares right back with cold, eggy eyes, as if she can tell what I'm thinking.

I look away quick, first at my shoes, then out of the window. But I can feel her staring at me. She done it all the way to the end of the railway line. It was horrible. Like she was putting a curse on me or something. Maybe she did. Looking back at what happened shortly after, someone must have done.

. . .

I'm knackered by the time we get to Lena's. Terry's wide awake though, because he had a kip on the train. He's in a really silly mood, swinging off Dad's bag while he's trying to carry it.

"Pack it in, Terry. No! Stop arsing about." He goes as if to clip him round the head but his hand never connects. It still sends shivers through me though.

"You better behave round your Auntie Lena's or she'll give you a slap."

"She won't."

"How do you know? You've never met her. She will if you're a naughty boy."

"She won't."

Terry can be really lippy sometimes. He gets away with it because he's cute. He won't always be though, will he? I wonder if Dad will change towards him then, hit him and that? We're just coming up to the police station and Terry's still mucking about. My dad points to the nick.

"You don't behave, you'll end up in prison and all you'll get to eat is bread and water."

"I like bread and water."

"Ah," says my dad, "but it's stale bread and the water's in a dirty cup and there's no toilet or nothing. You have to go in a bucket."

Terry doesn't look too bothered. "Good," he says, "I like buckets."

We get to my Auntie Lena's house. It's a prefab, just a little bit further than the police station. She doesn't seem all that pleased to see us.

"Oh . . . you're here then?"

Her hair is in rollers and she's wearing a dressing gown. Terry pushes past her into the front room.

"Terry!"

Dad apologises for him. "Sorry about that, Lena. He'll calm down in a minute. Can we come in, then?"

"Haven't got any choice, have I?" she says. "I haven't got much in though."

She goes into the kitchen and puts the kettle on. My dad introduces me.

"This is Mick, Lena."

"Oh, yeah?" She doesn't bother to look at me. "If he wants to go outside he can. My three are out there somewhere."

I go into the garden. It's tiny. There are no other kids there. They must have gone out. I sit on the wall and play with my spud-gun, firing little bits of broken berries at some empty milk bottles. *Ping! Ping! Ping!*

An old boy looks over next-door's fence. He must have been bending down weeding or something. I never saw him come out of the house.

"Alright, son?" He seems quite friendly. "What's that you got?"

"Spud-gun."

"Yeah? Want some ammunition?" He tosses me a little, green potato. It's still got mud stuck to it. I flick the mud off and go to bite a little chunk out of it, for a bullet.

"Oh, no," he says, "you mustn't eat them green, they're poisonous. Here, spit it out and I'll get you a knife."

I gob the potato out on the grass. It tastes revolting. I wonder if I'll die?

"Mister . . . will green 'tater kill you even if you don't swallow it?"

"Just a minute . . ."

He goes into his shed and comes back. I'm still spitting, just in case.

"What d'ya say, mate?"

"Will a green potato kill you if you just lick it?"

"You'll be alright. Might give you bellyache and the runs at worst."

He gives me the knife. It's a lovely one. Silver, with a little pattern carved in it. Very old, I should think. The blade's not a bit stiff though. He must look after his stuff. I cut the potato up into little cubes.

"I'll have it back when you're finished," he says. "It's my gardening knife. Staying at your auntie's, are you?"

"Yeah."

"How long for?"

"I dunno."

"Only her cat keeps squatting on my lettuces. See all those little sticks?" He points to a patch of lettuces at the bottom of his garden. It's full of iron sticks with wicked points on the ends. "I put those spiky railings in so it couldn't squat and it still manages."

"Does it?"

"Straight up. Mind you, they didn't cost me nothing, the railings. I found them in a lake in a park and stuck them on my cart."

The word "cart" jolts me awake. Who has a cart? A rag-and-bone man, that's who. He doesn't look anything like the rag-and-bone man in my dreams though. But then dreams play funny tricks on you. And anyway, the dream rag-and-bone man is at least five years younger than this bloke. I can't ask him outright who he is, can I? So I use my cunning.

"Have you got a horse?"

"No. Have you?"

"No."

He scratches his chin, goes over to his shed and gets a hoe out and hoes a row of beans. Then he walks back over to the fence towards me and takes his hat off.

"I'd like another horse, but where would I put it?" he said.

If he'd like *another* horse, he must have had one once, so he could still be the rag-and-bone man.

"What sort of horse did you have?"

"A mare," he says, "called Misty. Great big girl, she was. Lovely."

"Could she pull a cart?"

"Oh, yurrr. She could pull a cart alright. She pulled my cart."

He puts his hat on again and starts to walk off. It's all adding up. He had a cart. Now all I need to know is if he's got a daughter, about five years old. So I blurt it out.

"Have you got kids?"

He stops. Takes his hat off again and holds it to his chest.

"We had Alan, but he died when he was tiny. Oh, dear. Never mind."

"Why? Did he eat green potatoes?"

"No. He got stuck when he was being born."

"Stuck where?"

He wipes a dewdrop off his nose with the back of his hand.

"You don't want to know."

He puts his hat on, turns his back and hoes another row. That's it then. He's not my man. Then he suddenly puts down his hoe, pulls up a thistle and walks over to me again.

"Then we had Irene. She loved Misty, did Irene."

Irene? Not Eileen? They must have changed her name after Mum sold her so she'd never find out who her real family was!

"Course, she's long gorn."

He looks up at the sky and wrinkles his nose. Oh, no. I can't bear it.

"What, Irene?"

"No, the horse."

"Thank gawd for that."

I can't help saying it, I'm so relieved the horse is dead, not the girl. The man looks really hurt.

"I loved that horse," he says. "How would you like it if your horse was carted off and turned into glue by the rag-and-bone man?"

I tell him I know how he feels. I tell him the same thing happened to my baby sister.

"Terrible," he says, "terrible what goes on. Give us my knife back, son. I want to make some earwig traps for my dahlias."

I give it one last go, just to be sure in my head. I lean over the fence and ask him, "Do you know any rag-and-bone men?"

"No. Do you?"

"No."

"Nor do I," he says. Then he goes off into his shed and shuts the door.

My Auntie Lena calls me in. "What are you talking to him for?" she snaps.

"Who?"

"Him next door. The coalman. He didn't ask you to stroke his ferret did he?"

Oh, so he's a coalman. No wonder his hat was that colour.

"I never knew he had a ferret."

"He hasn't," she says very loudly, in the direction of his shed, "dirty old man."

I don't know why she was being so horrible about him. He lent me the knife and everything. Gave me the potato. I reckon she's got him all wrong.

Terry's already gone to bed. Dad sent him because he was being a nuisance and Lena's got a lot of china ornaments. I have my tea with her two sons, but they don't say nothing. They just keep kicking each other in the leg and giggling, like they're a bit backward or something. I never saw the daughter. Lena said she'd most likely gone down Wood Green with her boyfriend.

There's nothing to do here. Dad and Lena are arguing. I hover about by the sink, playing with the washing-up. I think they're arguing about Mum, but every time I walk in, they go quiet.

"Yes? Can we help you?"

I walk sideways down the narrow hall to the bedroom. There's a camp bed, a single bed and squashed between them on the floor is a mattress for me and Terry to share. No sheet on it or nothing. He's sleeping across it sideways. I can tell he's been crying because his cheeks are all shiny where they've made a trail through the dirt. Nobody's bothered to give him a wash.

I take my shoes and trousers off and pull the blanket over us. It's really scratchy and I'm itching like mad. I keep thinking about the coalman. I was hoping so much he was the rag-and-bone man. All the time I was talking to him, in the back of my mind I was thinking, any minute now, Eileen will come out into the garden. I was waiting and waiting, but she never came. Pity that. He was a nice man. He would have made a good father for her, I think. He would be kind and love her very much, because his baby son had died.

If she lived with them, Eileen would never be cold like me and Tel because he'd have all that free coal. And she'd never be hungry because he grows his own vegetables. Beans and that. Lettuces.

I'm thinking all this and I'm drifting off, and before I know it, I'm having this dream about a dead horse on a cart, being pulled along by a load of ferrets, and driving the cart is baby Alan. Then Auntie Lena's cat runs out of the lettuces and the cart screeches to a halt and throws the baby between some spiky railings so its head is trapped. The coalman keeps saying, "It's an earwig trap!" and I'm trying to pull the baby out by its feet and it's screaming and screaming and its neck is getting longer and longer . . .

"Don't do that. Its head will come off . . ."

Then there's a loud pop. And I wake up. My heart's thumping. The mattress is soaked. Lena goes mad in the morning when she finds out.

"Harry! I can't have this, Harry. You'll have to get some-where else to stay. I'm not putting up with this all the time."

She's almost in tears. Dad dogs his fag out on his tobacco tin.

"Yeah, OK, Lena. I'll sort something out, alright?"

She folds her arms.

"When?" He picks Terry up and goes towards the front door.

"Mick, put your stuff in the bag," he says. "I'll be back in a couple of hours."

I spend the rest of the morning in the garden, stroking the coalman's ferret. He did have one after all. It was called Alan. He kept it in the shed.

thirteen

Later that afternoon, Dad comes back for me. He ain't got Terry with him. I ask him where he's been.

"Up your Nan's."

"Nan who?"

"Nan Chadwick," he says. "You know. Your mum's mum."

I don't know. I've never seen her, don't think. Maybe I did when I was little, but I don't remember. That must have been the nan who phoned Mum up when we were playing cricket that afternoon.

We walk round to her house in Roden Street. Dad tells me he's seen Mum and she's had the baby. It's a boy called Gary. I ask him when she's coming home but he's not sure. He says there were complications.

"The baby is alright though, isn't he?"

"He's lovely." Dad grins. "He doesn't look a bit like Terry though."

"Does he look like me?"

"I bloody hope not." Then he laughs. He's only joking. Just having a laugh.

"Why did she call him Gary?"

"After Gary Cooper, I think. She's always liked him."

He knocks on Nan's door.

"That you, Harry?"

"No. It's your fancy piece."

She opens the door.

"I don't think that's funny," she says. "How can you joke at a time like this?"

Dad's face changes. I've seen that look before. Just the once.

"Don't you have a go at me," he says, "you cow! You had to stick your oar in, didn't you? We could have sorted it. Upsetting Connie like that, you could have lost us that baby."

"Don't you . . . dare!" she hisses.

My dad mumbles something and looks at his shoes. Nan looks me up and down, grabs my shirt and stuffs it into my trousers, then she yells upstairs, "Min! Fred! They're here."

She marches us into the front room. There's an old man sitting in one of those wing chairs.

"Mick, this is your grandad Charlie. Stand up straight, boy."

Funny being introduced to your own grandad like that. Grandad Charlie looks up from his paper and nods at me, but he don't say nothing. He's studying the racing pages.

"I reckon Red Dawn for the two-thirty," says my dad.

"Charlie doesn't gamble," snaps Nan.

Minnie and Fred arrive from upstairs.

"Min's your mum's sister," Nan explains. She pulls a face when she talks about my mum, like she's got a nasty smell under her nose. She never bothers to tell me who Fred is, so I'm supposing he's married to Min. Nan goes into the kitchen and starts clattering about, then she puts her head back round the door.

"Where are the children? I want them all here . . . now!"

"They're coming," moans Min. Then she turns to my dad. "Are you seriously saying you didn't know anything about all this, because I find it very hard to believe."

My dad looks daggers at her. "Are you calling me a liar, Min?"

"No."

"Yes you are. You're calling me a liar."

"Shut it!" says Nan. "Who takes sugar?"

She puts a tea tray down on the table. It's got a posh teapot, milk jug, bowl for the sugar and everything. And biscuits.

The door opens and in comes Janice, who must be about the same age as me, and Brenda, who's much older. About fourteen, I reckon. Janice looks at me and giggles.

"Janice, don't pull silly faces. Give your cousin Mick a biscuit," says Nan. Janice picks one up and waves it at me. Nan slaps her hand.

"Not with your fingers, girl! Pass the plate. Honestly, Minnie, she's running riot, that one."

Min's glaring at her.

"Don't start, Mum."

Nan looks round. "Where's Jean? I asked everybody to be here, didn't I?"

"She's coming," says Fred. "She was getting ready to go out."

"Not with a boy, I hope," Nan mutters.

The grown-ups all sit down on chairs. Us kids sit on the floor. Everyone's staring at me in silence. I don't know where to put myself, so I just try and eat my biscuit nicely. I dip it in my tea, but I leave it in there too long and when I take it out, the bottom half plops back into the tea and sploshes my glasses.

Janice giggles again. Nan's just about to have a go at her when Jean arrives. She's about sixteen and really nice.

"Hello! Sorry I'm late, Nan. Hello, Harry. Hello . . . Mick, isn't it?"

"Harry's just going," says Nan.

Dad looks a bit surprised because he hasn't even finished his tea. He drinks it quickly and gets up.

"Alright, Mick. I'll have to leave you with your nan for a couple of days until I can find us somewhere to live."

"What? Are you buying somewhere with the winnings?"

"Ha!" scoffs Minnie.

Nan's face sets hard.

"I don't believe this," she says. "Haven't you told him, Harry?"

"He doesn't need to know," Dad says.

"For crying out loud!" shouts Minnie.

Uncle Fred steams into her. "You keep out of it!"

"Stuff the lot of you," Dad says and he stands up. I think he's going to lump Uncle Fred for a minute. Uncle Fred sinks down into his chair and puts a cushion in front of his face.

Nan throws Dad's jacket at him.

"Go on. Get out, Harry."

She walks behind him to the front door.

"I never knew anything about it, Nan. Honest," I can hear him saying.

"So you say."

She shuts the front door in his face. I can't believe Dad's left me like this. Nan comes back in.

"Right," she says, pointing to the kids, "you lot, take Mick upstairs and watch telly. Go on. We're talking down here, so don't come down until I call you, do you hear?"

"Yes, Nan."

"I'm off out," says Jean.

"It better not be with a boy!" Nan calls after her.

Janice takes my hand and we go upstairs. I'm so excited by the idea of a telly and all these new cousins I forget about Dad's ruck with Nan for a minute.

"Come on," says Janice, "it's *Wagon Train*. Do you like *Wagon Train*?"

I tell her I've never seen it.

"Haven't you got a telly then?"

"Not yet. We'll get one when we get our new house with our pools winnings."

"You never won the pools," she says. "I know you never."

"Shut up," says Brenda. "Stop talking over it. I can't hear it."

Wagon Train is all about cowboys. It's really good. Me and Janice pretend to have guns and shout "Peeow! Peeow!" whenever we see an Apache. I wish Terry was here. He especially loves cowboys and Indians.

"You're really annoying me," Brenda groans. "I'm going to have a bath and don't you dare come in, Janice."

"Ugh!" says Janice. "Why would I want to, pointy-bra?"

Brenda goes bright red.

"Shut up. I'll tell Mum if you call me that again."

Brenda looks like a woman almost. She's not my type, but she's got a bra and everything.

"Pointy-bra! Pointy-bra!"

A bit later on, Brenda comes back with a towel around her and tells me it's my turn to have a bath.

"Ugh," says Janice, "you've got to go in it after Brenda. She pisses in it."

"I do not!" She grabs hold of Janice's ribbon and tries to yank it out. Janice kicks her in the leg.

"Ouch, you little cow! Mum . . . Mum! Janice's kicking me!"

"Pack it in!" yells Minnie, from downstairs.

Janice pulls away from Brenda and grabs my hand. "Come on. I'll show you where the bath is."

She seems very fond of me, this Janice. She takes me down to the scullery. There's a big, white tin bath full of scummy water. She feels it with one hand.

"It's quite warm. Take your clothes off."

I wait for her to leave, but she doesn't. She bends over and starts unbuckling her shoes.

"I'm glad you're staying," she says. "I like boys but I don't like girls. Have you got any brothers or sisters?" She takes her dress off, right over her head.

"I've got a brother called Terry and Mum's just had another baby called Gary but I haven't seen him yet."

"Oh yeah, she's in prison, isn't she?" says Janice.

"No." I laugh, unbuttoning my shirt. "I did have a little sister called Eileen once but I'm not sure what happened to her."

"How come?" She's standing in her drawers, watching me get undressed. She shuts the scullery door.

"I think my mum might have given her to the rag-and-bone man."

"Really?"

"Yeah. She was a bit short of cash in them days."

"I know. She came to borrow some off Nan, but Nan never let her have any," says Janice. "They had a row."

"When?"

"Ages ago."

She rolls her drawers down and kicks them across the floor.

"Get in then, Mick."

I've never had a bath with a girl before. I'm shivering. Maybe it's the lukewarm water. Janice shakes a soggy box of soda crystals into the bath and swishes them. They won't dissolve.

"Let's pretend they're diamonds," she says. "Make me a necklace."

She hugs her knees and sticks her chest out. She doesn't have nothing there. Just two little flat pennies. I pick out some wet soda crystals and stick them to her skin, all round her neck. It doesn't look half pretty.

"There."

She closes her eyes. "You can kiss me now."

"What if someone comes in?"

"They won't."

I slide myself along the bottom of the bath towards her, until our bellies are touching. She's so soft. I'm going to kiss her on the cheek but then I think, no. I'm going to kiss her like they do at the pictures. Then she'll think I'm more grown-up.

She stays still for a while, with her eyes shut, like she's out of breath. Then she starts tickling my foot. Then she makes a grab for me. I shriek and fall back in the water. She's howling with laughter, splashing me in the face.

"Let go, Janice! Let go!"

And she's squealing, "I thought it was your . . . toe!"

But it ain't, and she knows it. We're both laughing so much we don't hear Nan come in. She never says nothing. She just puts her hands under Janice's arms, pulls her out of the bath and drags her out of the room backwards. Janice is yelling blue murder and giggling at the same time. A door slams. There's a loud slap. Then silence.

I sink under the bathwater and hold my breath.

fourteen

I'm upstairs watching Auntie Min's telly when Brenda puts her head round the door.

"Mick, your dad's downstairs. He's in Nan's Everything Room."

At last, he's come to take me away. I've wet the bed again. No one's said anything yet, so I'm thinking, now Dad's here we should be gone before anyone finds out.

"Be down in a sec, Brenda. Just watching the end of this."

I almost don't want to go home because we ain't got a telly and I'd love a telly. Even Pete's mum and dad never had a telly. I'll have to try and talk Dad round to getting one. I'll say it's for my education because you can learn ever such a lot from it. How to make a pot out of clay and that.

I pass Janice on the stairs. She's putting her roller skates on. I ask her if she's alright.

"Did Nan give you a smack, Janice?"

She smirks. Then she sticks her tongue out and whooshes her skirt up, flashing her knickers.

"Wouldn't you like to know?" she grins. "'Bye!" She clatters off down the hall and disappears.

Nan puts her hand on my shoulder. She's got a nasty habit of creeping up on people. I never know where she's going to pop up next. It's making me quite nervous.

"He's in there," she says, pushing the door open. "Go and say hello."

There's a man in there I've never seen before and my grandad. I look round for my dad, but he don't seem to be here. Then this other man says, "Hello," and I say, "Hello," and then I ask Nan where Dad is.

"This is your dad," she says. She pats the settee next to the man I've never set eyes on before. I'm not sure what she's getting at.

"But I've got a dad."

I look at my grandad to see if he'll get me out of this, but he's looking up at the ceiling. I stare at the man on the sofa.

"You're not my dad."

He stubs his fag out and looks me in the eye.

"Yes, I am. The dad you call Harry, well, he's your stepdad." I can't figure out what he means by this.

"No, he ain't. Is he, Nan? Who is he?"

"He's Harry Stokes," says Nan, "and you're Mick Stokes."

"No I ain't! I'm Mick Spicer. Look, it says so in my jumper." I pull at the label in my jumper neck. Mum wrote my name on it so I wouldn't lose it at school.

Nan shakes her head. "I don't care what your jumper says. Someone should have put you straight a long time ago. Like your mother." Then she spits over her shoulder.

I couldn't believe she done that. Everything in her house is so clean, you wouldn't think a lady like her would spit.

"Do you remember Shirley and Glen?" she says.

"No. Who are they?"

Nan and this other man look at each other. The man seems to want Nan to explain. She sighs. "They're your brother and sister."

I shake my head. "No. I've got a brother and I've got a baby brother. Terry and Gary."

Nan throws her hands up in the air. "Oh!" she wails. "She's never called it Gary! Did you hear that, Charlie? She's called it Gary. What for?"

My grandad shakes his head. "Never mind that. Tell him. Tell him what you were telling him. Put the poor little beggar out of his misery."

"I am doing," she says. And she sat me down and told me Harry Stokes and my mum were married and that Glen was born first, then Shirley, then me. The man on the sofa was listening and nodding to all this, dead interested, almost as if he was hearing it for the first time too.

"Then Harry Spicer came swanning along and your mother ran off with him."

"Cow," says Harry Stokes.

"No, she never," I says. "I was there. We met Harry Spicer at the station. He just come out of the army."

"No, he never," says Nan. "He was in the army, but he'd been out a while, hadn't he, Charlie? . . . Hadn't he, Charlie!"

Grandad never looks up. He seems a bit bored by it all. Wants it to be over so he can get on with his paper, I think.

"Oh, yeah."

"She just liked the uniform," whines Harry Stokes.

"There's nothing wrong with the uniform," says Nan. "It's who's inside it bothers me."

They argue amongst themselves. This isn't for real. They've all gone mad. In a minute, I shall wake up in the room I share with my cousin Jean and I shall go and look for Janice and I shall ask her if she's got another pair of roller skates I can borrow and . . .

"We had the Salvation Army out looking for you, Mick!" Nan says. "Do you hear? We were worried sick. There was your dad with Shirley and Glen to look after, and your mother runs off with Harry Spicer and leaves them. We're still not sure why she took you. Do you know, Harry?"

"Him being the youngest, probably," says Harry. "He was a lot younger then."

It's like I'm not here. They're talking at me and over me. I've got a feeling they even think it's partly my fault. Probably all my fault. That Harry keeps looking me up and down. I don't look anything like him. He's wispy and pale and tight all over, with big lips and these thick, blonde eyebrows. He keeps arching them. I really don't like the way he does that. He looks a bit like a puppet. No wonder Mum left him.

"Can I go home now, Nan? I want to see Mum."

"Well, you can't. You know you can't."

"I can. I can get a bus to the hospital and see her. Dad gave me some money."

"No, I never," says Harry Stokes.

"My dad, Harry Spicer . . ." I explain. But it just comes out as a whisper.

I show Nan a handful of cash which I fish out of my pocket. I drop sixpence on the carpet. Her eyes meet mine. They seem to well up. Then they go steel-grey again. She picks up the sixpence, puts it in my hand and folds my fingers back round the pile of thruppennies.

"Don't throw good money after bad," she says. "Your mother's not in the hospital. She's inside. She's doing a twelve-month stretch in Holloway." She looks genuinely surprised that I don't know this.

"Didn't he have the guts to tell you? Typical Harry Spicer, eh, Charlie?"

Grandad is busy separating the back pages of his paper. "Oh, yeah. Yeah. Typical Spicer."

I can't believe Nan's saying all these wicked things. I don't want to believe her and I wouldn't if it hadn't been for what Janice said last night. She'd said Mum was in prison and I thought she was just being daft. I never thought nothing of it, it was such a stupid idea.

Then I think about Eileen. Maybe Mum murdered her. Maybe the police caught up with the rag-and-bone man and found the evidence. My knees buckle. I sit down hard on the rug. I've been standing all the time listening to them and I haven't got any blood left in my legs.

"Sit down. Good idea," says Nan. "I haven't finished yet. Don't look at me like that, Charlie. I'm not being hard. The boy's got to know, you said so yourself."

She tells me Mum came and stayed with her for a couple of days a while back. While I was at Pete's.

"Gave me all these hard luck stories," she says. "Then, when I was at church, she took my chequebook, went up the bank and stole a hundred pounds off me."

Suddenly, Grandad sits up straight and takes a deep breath.

"She never would have if you'd lent her the money."

"After the way she's carried on, you must be joking," says Nan. "You were always too soft on her, Charlie. That's why she's ended up like she is. You wasn't like that with Minnie."

Grandad gets out of his chair. Nan looks quite scared for a second, but he just farts softly, fans the air with his paper and walks out of the room. She sticks two fingers up at him behind his back. Harry Stokes giggles and Nan turns on him.

"You're as bad," she roars. "If you hadn't been so flaming weak this would never have happened."

He opens his mouth as if to have a go at her, but nothing comes out. He crosses his legs and turns to face the wall, like he's sulking. It's all gone quiet. I can't move my arms or legs. All I keep thinking is, why would she rob her own mum if she's won the pools? It doesn't make any sense.

"Mum wouldn't have nicked off of you, Nan. She won the pools."

"Pardon?"

"She won the pools."

Nan scoffs and shakes her head. "No, no! She never. She pretended she'd won them, so when she turned up at Southend with more than a few quid it wouldn't look out of place. Harry Spicer fell for it."

"Or so he says," says Harry Stokes.

"No, I believe him," says Nan. "Charlie don't but I do. She's a crafty cuss. She'd already heard the pools results on the wireless and filled in the eight draws, then when he was sitting there looking at the paper, she asked him to check them out. Course, as he was marking them off, they were all coming up and he really thought she'd won."

"Is he stupid or what?" says Harry Stokes, picking his teeth.

"Since when has that been a crime?" says Nan. "Better to be stupid than rob your own mother, the conniving little cuss. The police couldn't believe it when I told them."

I'll never forgive her for that. How could she grass my mum up like that? It wasn't a big crime and I bet Mum would have given it back if she'd asked nicely. She'd never have taken it unless she was desperate.

Alright, I don't know what went on. I was at Pete's. But I can't helping thinking it's more evil to rob me of my mum than it is to rob a hundred quid.

If only I'd known she was skint, I'd have stacked some more deckchairs and this would never have happened in the first place.

Minnie comes in. "Well," she says, "what's the score?"

"Mick's stopping here for a bit," says Nan. "Don't pull that face, Min. The wind might change."

Min's fuming. It's clear she don't want me there. "Mum, I've got three of my own to look after," she says.

"One more's not going to make much odds," says Nan. "Jean don't mind sharing anyway, what are you moaning for? If it wasn't for me and Charlie none of you would have a roof over your heads . . . alright?"

She says she's going to take me to meet Shirley and Glen next. They won't know me, I don't suppose. But then, I don't know me either. Not any more.

fifteen

Nan found the wet sheet, but she didn't seem all that bothered about it.

We catch the trolley bus from the Nag's Head, just me and her. Janice wanted to come, but Nan wouldn't let her. I think Janice's probably off her rocker. She's not a bit scared of Nan. She doesn't seem to care how often she gets a slap and even when Nan threatens her with Grandad, she just laughs and runs off.

Everyone else is terrified of him, Brenda, Jean, even Nan. She hardly speaks to Charlie and she's always pulling faces behind his back and sticking two fingers up, but I can tell she's nervous of him. On the rare occasions when he barks at her, she goes quiet and her lips disappear.

We're rattling down the Caledonian Road now, off to meet the brother and sister I never knew I had.

"Don't you remember Shirley tipping you out of that little cart?" she says.

"No. How old was I?"

"You'd have been about two at the time. Shirley's what? Twelve? That'd be about right. She was running down the street with you in this little cart Glen had made and she said the cartwheel hit a brick and you flew out and landed on your nose. Your mum had to take you up the hospital. Fancy forgetting a thing like that."

I think hard, but I still can't remember.

"There's the scar," she says, pointing to the top of my nose, "under your glasses."

I take my bins off and feel the little dent. Oh, yeah . . . here it is. So that's how I got it. I thought it was just something I'd been born with. Just goes to show how little you know about yourself. Nan's staring at me.

"What? Have I got something on my face, Nan?"

"No, it's not that," she says, "but you don't half look like your mum without your glasses on. I never noticed before."

I put my glasses back over my ears.

"That's better," she says, "only I don't want to be reminded, so you keep them on."

"What, even in bed?"

"No. You can take them off bedtimes."

"Thanks . . . Nan, what's Glen like?"

"He's fifteen. That's what he's like," she tuts. "He's all mouth and trousers. I keep telling your dad that lad will end up in Borstal, but he don't take any notice."

"What, Harry Spicer?"

"No, get it right. Harry *Stokes*, your real dad. It's no good to keep saying Spicer."

"But I like Harry Spicer."

"I know," she says, "but that don't change anything."

I don't think she likes Harry Stokes much. In fact, I think she hates him. She called him weak. She said if he hadn't been so weak, none of this would have happened. Meaning my mum would never have left him, I suppose. Also, I noticed when he come round she gave him a cup of tea but she never gave him a biscuit, and that's always a sure sign. She gave Harry Spicer a biscuit. The bus stops.

"Does it look familiar?" Nan wants to know.

It's just like it looks in the Eileen dream, only there are no girls skipping and no rain. This is the place where I marched up and down in the wet gutter.

"I had some red wellingtons."

"They were Janice's. Your mum cadged them off Minnie. Janice didn't half kick up a stink. She loved those wellingtons."

This is Tillock Street, the street where I was born. Straight ahead is the corner where the rag-and-bone man's horse comes charging towards us. I can hear the sound of the hooves in my head even now and the rattle of the cart with its big, ugly wheels grinding to a halt outside number . . . thirty-nine.

"Is that it, Nan? Number thirty-nine?"

"That's it."

It's a bomb-site. There are piles of rubble at one end of the street where Hitler tried to bomb King's Cross Station and missed. It must have been like that when I was little, but I can't remember.

"It's a pity we never found you earlier," says Nan, "because your Nan Stokes wanted to see you before she died. She only passed away last year."

"Sorry." The nan I never met, dead already.

"You did meet her," says the Alive One.

I'm beginning to think there's either something terribly wrong with my memory or she's making all of this up. I ask her what Nan Stokes was like.

"Best not speak ill of the dead," she snaps. "I couldn't stand the woman."

The house in Tillock Street is like all the houses up the street, built over three floors. Basement, ground floor, first floor. Nan's got her own key.

When we get in, Nan grabs Harry Stokes's kettle and asks Shirley to show me round the garden, telling me all the names of the flowers.

"That's a lupin, those are roses, those are pinks . . . those are . . ."

It's all going in one ear and out the other. I follow her, watching her all the time, trying to see if she's like me. Or like Mum. She's nothing like Terry.

"What are you staring at?" she says. "I'm going to tell you about the flowers."

"Where's Glen?"

"What do you want him for?" She says it really angrily.

"I dunno. I just wanted to say hello and that."

"You're supposed to be saying hello to me. You don't even remember me, do you?"

She screws her face up, grabs a bike which is leaning up against the shed and pedals off, almost running over my foot. I try talking to her, but she's not having it.

"That's a nice bike."

"Don't bother yourself," she shouts. "It's bad enough having one brother."

I'm standing in the garden like a lemon when someone creeps up behind me.

"Alright, Mick?"

I whip round and there's this lanky-looking bloke. It must be Glen, only I never expected him to be a Teddy boy. He's smiling at me, showing all his goofy teeth, and he's got thick Brylcreem on his hair, combed back in a DA with a quiff at the front.

"Alright . . . Glen?"

He's still smiling at me doing a sort of bobbing thing with his knees, like he's about to do a dance. He takes a comb out of his back pocket and runs it through his quiff.

"What you been doin' then?" he asks.

I think, since when? Where does he want me to start? There's almost me whole life's-worth to catch up on.

"This and that."

"And that and that and that," he grins.

I'm not sure if he's taking the mick or just trying to be funny. Either way, he seems OK.

"I'm working," he says. "I don't go to school no more. I'm a bricky's labourer."

"Oh, yeah?"

"I build lots of walls. It's alright as it happens."

I tell him about my job on the deckchairs. He nods as if he's listening, but he's thinking about other stuff.

"I can't get over you," he grins. "Last time I saw you, you was only this high." He points to his knees. He's wearing drainpipe trousers and these huge shoes. They make his feet look massive.

"They're my brothel creepers," he tells me. "Nan hates 'em."

I laugh. "Nan hates everything."

"What's it like living there?" he says. "Does she make you go Sunday school?"

I snort. "I ain't going Sunday school."

"Wanna bet?"

Just then, Nan calls us in for tea. She's slicing up an angel cake and glaring at Harry Stokes.

"Just as well I brought this," she says, hacking off another slice. "You knew we was coming. You haven't got a dry tea towel or so much as a packet of biscuits. Where's Shirley?"

"She went off on her bike."

"Why did she? You never upset her, did you, Mick?"

"Everything upsets her," says Glen.

"Soppy little tart," says Harry Stokes. "I told her to get biscuits."

Nan slaps the angel cake onto some plates and pours the tea. Nobody says much. All I can hear is tea being sucked and teaspoons clanking and the soft *duff, duff, duff* of Glen's brothel creepers as he practises a bit of fancy footwork.

"Rock and roll," he keeps saying to himself, "rock and roll."

There's a baby photo on the sideboard, stuck behind a china dog. I go over and have a closer look. It's so dusty, I can't make much out, so I pick it up and blow the dust off. Nan barks at me.

"Put that down."

"Why? I'm only looking."

"You might break it."

I wonder who the baby is? It looks like me, but then lots of babies look like me only without the glasses.

"How old was I there, Nan?"

"That's not you. Put it down. You're getting cake all over it."

It's hard to tell if they're girls or boys at that age and I can't see much of it, just its little face poking out of a blanket.

"Is it Shirley?"

Nan snatches the photo and gives it a rub with her hanky. "No, it's Eileen. You won't remember her."

She puts the photo back on the sideboard. I feel sick. I can't take my eyes off the baby in the blanket. It's as if she's looking at me. She's smiling.

"She'd have been about three months there," says Nan.

"Four months," says Glen, twirling on one heel.

Harry ain't saying anything. He's just watching me. I wish he'd stop staring at me like that. I've caught him doing it a couple of times now.

"Could have sworn it was three," says Nan.

"It must have been four," says Harry, "because she went in November, didn't she?"

Everybody nods in agreement. Every one of them knows where Eileen is and nobody's bothered to tell me. Maybe I'll be able to see her soon. Maybe I can wangle the rag-and-bone man's address out of Harry Stokes.

"Where did she go?"

He takes a drag on his fag and glares at me. "Are you trying to be funny?"

"No. I just want to know where she is, that's all."

"Finchley," he says, jerking his thumb in the direction of Finchley, I suppose.

There are some quite nice places in Finchley. I hope she got to live in one of the big houses with a nice garden and everything. Maybe she's even got her own bike.

"Can I visit her?"

"I don't know where she is exactly," says Harry Stokes.

Well, he would say that, wouldn't he? He's probably ashamed he never had the money to keep her. I bet Mum never forgave him for that. That'll be why she left him. Nan is giving Harry Stokes a filthy look.

"I know where she is," says Nan, "and I don't know why she had to go all the way over there. I never did understand that."

"Connie's idea. Not mine," he says.

Now he's trying to pin the blame on my mum. Just then, Shirley comes back. Nan tells me to put my coat on.

"Oh, you're not leaving are you?" she says, nastily.

I tell her we're going to visit Eileen. She looks a bit surprised.

"Oh," she says, looking at her shoes. "Give her my love." Then she runs out of the room, up the stairs and slams the door.

"Moody cow," says Harry Stokes.

Glen turns on him.

"You always have to pick on her, don't you?" he shouts.

"What?" squeaks Harry Stokes. "Now what am I supposed to have done?"

Glen storms out of the room. Nan ties a scarf round her head and grabs her handbag and her biscuits.

"Ready, Mick?" She straightens my coat, makes me pull my socks up, then marches down the steps onto the street. She's another one who likes people to swing their arms when they walk.

"Chest out, shoulders back," she bellows. "Quick, march."

It's like that all the way to the bus stop. When we get on the bus, I suddenly wish I'd got some money to take Eileen a present. I wonder what she'd like?

"Flowers," says Nan, "but we won't give her any today because she's still got the ones I gave her. Carnations last for weeks."

"Yeah, but they won't be from me."

"That doesn't matter. She's not going to mind, is she?"

The bus conductor stops at our seat.

"One and a half to the cemetery," she says. She gives me the ticket to play with. I roll it up and pretend to smoke it.

"Don't do that," she says, and slaps it out of my hand.

"Is it much of a walk to Eileen's?" I ask.

"What?"

"Is it much of a walk?"

The bus pulls up by the graveyard. Rows and rows and rows of headstones. There's a hell of a lot of dead people.

"It's not far," Nan says. "You go down a little path and there's a little cherry tree on the left."

She goes through the gates. Obviously knows the short cut to Eileen's place. I'm so excited, I think I'm going to puke. All this time I've waited to see her and today's the day! I just wished I'd got nicer clothes, because if she's dead posh she might turn her nose up and not want to know me.

"Wooooooo . . . Spooky here, isn't it?" I grin, pretending to be a ghost.

{144}

"It's peaceful," shouts Nan. "Have some respect."

Then she stops. "Eileen's over there." She points.

I squint into the distance, but I can't see anybody. Maybe she's hiding behind a tree or something. Playing a game.

"I can't see her."

"Of course you can't, you twit. She's six feet under, isn't she?"

"What? Nan! . . . She's what?"

Nan stops. She takes one look at my face and her legs give way. She steadies herself on the headstone.

"Oh my God," says Nan, "you poor little bastard. Excuse my French." She crosses herself. "I thought you knew."

She kneels down at a doll-size grave and rearranges a few dried-up carnations in a tin vase.

"She died of pneumonia," she said. "Six months old, bless her."

There's a little wooden cross with a number on it and a photo. Rain has got into the photo and smeared her face, but I can see it's a baby girl with wispy blonde hair, a bit thin on the sides. Not as pretty as I'd hoped. Didn't recognise her in fact. I'd been expecting something quite different. This is a stranger.

"So sorry you didn't know," says Nan.

"It's alright," I say. "It's not like I knew her."

I feel cold and empty inside. I'm sad for the baby who died, but to me, it isn't Eileen. Not the Eileen I've been living with in my head all this time. She is still somewhere waiting to be found.

"She's better off where she is. God's looking after her," says Nan. "I dare say he'll make a better job of it than certain people, mentioning no names."

"Why did God give her pneumonia in the first place, then?" I don't believe in God any case.

"God didn't give it to her. A germ did."

"Yeah, but who made the germs?"

"The devil. Which reminds me, you're going to Sunday school from now on." She gets up and brushes some mud off her coat.

"It will do you good," she says. "I don't suppose you've set foot inside a church, have you?"

I shake my head.

"It shows," she says. "You need guidance, you do. And while you're there maybe you could say a few prayers for your mother because I'm beggared if I'm going to."

She blows a kiss to Eileen. "Bye-bye, my darlin', see you soon," she says.

All the way to the bus stop she's moaning about how they don't keep the place as nice as they should.

"The grass wants cutting," she says, "and the weeds! Did you see all the weeds?"

I hate violence, but if she doesn't shut up in a minute, I'm going to push her off the bus. God or no God.

sixteen

So here I am, settling down to life back at Nan's. Nothing else can shock me, I don't think. I've been adding it all up. My mum's in the nick doing a stretch. My dad's not my dad. I've got a new older sister and a brother who's a Ted. I've got a little dead sister and a new baby brother who I haven't even seen and I've got more aunties and cousins than I know what to do with.

Oh, and Nan was right. There is a God. I know this, because the night after we visited Eileen's grave I shut myself in the scullery where the bath is and came over all funny. Kind of crying and laughing at the same time.

I was gutted at not finding Eileen alive, and embarrassed that I never knew she was dead in front of Nan. At the same time, the whole thing suddenly seemed hilarious, stepping back from it a bit.

I kept going over what Nan and I said to each other on the bus. About me wanting to get her a present and Nan saying "flowers." I thought flowers was a stupid idea at the time. I wanted to get Eileen a skipping rope. A skipping rope! I wished I'd said it on the bus now about getting a skipping rope. I'd love to have seen Nan's face.

Anyway, I'm laughing my head off in the bathroom when just as quickly it turns into a weird gulping and crying and I'm saying, "There is no God. There is no God," over and over again.

Then I can hear Janice coming down the corridor. I don't want her to hear me sobbing, so I turn the taps on full to cover my noise, only . . . no water comes out! At first, I think maybe I've turned them the wrong way, but that's not possible. I'm panicking now, shaking the taps, sticking my toothbrush handle up them to see if there's a blockage. There isn't. There is just no water coming out. Janice bangs on the door.

"Mick, let me in. Mick."

I don't want her to see I've been crying.

"I know you've been crying, Mick."

I tell her to go away, but she won't.

"Go on, let me in. If you don't I'll kick the door down."

She starts toeing the door. At this rate, she'll have Nan down here, so I let her in. She puts her arms around my neck.

"Sad boy," she says. "Kiss me."

"Get off . . . Look, there's no water coming out of the taps."

"You haven't turned them on," she says.

"I have."

I turned them off, then on again. "Watch . . . on . . . off . . . no water!"

I told her what I'd been saying about God and she said it was more than likely not the hand of God stopping the water coming out, but most probably the ballcock was stuck and that we ought to ask her dad to have a look at it, because he's a plumber.

As it turns out, she was right. The ballcock was stuck, but Uncle Fred said it was very odd, because when a ballcock gets stuck it always gets stuck in a downwards position, not up, and this one was definitely stuck up.

"Almost as if someone was holding it," he said, wiping his wet hand on his trousers. After that little incident, I promised to go to Sunday school with less of a fight.

It's as boring as hell but I'm hedging my bets. Anyhow, I can't get out of it even if I want to, because they give you a sticker every week. You have to put it in a little book to match up with a story and Nan always checks to make sure I've done it.

She's a bossy old cow. She's got all these rules. Rules for when I come in. Rules for when I go out. Even rules for how to comb my hair. It's like being in the army. She loves the army. Bound to, I suppose, what with Grandad having been a lance corporal. He served out in India under Lord Mountbatten according to her.

Grandad Charlie's ex-service now of course, but he's still got his routine, same as he done in the army. Up at six on the dot, breakfast at seven, go for a crap at seven-fifteen . . . you could set your clock by him. I call him the clockwork man.

He works for the LEB in Holloway Road as a doorman, but he still wears his army uniform to work. He's got loads of flashy medals across his tunic. I'm not sure what they're all for, mostly for doing stuff in the First World War.

My mum was born out in India, Nan tells me. They had servants and everything. Big posh house overlooking the jungle . . . nice verandah.

"We had class," she said. But she never told me why we hadn't got it no more. She just said if I carried on the way I was, I'd end up in Borstal. If I dropped my angel cake on the floor, I'd end up in Borstal. If I slammed the door, I'd end up in Borstal. If I farted, I'd end up in Borstal.

I think I'm doing alright, actually. I've started school at Pakeman Primary and I've already made a couple of mates, Tommy Corbett and Andy Harris. We have a right laugh. We're all in the Lifeboys. That's what you go in before the

Boys' Brigade. I didn't want to join. Nan made me, but I'm glad in a way. It's only once a week after school every Tuesday and although some of it's a bit poncey, we get to play football and rounders.

Anyway, one Tuesday after Lifeboys, Andy Harris says, why don't we all go up to Hampstead Heath on the scrapcart and do some knife-throwing? Sounds like a great idea to me. We've made this really good scrapcart out of some old pram wheels, a plank of wood and a lump of rope. We had awful trouble getting hold of a bolt but Tommy found one in the end. I've got a feeling it came off his kid brother's pram but he never owned up. Not even when the front wheel fell off.

I've got a really good knife that I've been using for my Airfix kits, so I'm fixed up. The only thing is, Nan wants me home straight after Lifeboys and in bed by nine. Nine, I ask you! Mum never bothered what time I come home, but when I told Nan that, she said if I didn't go to bed at nine . . . you've got it . . . I'd end up in Borstal.

"Yeah, but we're not going up the Heath till then," says Andy.

There's only one thing for it. I plan my great escape. All I have to do is pretend to go to bed, then I'll climb out of the window and shin down the drainpipe. Then, when my mates have gone home, I'll climb back up the drainpipe and get back into bed and Nan will be none the wiser.

I tell Andy and Tommy to meet me by the Angel at half past nine.

Nine o'clock, I say goodnight to Nan. At five minutes past, I have to get rid of Janice. She won't go, unless I promise to feel her bum.

Eight minutes past nine, I'm opening the window, trying not to let it creak. Nine minutes past, I'm clinging onto the drainpipe and wishing it was stuck to the wall properly. It's a long way down and the paint's sticky for some reason. I've got a thumb full of pigeon-shit mixed with blackberry pips.

Fifteen minutes past nine, I'm still clinging to the pipe like an idiot because Nan's come out to empty the tea leaves down the drain and if she looks up, I'm as good as dead. She goes back in. I'm just about to slide all the way down when she comes back out again with a kettle full of boiling water and a box of soda crystals, both of which she tips down the drainhole.

She goes back in. I skid down the drainpipe, taking a big lump out of my hand on a ragged bolt.

Nine twenty-five, I'm legging it down the road towards the Angel, triumphant, where Andy and Tommy are waiting with our cart.

"Thought you was never coming," says Tommy. "Get in. You're steering." And we're off.

Our knife-throwing evening down Hampstead Heath is such a good crack, we decide to repeat the whole thing the next night. Tommy's got a better knife he wants to try out. He was using his fishing knife which is alright, but it's a bit heavy and the blade wants sharpening, so he wants to see if he can thrash us with the knife his dad uses to clean his pipe.

So we're all set for same time, same place tomorrow. I bus it down to my dad's after school and blag a really good penknife off Glen. Then I spend the rest of the afternoon buffing it up with a bit of emery paper.

I eat my tea nice and quietly. Every so often, when Nan's watching, I screw up my eyes and rub my head. At about half past eight, I tell her I'm going to have an early night because I've got a banging headache. She says, "Oh yes? Got a maths test tomorrow by any chance?"

"No, Nan. I think it's my glasses. I've got eye strain looking at the blackboard."

"Sit at the front then."

"Oh yeah. Good idea."

"It's yes, not yeah. Put a cold flannel on your head."

I go upstairs slowly, looking desperately ill, clutching my head. Janice is laughing at me.

"Shut your face, Janice. I'm not well."

She sticks her tongue out. "Liar."

She follows me up the stairs. "Can I come up the Heath with you, Mick?"

"No. Shut up. I'm not going up the Heath."

"Feel my bum."

"No. I'm not well."

"I'll tell Nan." She cups her hands to her lips as if she's going to yell.

"Don't you dare, Janice!"

I put my hand over her mouth and she grabs hold of it and shoves it up her dress. I'm getting fed up with this.

"Hurry up," she says, "or they'll go without you."

Nine twenty-five and I'm climbing out the window. Nine twenty-six, I've landed at the bottom of the drainpipe. Nine twenty-seven, something hits me very hard on the side of the head. It's Nan's hand. She's been waiting for me at the front door.

"Ouch!"

"There's a headache for you!" She chases me back inside, slapping the backs of my legs. "What do you take me for, you little sod? You ever do that again and you'll be in big trouble. I'll tell your Grandad Charlie to take his belt off to you. Get upstairs!"

The backs of my legs are covered in red, raised fingermarks. I can even see where her wedding ring got me. I get into bed. A bit later, she comes in with a hammer. At first I think she's going to hit me with it, then she takes a nail out of her mouth and bangs it into the window frame so I can't open it.

So that's that. I can no longer get out of that particular window. Luckily, I can squeeze quite easily out of the one next to it.

It's nine forty-five and I'm crawling across the little clay roof with Glen's best knife in my teeth. The coast is clear. By the time I get to the Angel, Andy and Tommy are just about to leave. Andy's none too pleased.

"It's too late to go up Hampstead Heath now. Where was you?" he says.

I tell them about Nan nailing the window down and they think it's hilarious. They want to know how I'm going to get back in and how many lashes I'll get off of Grandad Charlie's belt if Nan catches me.

"Does he really belt you," Tommy wants to know, "with his belt?"

"Na. Not yet anyway."

"I bet it hurts," he says. "I bet it makes blood."

I tell them about Grandad Charlie taking forty German prisoners during the war. He often tells me about the war after I've been down the offy for him. I get him the same thing every night, two brown ales and four stingoes. Tommy loves hearing about the war.

"Did your Grandad Charlie kill all forty Krauts?"

"Na . . . he only had a rifle. By the time he'd got to the top of their trench, they'd run out of ammunition. They were just sitting there with their hands up."

Tommy thought about this.

"Did he get a medal?"

"Yeah. He did."

"Even though he didn't kill any?"

"Yeah. He got loads of medals."

"I'd have shot them," says Tommy. "He could have shot a few of them, at least."

I tell them about the bullet hole in Grandad Charlie's top bicep. A German bullet went right through him and come out the other side.

"See," says Tommy, "they didn't think twice about shooting him, did they?"

I try to explain they weren't the same Germans, but he just says, so what? Then he wants to know all about the bullet hole. How big is it? Big enough to put a pipe-cleaner through or a carrot? He's quite bloodthirsty at times, is old Tommy.

"Come on," says Andy, "where are we gonna go? I've got to be back in less than an hour."

"Spaniard's Wood?"

"Too far."

We put our heads together and decide to go over the flats in Holloway Road. We'd never been before, but Tommy said one of his mates had been and it was good, because there were kids' swings you could lark about on and at that time of night there wouldn't be any little kids or grown-ups around, so we could have one of Andy's fags.

Andy smokes more than anyone I know. He pinches them out of his mum's handbag.

"I'd buy my own," he says, "but I get rubbish pocket money. How much do you get, Mick?"

"Depends."

The thing is, every Saturday, Auntie Minnie makes all the kids line up and wait for it. So there's Jean, Brenda, Janice and then me, tagged on the end. We all have to put our hands out and then Uncle Fred comes down the line, doling out the money. He gives me a shilling.

"Herey'a."

"Thanks."

But he never smiles, the miserable bugger. It's like he begrudges me every penny. Once, I missed the line-up because

I woke up late and he never bothered to give me my shilling later. I think he wanted me to grovel for it, but that's against my rules. Either he hands it over nicely, or he can stick it.

"So sometimes you get a shilling and sometimes you don't?" Andy wants to know.

"Yeah. And also my grandad gives me all his change on Sunday afternoon after he's been up the pub."

"What, all of it?"

"Well, say his drink cost one-and-eleven, right? He gives me the penny change."

When we get to the swings, I show them the ring I've bought with my pocket money. You fill it with water and squirt people in the face with it. Tommy thinks it's the bee's knees.

"Where'd you get it?"

"Woolworths."

"Swop it for an Embassy? Go on."

I quite fancy a fag. I haven't had a proper one in ages. Harry Spicer always had roll-ups, didn't he? So did my real dad.

"I'll lend it you."

Andy takes the ring and studies it.

"Give us a fag then."

"I've only got one."

All three of us share it. It's lovely having a puff in the dark until Tommy bums the end and makes the fag all soggy.

"I can't help it, it's too small to hold, I'm burning my fingers," he laughs. Then he pulls what's left of the fag right inside his mouth and shuts his lips. Then he sticks it out again.

"Want some?"

"Ugh! You rotten git!"

We try to tip him off his swing. I'm trying to undo his hands and Andy's got him by the ankles and we're making so much noise, we don't see this big geezer and his mates until they're almost on top of us. Tommy spots them first.

"Mick . . ."

"What?" I'm still laughing and trying to get him on the floor.

"Behind you."

"Oh, yeah?"

Then I catch Andy's face. It's gone white. He's holding onto the swing pole and trying to look tough.

I turn round. The big geezer's got a really nasty look on his face.

"What you looking at?" he says.

"Nothing." I sit down on my swing and look away.

"I'm talking to you."

Andy and Tommy start edging away. There are three of us. And he's so big, there's three of him an' all. Plus his two mates. I twist the chain on the swing so it turns me in the opposite direction. Bad move. He kicks the swing and the chain unravels, spinning me to face him, then away, then to face him again. Then he grabs me by the shirt, picks me up off the swing and slams me against a wall.

"This is our fucking camp, alright?"

I look for Andy and Tommy. They're legging it across the grass. He slams me so hard, all the wind is knocked out of me.

"I said . . . alright? Alright? Al" — *slam!* — "right?"

"Yeah . . . alright."

I slide to the floor, but before I get there, he kicks my legs away. I curl into a ball and he kicks my head in, very slowly. Very, very slowly.

"Get it?" . . . *Boot!* . . . "Do you get it?" . . . *Boot!* . . . "Whose swings are they?"

"Yours."

They're his alright. He's the Hard Man of the Swings. I am the shit beneath his shoe.

seventeen

It's been months since I got beaten up and I've still got a dicky ear where the Hard Man kicked me. Nan keeps dripping warm lard in it and my earholes smell permanently of bacon. She don't know what happened to me. I said I fell out of a tree. The only people who know apart from Andy and Tom are Janice and Jean.

Janice heard me crawling about outside after the duffing up. There was no way I could climb back up the gutter. I was all done in and covered in blood and I'd been sick. Andy and Tommy helped me a bit of the way, but they scarpered when they got near my house in case Grandad clocked them one with his belt.

Janice saw me out of the bedroom window. I was on my hands and knees, dying. I'd lost a lens out of my bins as well. I didn't realise at the time. I thought I'd gone blind in one eye.

"Mick? . . . Blimey!" she says. "Stay there!"

"Get Jean . . . don't tell Nan."

"What?"

She can't hear me but she runs off to get Jean anyway. They sneak downstairs and bundle me up to the bedroom.

I stink to high heaven and I'm covered in mud. Janice holds

her nose and wants to know if I've done one. I tell her it's dog's muck but she don't believe me.

Nan wakes up when we go past her room and calls out, but Jean fobs her off.

"Only me, Nan. I left my magazine downstairs."

"Is Mick in?"

"Yeah. He's in."

I'm still sharing a room with Jean. She gets a bowl of water, washes me down and puts some stuff on my cuts. She wants to know who done me over, but I won't tell her. I'm more concerned about my pants at the time, but she says it doesn't matter.

"Everybody does that when they're scared, Mick. Even the Queen."

She folds them in half, puts them in a brown paper bag and gives them to Janice. Janice pulls a face.

"I don't want them! What am I supposed to do with them?"

"Put them in a bucket of water and put the lid on and Janice, don't say nothing to Brenda, OK?"

"Why not?"

"Because she'll tell Mum and Mum and Nan will have a row and Mick's got enough on his plate, don't you think?"

Nice of her to stick up for me. Nan and Min have already fallen out over me staying here and Brenda hates me because I play with Janice. Jean's lovely. She patches me up and lets me sleep in bed with her. I like that. She usually sleeps in the nude, but when I'm with her she never, which is a bit of a shame because she looks so nice with nothing on. Instead, she undresses behind the door and comes back out wearing a white, shiny slip and a pair of white knickers. Every time she rolls over in bed, she rustles.

I tell her I wish I could sleep like that every night. With her, in her bed. She holds me while I cry it all out.

"I want M-M-Mum."

"I know."

"I miss Terry."

"I bet you do. Shh . . . it'll be alright."

No one's ever held me like this before. Not my mum, no one.

"When's Mum coming home?"

"Not long. When she does come out, I'll take you to see her, alright?"

"Alright."

"Don't tell Nan though. Come on, give us a smile." She wipes my face with the sheet and rubs the snot off her slip.

"Go to sleep now."

"My head hurts."

So she sings to me like I'm a baby. But that's how I feel, like a baby. I hoped I was starting to rise above it all. Getting my act together. I've got mates. I've got a bit of money. Enough to eat. I'm doing alright at school. I'm just about managing reading and writing and if I can't spell a word, I just do a squiggle, like joined-up writing. That way, the teacher just thinks I've got bad handwriting instead of thinking I can't spell.

"I don't understand why he hit me, Jean."

"Maybe you was on his territory."

"Yeah, so? I never done anything to wind him up. Why did he have to hit me?"

"Because he's a lad. You either do the beating or you get beaten up in this life, Mick."

I never hit anybody. I hate violence. Especially the sort that comes out of nowhere. I don't mind the boxing. That's not violence, that's different. I watch it on Nan's little Ferguson telly and it's great, because the blokes don't mean nothing by it. It's a skill. Afterwards, they shake hands and everything's fine. I've been watching the boxing more and more since I got beaten up. Afterwards, I have little jabs at myself in the mirror when no one's looking.

I'm not going over the flats again. Not yet. I've made up my mind to get hard, because I'm never going to be on the wrong end of a fist again. I've tried it and I don't like it. I'm not going to pick a fight, but if someone wants one, he can have it.

I'm helping Nan put the ham sandwiches out in her front room when Andy and Tommy pedal past the window on new bikes. They've both got brand new push-bikes for Christmas, lucky gits. I got some quite nice things but I never got a push-bike.

"Hey, Mick. Coming out?"

"Can't. Nan's having a party."

"Can we come? Go on, give us a sammidge!"

Nan bangs on the window and yells at him. "Clear off, Tommy Corbett. And you, Harris!"

They pull faces and pedal off, waving. I wish I could go with them. It's stuffy in Nan's front room. It's her best room. No one is allowed in it the rest of the time. It's got a piano, sideboard, cabinet, the works. There's a thick carpet in the middle of the room and the floorboards are polished round the end. I've never seen a room so posh. I help myself out of a little dish while she's not looking.

"Mick! Fingers out of those nuts!"

There must be loads of people coming tonight, judging by the amount of food Nan's put out. She's in a foul mood, getting it all ready. Minnie's refusing to come to the party, Uncle Fred and Grandad have gone up the Favourite to get out of the way, Jean's been rolling out pastry all afternoon and Brenda and Janice are about to come to blows.

Nan says she's going to bang their silly heads together. She's just about to do it when someone knocks at the door.

"That'll be my Terry," she says. "Let him in, Jean."

"Can't, Nan. I'm covered in pastry."

"Janice, then . . . Open the door."

"Why me? Why can't Brenda?"

Nan slaps the table with her hand and all the mince pies jump up in the air.

"Will one of you open the flaming door?"

Janice and I open it together, and there, standing to attention on the doorstep, is this scary-looking soldier with a shaved head and a uniform. He stamps his feet, salutes us both and says hello. Then he marches into the kitchen.

"Terry!" smiles Nan, and her face goes soft. "How lovely. Come here, son!" She holds her arms out and he gives her a cuddle.

"Merry Christmas, Mum."

Turns out he's my mum's little brother. She must have called my brother Terry after him. He's on leave from the Paratroopers. Janice says I should show him my Airfix planes. He's really into Airfix, apparently. I haven't got many models, because even the cheapo ones cost one-and-six. I've only got a couple of the really good ones that cost three bob and one of them I haven't even made yet. Glen and Shirley give it me for Christmas. Mind you, I think it was all from Glen really, because when I thanked Shirley for it she said, "What Airfix kit?"

She doesn't like me, I can tell. Maybe it's because she doesn't want my real dad to give me any attention. She wants it all for herself.

From now on, the door knocker never stops. I've never seen so many people in one room and they're all my relations on my mum's side. Not that anyone mentions her to my face.

There's a man smoking a fat cigar standing with a woman. Nan tells me it's my auntie Kitty.

"She's another one of your mum's sisters," Janice whispers. "She lives up Archway off Junction Road near the Drum and Monkey."

"Who's the bloke with her?"

"That's Uncle George. He used to be a boxer."

It looks like it too. A bit later on, after he's had a few sherries, he takes his jacket off and lets me feel his muscles.

"Feel that . . . I was a south paw," he says, "like my boy."

He throws a few punches in the air and makes the sound effects. His son, Little George, is puffing himself up and doing a few jabs on his own.

"I'm training him up," says his dad. "Aren't I, son?"

"Yuh," says Little George. "Fancy a spar, Mike?"

"It's Mick."

I did as it happens. I fancied giving his smug face a slap, but I hate violence. And he is family. He's my cousin whether I like him or not, so I try and get out of it.

"No, you're alright. Anyway, I ain't got no gloves."

He doesn't give up though, Little George. "Dad's got some in the car, haven't ya, Dad?"

Next thing, Big George has stubbed his cigar on the bottom of his shoe and gone out the front to get two pair of gloves.

"Go on, punch him in the nose," says Janice. "He's getting on my wick."

Nan's none too pleased when she gets wind of what's going on.

"Oi," she says, "not in this room you don't. It's Christmas. It's supposed to be Peace on Earth, Goodwill to all Men."

"I'm only going to show him the ropes," says George.

Nan folds her arms and wags her finger at him. "Not in my house you don't. That's my best tablecloth and glasses."

Then Grandad Charlie rolls in. He's had a few by now.

"They're only having a laugh," he says. "Let them hit each other if they want to. It's Christmas, innit?"

Nan stomps off to make tea. She sticks her fingers up at him from behind a tea towel. Janice is wetting herself laughing, which winds Nan up even more.

"It's alright, Nan," says Kitty. "George, don't you dare! You'll have that trifle over and all them cups. Go out in the garden!"

Next thing, the two of us, me and Little George, are standing eyeball to eyeball, all gloved up. He's quite big, as it happens, despite being called Little. Big George starts telling me how to put my guard up, and how to throw a punch and move about. Little George is warming up, dancing up and down like he's got a feather up his crack. Then Uncle Fred comes staggering down the path eating a jar of pickled walnuts.

"Right," says Uncle George, "you two have a go and I'll be the ref. Take your hat off, Mick."

I forgot I'm still wearing my hat. It come out of a cracker earlier. It's a green crown, made out of tissue paper. There was a plastic soldier in it an' all, and a joke about a chicken.

"Ready, Mick?"

Uncle Fred totters into our "ring" and sits down with a soppy smile on his face. Uncle George drags him under a tree by his braces.

"Get out of the way, you silly old git."

I hang the crown over a tree branch and take my position. We start sparring. Little George is quite tasty. He throws a few punches and they connect. It don't hurt much, though. What it does do is make him a bit cocky.

"Come on, Mick," says Big George, "try and throw a few jabs!"

So, I went two left jabs, came straight across with my right and *blam!* hit him square on the button with such force his head went back and bounced off the shed door.

I KO'd him.

"Fucking hell!" says Uncle George. "Where'd you learn to do that?"

I was as surprised as he was.

"Off the telly, I suppose."

I put my tissue-paper crown back on and pull it over my eyebrows. I'm King Mick.

"You should take it up." He's so excited he don't even seem to notice Little George rolling about on the floor with his eyes all crossed.

"You'd be good! I'll train you!"

I tell him I don't really like bashing the hell out of people, but he won't let it drop. He follows me about at the party like a puppy. Every time I turn round, I fall over Uncle George, bobbing and weaving. I'm standing with my auntie Joyce, having a natter and a bit of cake, when he puts his arm round me. He squeezes me so hard I spit my mince pie out.

"How about it, Mick? Go on. Give it the old one-two. It'll make a man of you."

"Oh, leave him alone," says Joyce. "He's only ten, George." George tries to get Joyce's husband, Adam, on his side.

"Adam . . . tell him will you? Why waste a talent like that?"

Adam's a milkman. He's nice-looking. Tall and well-built with blonde hair. He done all Nan's garden for her. Put the turf down, made a concrete path and knocked a few doors out. He even made a partition so you could walk through the hallway straight into the garden.

"He doesn't want to get into boxing," says Adam. "He wants to get into plastic. That's where the future lies."

"What are you on about?" says Joyce. "What's plastic got to do with anything?" She's Mum's youngest sister. She must be about twenty, I reckon. Sometimes, when she comes down to Nan's to watch telly, I put my arm round her. She used to sit really stiff at first, like she was shy or something, but after a while she got used to it.

She's always having a go at Adam about being too friendly with his customers but he just laughs, and then she says, "If I ever catch you, that'll be your lot. I mean it, Adam."

We all thought she was joking.

Come the New Year, Auntie Min put another single bed next to mine and Jean's, and Auntie Joyce moved in with us. I never saw Adam again. When I asked Joyce what had happened to him, she just snapped, "He delivered more than he should have to a woman called Avril Wardby."

"What? More eggs? More milk? . . . What?"

Then she said, "Oh, shut up!" and burst into tears. So I kept my nose out.

eighteen

Most Fridays, I go round to see my dad. One time, I took Janice with me. She wanted to listen to some of Glen's records but he wasn't in and nor was Shirley. As it turned out, nor was my dad. He was working late, so we just let ourselves in with the house key. It's tied to a piece of string hanging on the other side of the letter box.

We didn't do much. Just had a piece of bread and butter and listened to the radio. Then Janice says wouldn't it be a laugh if she tried Shirley's shoes on. I tell her not to, but she goes upstairs anyway and keeps coming down, wearing different things and doing silly walks. I'm trying to listen to a quiz thing and she's really getting on my nerves.

"Take that hat off. Shirley will kill you."

"No . . . I've got her drawers on and all . . . look!"

"No thanks. I'm listening to this."

She sticks her tongue out. "Bor-ing."

Then she kicks Shirley's shoes down the stairs, one after the other. *Clomp, clomp, clomp.* I tell her to pick them up.

"No, you pick them up."

"No, you! You sound like Nan."

She flops down in my dad's chair and kicks her legs up and

down, giggling and going "bla bla bla" so I can't hear the radio. I get out of my chair and go upstairs, picking up the shoes and shouting at her.

"I ain't bringing you again."

"I don't care. Bor-ing."

She's left Shirley's clothes all over the floor. Pulled out great drawerloads of socks and pants and everything. I put them all back, trying to make sure none of the pants go in the sock drawer. Quite nice, some of the pants, but because they're Shirley's and I don't like Shirley I'm not as interested in them as I might be.

Janice creeps up behind me.

"I'm telling," she says. "You're looking at Shirley's drawers!"

I slam the drawer shut.

"I want to go now," says Janice. "Can we go now?"

"I want to wait for Dad. He'll be in soon."

She pulls at my arm. "But I want to go. It's half past eight. Come on! If you don't I'll empty all the drawers again."

So we leave. Janice is turning into a really bad girl. Scared of no one. Auntie Min can't do nothing with her and Uncle Fred spends all his time down the club. Nan says Janice is going to get into serious trouble one day, and for once I reckon she's right.

I never asked her to come the next time I went to my dad's. I prefer to go on my own. It's only one stop on the tube from Holloway to the Caledonian Road and I never pay. What I do is this. I run down one lot of emergency stairs and up the other, so I don't have to hand in a ticket to the collector. Then, when I come out of the Cally tube, I cross the road to Pentonville Prison, climb up the wall and walk all the way along it on the top. Then I jump down the other end.

It's a bit like an assault course. Just something to do. And it helps to build my legs up because I'm trying to get hard, aren't I? Either you beat, or you get beaten.

I hope Glen's in, because sometimes he give me a couple of bob. And if I chop up some firewood, Dad gives me money an' all. Mind you, I must have chopped him up a couple of months' worth of fires by now. He hasn't got anywhere to put all the logs.

I love doing it though. It's knackering, but it makes me feel strong and peaceful somehow. I'm sure my biceps are growing. Glen says they ain't, but that's just because he's trying to act smart in front of his bird. Gives him an excuse to show her his muscles, I suppose.

Glen's always got a girl there when I go round. It's never the same one though and he always gets rid of her before Dad comes home. Can't wait until I'm his age. He's alright, is Glen. Gives me fags and lets me listen to his records whenever I want.

Anyway, I get out of the tube and I'm walking along when I hear this car tooting softly and there's a car crawling along the kerb. Someone winds the window down. I keep walking.

"That you, Mick?"

It's Harry Spicer. He stops the car and opens the door. For a minute, I think he's come to take me home, just like he did when Mum won the pools. Only she didn't win no pools, did she? Second thoughts, I know he ain't going to take me home. I've learned to read faces now.

"Get in the car, son."

And I'm not his son, but I get in anyway, because I've missed him. I never realised quite how much until I saw him sitting there like that. I go and sit next to him. We talk about this and that. I tell him I'm going round my real dad's.

"Your real dad's, eh?" he says.

"I wish you were my dad, Harry."

"Sorry about that. I should have told you. I just never got round to it. It's alright though, isn't it? You're alright, aren't you, round Nan's?" He gives me a Mars bar.

"It's not so bad. Where's Terry?"

I turn and look in the back of the car, wishing he was there but knowing he won't be. "He's at school."

I can't believe he's old enough to go to school. I've missed a great chunk of him. "Where's Mum?"

He never said where she was, he just said she was alright and wanted to know how I got on with Harry Stokes.

"Alright, tell her. I'm going round there to chop wood for him and that."

I wish I'd never met Harry Stokes. I wanted it to be like it was. Me, Harry Spicer, Mum, Tel and Gary. I've never even seen Gary.

"When can I see Gary?"

"Soon."

"Is Mum out of . . ."

"Yeah."

"When can I see . . ."

But he never lets me finish. He puts his finger to his lips and starts fiddling in his pockets. He counts some money into my hand.

"There you go, three . . . four-and-sixpence . . . five bob."

I suppose it's meant to be a sweetener, the money. I sit and look at it. There was no need to give it me. I'm happy enough just seeing him again. He starts the engine up.

"I'll see you later," he says.

"Are you going?"

"Got to, mate. Mind how you go."

"See you, Dad."

I realise what I've said is wrong as soon as I say it . . . Dad. He looks gutted for a second, then his mouth goes back to normal. He smiles at me. I get out of the car.

I wave until the car turns the corner and I keep waving long after it has gone, hoping in the back of my mind that if I wave hard enough, he'll see me in his mirror and reverse all the way back up the road and say, "Come on, son, I'm taking you home. We have won the pools really. We were just having a joke."

Only he never. He rode off into the sunset, just like the cowboys.

I carry on down the road, feeling really low, when Andy Harris screeches to a halt and does a wheelie onto the pavement.

"Wotcha, Mick. Guess what?"

"What?"

"Me and Tommy's found you a bike. It's a good'n!"

I've always wanted a bike. Nan keeps saying I can use Jean's old one, but it's a girl's one and I don't want it. It would do at a pinch, but not for riding out with my mates. They'd die laughing.

"Where'd you find it?"

"Borrowed it from Finsbury Park. We didn't nick it."

"Honest?"

Andy scratches his head. "Don't think we nicked it anyway. It was just lying under some trees and we waited over an hour and no one came to get it so we reckon either the owner forgot it or he died or something."

"What colour is it?"

"Same as Tommy's. And the brakes work. Come and see it."

I really want to. I'm desperate for a bike. But I'm desperate to get to know my real dad as well. I've got to learn to like him and get him to like me because Harry Spicer don't want me any more. He likes me, but he don't want me there, I can tell.

"Can't. I'm going round my dad's."

"What, Stokes or Spicer?"

"Stokes. Spicer gave me five bob though. I saw him just now."

"Give us it for the bike," says Andy. "Then if your nan asks, you can say you bought it off us. Otherwise she might think you nicked it."

I offer him three shillings for it.

"Three-and-six and I'll bring it round your house tomorrow," he says.

It's a deal. By the time I get to my dad's, it's about half past four. There's no way he'll be home yet, so I let myself in. I'm pretty sure the house is empty, so I walk down the hallway towards the kitchen to make a cup of tea.

Suddenly, Shirley appears on the stairway from the basement and starts pushing me back down the passage. I'm laughing at first.

"Get off. I want a cup of tea. What are you doing?" But when I see her face, I can see she's mad at me. She's almost in tears. I can feel her nails digging into my stomach.

"Go . . . back! Go . . . back!" she screams.

"What? What have I done?"

"You . . . get . . . back!" She pushes me with such a shove I end up on the floor.

"Shirley! Get off . . . ouch . . . you bitch!"

I know I mustn't hit her, but she's biting me. I push her face away with my palm, talking to her like I'm trying to calm down a dog.

"No . . . no . . . stop it . . ."

She tears at my hand with her fingers, and when I grab her wrists, she starts kicking me in the thigh. In the bum. In the nuts.

"Right, Shirley. You've asked for it now."

She's strong though. She's a lot bigger than me and I daren't smack her one, or I'll have my dad to reckon with. Anyway, she's a girl. I just keep pushing her away, trying to limit the damage, and she just keeps saying over and over, "Thief! Thief! Thief!"

I can't think why she's saying it. I'm going over and over in my head what it could possibly be that I'm supposed to have done. At first I think maybe she's angry about Janice poking about in her wardrobe, but I'm sure I put everything back properly.

"What do you mean, thief? Eh? I haven't nicked nothing."

I push her away again and my shirt rips right down the front.

"Shirley! Look what you've done, will ya?"

"So? You're a thief! Just like your mother."

She gobs in my face. I can feel the rage boiling up in me like a kettle. My hands are curling into a fist. She's down on the floor, snarling at me and panting. Then the key turns in the lock and she scuttles back down the basement stairs, screaming.

Harry Stokes slams the front door. Shirley slams another door. Then the basement window opens and shuts. She's done a runner. Dad stares at me. My shirt's hanging off me in rags and I'm sitting on the floor, shaking with anger.

"What's happened to you?" he says.

"Shirley just went for me."

"Did she? Shir-lee!"

He goes down into the basement and pushes the door open, but she's flown. He comes back, puts his hands under my armpits and pulls me up. He's not very strong.

"Are you alright?" He says it in a sing-song way, a bit like a little girl.

"Look at my shirt, Dad! She done that. I don't know what's got into her."

He tells me it's probably about the money that went missing last Friday.

"What money?"

"There was two bob for the gas meter," he says. "I left it on the shelf but it wasn't there when I come home."

I remember seeing it now. I thought I'd better come clean.

"I saw it when I come round here with Janice, but I never took it."

That's one thing I never do, take money off someone I know. Nobody likes a thief. Dad's puppety eyebrows almost disappear off the top of his head.

"Janice was with you?" he says. "Must have been her then. Course it was."

She must have put it in her pocket when I was tidying up Shirley's things. Little bitch. No wonder she wanted to go home before my dad came back.

"Shirley must have thought you took it, Mick."

"I never."

"I know that. Trouble is, I thought it must have been Shirley." He pulls a face. "I belted her one."

I feel sick inside. Shirley's never going to talk to me again now. I want to tell her I know how it feels to be smacked about when you ain't done nothing. It's all Janice's fault. Harry Stokes offers me a biscuit. He's staring at my chest where the shirt's all ripped.

"You wanna watch that Janice. It's not the first time," he says. "Do you want me to give you a strip wash? Get the dust off?"

"It's alright. I'll be chopping wood in a minute, won't I? I'll get filthy again."

"Alright then," he says. "After, maybe."

I go into the yard to chop the wood. I take what's left of my shirt off, swing the axe over my head and bring it down hard. *Whump!* The two halves shoot off in opposite directions. Harry Stokes sits on the step and watches me, rolling a fag.

"Your muscles are coming on," he says, "in your arms."

I swing the axe again, standing nice and square to the log, so I look taller. So he'll be proud of me. I bring the axe down again. I can feel him watching me.

"How's school?" he says, just making conversation.

"Bit boring. Got my eleven-plus coming up."

"Yeah? Doesn't matter though, does it? You'll be going in the army, won't you? You don't need to get into no poncey grammar for that."

"I hadn't thought."

I don't want to go in the army at all. Why should I? I'm not sure what I want to do, but it ain't that. I don't want to shoot people I don't even know. I hate violence.

"You'd look good in the uniform. Don't you like the uniform?"

"Not really."

"I do."

"Was you in the army, Dad?"

"No. They won't let you in if you're colour-blind. I'm colour-blind. I can't tell the difference between blue and green."

"So? You can see alright, can't you?"

"Yeah." He takes a drag on his fag then flicks it across the yard. "But I might have shot the allies instead of the enemy, because you can only tell who's who by the colour of the uniform in the heat of the moment."

I tell him I'd quite like to be a model-maker or a carpenter. Or maybe play a guitar, like Glen.

"You don't want to be like him," says my dad. "He's ugly."

Glen wears these really good jeans. Drainpipes, he calls them. I don't know how he gets into them, they're so tight. They look pretty good though, with his brothel creepers.

"Can I have a pair of drainpipes, Dad?"

"Ask your nan."

I know she'll say no.

"Oh, go on, Dad. I'll give you something towards it."

I show him what's left of Harry Spicer's five bob.

"Where'd you get that then?"

I almost tell him. I almost tell him how I've been talking to Harry Spicer and how Mum's out of prison and about Gary, but I decide to keep it buttoned. I don't think he's too keen on Harry Spicer.

"Uncle Fred gave it me. It's pocket money."

"I've got something for you. Want a bit of wood?"

I look at the pile of logs round my feet. "No thanks. Nan's got plenty."

He laughs and gets up. "No, not logs," he says. "Not for the fire. I've got some big bits you could do woodwork with. Want it?"

He goes over to the shed and staggers out with a cloth bag full of stuff.

"Any good?"

I root through the bag. It smells wonderful. All warm and sappy and damp. I brush the cobwebs off. There's some three-ply . . . even some balsa.

"Thanks! Oh, that's lovely. I know what I'm going to make."

"What?"

"A guitar!"

Just then, someone knocks at the door. Dad says it's his friend, Keith. He introduces me and Keith shakes my hand. It's a very small, dry hand.

"Hello, Mick. What have you got there?"

"Dad gave me some wood."

Keith looks at my dad and starts laughing. I dunno why. I tell him I'm going to make a guitar with the stuff. Keith says that's nice, because he's very musical. Perhaps I'll play him something on it when it's finished? I tell him I can't play yet. Glen's going to teach me.

"Oh, yes. Glen!" says Keith, rolling his eyes. "He of the wastepipe trousers."

"Drainpipe," says my dad.

"Whatever," says Keith. "Are we going into town or not? What is Mick doing?"

Harry Stokes helps me out of the yard with my bag of wood. "Going back to his Nan's, aren't you, Mick?"

"Dad, what about Shirley? Will you tell her about Janice?"

"I'll sort it. See you, Mick."

I thank him for the wood again and struggle up the path with my bundle. I can't wait to get started on the guitar.

"Mind you don't get splinters . . ." sings Keith.

Funny bloke, Keith. I can't quite work him out.

nineteen

Failed my eleven-plus. I came last of the lot, which is pretty amazing. I couldn't understand half the questions, never mind trying to answer them. Mind you, I've only been to school for about two years in all my life if you add up the days I actually bothered to go.

It's annoying, because recently, I've been to school more often than ever before, because of Nan. She gets to know if I cop off, because Brenda tells on me. So does the bloke in the offy.

The teacher reckons I only answered one question and I got that wrong. I just put a stroke of a pen by all the others. I've got a choice. I can either leave at the end of term and go to secondary modern, or stay on another year and retake the exam.

"What's the point, sir? I'll only flunk it again. I'm thick as a brick," I tell him. He looks out of the window and sighs. Then he opens the window. I think he's going to throw himself out for a minute, but he never. He just bangs the ash out of his pipe and sticks it back in his pocket.

"You're not thick, Stokes. You're lazy. There's a difference."

"Yes, sir."

"If you spent as much time on your homework as you did mucking about with that lunatic Harris and that nitwit Corbett, I believe you could almost be average."

"Thanks, sir."

Tommy and Andy failed too.

"What is it you want to do, Stokes?"

"What with, sir?"

"With yourself, lad. Any plans . . . ambitions, perhaps?"

I hadn't really thought. I didn't want to go in the army, that's for sure. Right now, all I want to do is go home and finish making my guitar.

"I'm talking to you, Stokes."

"Oh . . . I'd like to play the guitar, sir."

That seems to perk him up a bit.

"Really? Well, that's a start. Modern or classical?"

"Like Bill Haley, sir."

"Like . . . Bill . . . Haley."

He pushes his fingertips together and looks at me over the top of them. "I'd rather you became a petty criminal," he murmurs. "Go away, Stokes."

I decide to go up the shops to buy some guitar strings. Nan's given me the money. She's dead impressed with my carpentry skills.

What I done was this. I cut the basic guitar shape out of the three-ply, then I put four blocks of timber on the inside to get the distance. Then, I soaked some balsa in water and cut it into four-inch strips which I stuck round the outside. After that, I made a handle out of some two-by-one. I even made a bit on the end that holds the pegs that hold the strings.

"Very nice," Nan says. "You could be a carpenter when you grow up."

"Na . . . I want to be in a rock and roll band. I want to be famous." I pick the guitar up and dance with it, like Glen does.

"You have to spoil it, don't you?" she says. "Don't do that with your hips, it's rude. Why can't you be a famous carpenter instead?"

"Name one."

"Jesus Christ our Saviour."

"Bit of a short career though, wasn't it, Nan?"

She hits me round the head with a tea towel. "Wash your mouth out," she says. "He died for your sins."

I tell her I've never done nothing wrong in my life and that I couldn't think of a single sin. She isn't having it though.

"Everyone's a sinner," she says. "I was going to give you some money for strings, but I'm not so sure now."

"I thought Christians were supposed to forgive sins."

"That depends."

She never says what it depends on, she just puts her head down and carries on painting a model of a Ford Tee. She often does homework for a firm called Britons, up the Hornsey Road. She does it for pin money. I give her a hand sometimes.

"Oh, come on, Nan. I'll help you paint those Fords."

She shakes her head. "Not good enough . . . taking His name in vain. I dunno."

"Nan . . . see this guitar? I'll learn hymns on it. I'll play it at Sunday school. 'Jesus Wants Me for a Sunbeam.'"

She puts her brush down. Her eyes are narrowed to a slit, but she's kind of smiling even though I don't think she believes me for one minute about the hymns.

"Go on then. Get my purse."

Great. I go and buy the strings and the bit of metal I need to stick on the front to make the notes. Then I buy a bag of chips, have a fag and go back to school in the afternoon. When I get there, Andy collars me.

"Cramphorn's after you," he says. "Wants to see you in the playground, playtime."

"What for?"

"Reckons you called him a fat pig."

"No, I never."

He is a fat pig, but I never called him that. I never take the micky out of people. I learnt that a long time ago. Cramphorn deserves it though. He nicked a little kid's comb and flushed it down the toilet after games. Made him cry.

There are fights going on all the time at the moment. I've managed to keep out of them so far, because I hate all that. Fat Pig is different though. He's a bully. He doesn't know it yet, but I'm going to have him if he doesn't watch it.

All through Maths, he's screwing me, trying to make me scared. He's big, but he's all lard.

"What are you looking at, Cramphorn?"

"I'm gonna have you, Stokes."

He's asked for it now. I can't disappoint him, now can I? In fact, I'm so looking forward to it, by the time the bell goes, I'm almost in the ring, ready for the first round. The rest of the school have got wind of it by now and they're all milling about, waiting for something to happen.

Andy and Tom are nearly as excited as I am. They're running around like my managers. Fatty's henchmen are ahead of us, going over to the corner of the bottom playground, out of sight of the staffroom.

The entire school starts drifting over, pretending they ain't going anywhere. I take my jumper off and give it to Andy. Fatty's waiting for me. As I walk over to him, the crowd starts chanting.

"Bundle! Bun-dle!"

They form a big circle round us. Cramphorn gives me a mean look and spits his fruit pastille out.

I grin at him. He's so sure I'm going to lose. I'm standing about two foot away from him now. I lean forward and talk to him nicely.

"Ready, fatty?"

That gets him mad. He takes a dive at me. His right arm comes up to hit me, but I just stand there with both hands straight down by my sides. As he takes the swing, I move to the left about twelve inches and stick my right leg out. As he comes past, he trips over my leg, my right arm comes round and I smash him on the back of the shoulders with my forearm to give him more of a shove.

He goes flying and hits the deck. He don't move. I've winded him and he's skinned all his knees and elbows. I can hear them chanting, "Mick! Mick! Mick!"

Cramphorn lifts his head up off the floor. He's furious. "Right, Stokes. You're gonna get it now!"

"Cramphorn! Cramphorn! Cramphorn!"

He gets to his feet. I'm dancing about, I'm loving every minute of it. He takes another run at me, like a bull with its horns down, but I done the same thing. He fell for it again! Over the right leg, smash on the back and *whump!* I can't believe he fell for it twice. I'm cracking up laughing.

"Mick! Mick! Mick!" Cramphorn gets to his feet, knees pouring with blood. His elbows and hands are full of tarmac. He sinks back down again.

"Sir's coming Sir's coming Sir's coming."

The circle breaks up. Cramphorn's cronies bundle him into the boys' toilets. The other kids start patting me on the back, getting round me, like. Suddenly, they all want to be my mates.

"Alright, Mick? Stuffed him, didn't ya?"

"Did you see the state of Fatty? Stokes done him over."

I can feel them talking about me everywhere I go. Girls whispering behind their hands and smiling. First years asking for my autograph. I'm Top Dog now. Nothing ever felt this good before.

After that, I'm in constant demand for fights. I never start them, just go in to defend. If I see a kid picking on someone smaller than themselves, I go over, grab hold of them and say, "Oi! Pick on someone your own size or I'll give you a slap."

Usually, that's enough. They back down. However, there are a few animals who won't take no for an answer. Then there's the kids who get picked on, on purpose, just so they can get me into another ruck. In the end, I have to tell them all to behave, because it's getting ridiculous. Suddenly, everyone's got a little brother or sister some big bloke is supposed to have half-murdered and they all come whining to me to sort it.

I'm getting worn out with it. Enough's enough. I've had a good few fights now. Always clean ones. Two left jabs and a right cross, right on the button. It always finishes there, pretty much. It's not violence as such, I don't think. Not if someone's got it coming to them.

I'm glad when the weekend comes so I can forget about my responsibilities. Andy and Tom call round for me. We're going to play follow-my-leader on our bikes. Andy's already bagsied being the leader and shoots off towards Hornsey Road. We race off after him.

Now that my legs are so strong, I'm powering along, over-taking Andy, which makes me the leader. When I get to the traffic lights at Isledon Road, I stop at the kerb and decide to play a trick.

What I'm going to do is whizz straight across the road and then do a sharp right, because they won't be expecting that. Only neither does a bloke in a car. I didn't think to look right when I done it, just veered over and suddenly there's a dull thump and the bike comes away from underneath me and I'm flying up in the air.

It's all going in slow motion. I'm aware of a screeching noise and Tom and Andy shouting, then I land in a heap on the road. I don't feel no pain. It's just like watching a film, only I'm starring in it.

After a few seconds, I'm back in the real world. The driver of the car gets out and comes over to me. There's quite a crowd gathered.

"He just pulled straight out!" the driver's saying.

"Shouldn't have been going too fast," the woman says. "He's only a kiddy."

Kiddy, my arse, I don't know where Andy and Tom are. I'm worried someone will tell Nan and she'll have a go at me for not riding properly. She'd be on the driver's side. She always thinks it's me that's in the wrong. I sit up and rub my head. The woman makes me lie down again.

"You should keep still," she says, "in case you've broken your neck."

People are crowding round me, firing questions. What's your name? Where do you live? Can you hear me? How old are you? What's your inside leg measurement?

"Is my bike alright?"

"Never mind the bike, sonny."

There's a ball of knitted metal on the kerb with a couple of wheels stuck in it. Andy's rescuing bits off it, because it's going to have to be scrapped. The pump. The saddlebag. The front wheel. I wonder if the same thing's going to happen to me? He'll be going through my pockets in a minute to see if there's anything worth saving before I'm taken for scrap.

My knee's killing me. I can hear bells. An ambulance pulls up and two big geezers in uniforms get out. I shut my eyes. One of them pulls my eyelids up and looks into them.

"What's your name, son?"

"John." I told them that in case they went and got Nan.

"Where do you live?"

"I can't remember. My mind's gone blank."

"Alright, John. We'll just take you into hospital to make sure you haven't banged your head."

Then he turns to his mate. "Nothing much, Reg," he says. "Cuts and bruises."

The crowd seem really disappointed I'm not going to die. The driver wants to come with me in the ambulance, but a policeman's arrived and wants to have a word with him.

"It wasn't his fault," I call, as they slide me onto a stretcher and bung me in the ambulance. "I wasn't looking where I was going."

Don't want them going round Nan's!

They cart me off to the Northern Hospital. I feel a bit of an idiot lying down in this serious-looking vehicle. There's nothing wrong with me, I tell the man, but he says it's best to make sure.

"Are the sirens on?"

"No. You're not an emergency."

"Oh."

Charming. My first ride in an ice-cream van and they don't even put the sirens on.

I'm only in the hospital for about an hour and most of that I'm waiting to see the doctor. He looks in my eyes again and gets me to watch his moving finger. Then he feels me all over and gets the nurse to patch my knee up.

"You'll survive," he says. "Is someone here who can take you home?"

"Dad will. That's him over there." I point to the man who knocked me over. He's hovering about in Casualty.

"You can take him home now," the doctor tells him. "Any worries, just bring him back."

The poor bloke looks a bit surprised, but he gives me a lift anyway. He's still shaking so much, he almost goes into the back of a bus.

When we get to my house, he wants to come in and talk to Nan but I tell him not to. I've cleared his name with the police.

He ain't in any trouble, but I will be if she finds out. She won't let me have a bike again, that's for sure. He says he's sorry for the umpteenth time and then he drives off, really really slowly. He'd have been quicker walking.

Of course, Nan takes one look at me and starts giving me the third degree. I tell her I got my injuries rescuing a cat out of a tree. She likes cats, so she never had a go at me. I'm not her favourite person at the moment, because I failed my eleven-plus.

"You'll just have to go in the army, won't you?" she said. "Best thing for you."

That night, I tell my cousin Jean I don't want to go in the army. What am I going to do? If I'm so thick I can't even pass my exams, how am I going to get out of it?

"I'll help you," she says. "You're not thick. You just haven't been to school enough." She says I should go up the library with Terry and get some books and she'll learn me to read better.

"I'm not reading baby books," I tell her.

"I wasn't asking you to," she says. "Get something you're interested in."

"What, like model-making?"

"If you like. It's still reading, isn't it?"

"Thanks, Jean. You won't tell Andy and Tommy though, will you? In case they laugh?"

She promises she won't. She's got a job now, in Woolworths. She's good at maths and that, so she can give people the right change, no trouble. She's smart, is Jean.

Next Saturday, I go round my uncle Terry's flat and tell him what Jean said. He says he's game to go up there with me and show me where all the different books are. I've never been to a library before. I have a good look round before we go, in case one of my mates sees me. I don't want them to think I'm a swot.

That would ruin my image. If Fatty Cramphorn learnt I spent Saturdays in the library, it would be all round the school by playtime.

I can't believe how many books there are. And they're all in different sections so you can find them easily.

"What is it you're after?" Terry wants to know. "Murder, mystery and suspense or dirty ones?"

"Have they got dirty ones?"

"They've got everything."

I'm tempted, but I'd be a bit embarrassed reading those to Jean. Maybe I could get one for Janice. Jean and Joyce went out dancing the other night, and because they never come back until late, Janice got into bed with me and wanted to play mothers and fathers. I had to throw her out in the end. I still haven't forgiven her for nicking Dad's gas money.

"Have they got anything on Airfix kits, Terry?"

"Not as such, I don't think. They've got a load of aeroplane books though."

"How many books are we allowed?"

"Three . . . and as many as we can fit under here," he says. He's stuffing all these books inside his jacket.

"What? Do you nick them?"

"Shhhhh. You've got to whisper in the library, Mick."

I don't know why he had to nick them. They was free anyway. You could borrow them for ages and then you brought them back and swopped them for new ones.

"Yeah," he said, "but this way, if you bring them back late, you don't have to pay. They fine you if the books are back late."

We wander down the aisles and he stops and pulls out a big book with a hard cover.

"There you go," he says. "*British Warplanes.*"

It's a beautiful thing. Big pictures with all cross-sections showing the inside of the engine. I can't wait to get it home.

"Want anything else?"

"No, this will do. We can come back, can't we? Another day?"

"Yeah, alright."

It'll take me the best part of a month to read this one, I reckon. Terry's found a book about murderers.

"Bloody 'ell, Mick. Look at that."

"Ugh!"

There's a revolting picture on the cover. A zombie with its guts spilling out. Terry sticks it in his inside pocket.

"I'd better get some legit ones an' all," he says.

He pulls two out at random. One's got a picture of cakes on and the other's a medical dictionary, I think.

"I bet this one's got good pictures," he says, flicking through it.

He stops at a photo of a woman lying on a table with nothing on except a sheet over her middle. There's a bloke in a white coat cutting into her belly with a scalpel. All his mates are watching. I look away. I don't like that sort of thing. Then Terry finds a close-up of a diseased leg, all puffy and raw.

"Gangrene," he whispers.

I shut my eyes. My breakfast's going to come up in a minute. He laughs and snaps the book shut.

"You can have it after me if you want," he says.

The librarian stamps our books and we walk back to Terry's bedsit. I ask him if I can see his Airfix models.

"Ain't you seen them?" he says. "I thought I'd shown you."

"No. Janice told me about them."

He leads the way to his bedroom. Wow! He's got hundreds of them. Planes hanging off the ceiling on bits of cotton, army tanks arranged on little pans of sand, lorries, missile launchers and loads of little soldiers in various states of being blown up. They don't half look good. I can hardly speak for jealousy. He throws himself on his bed and looks at a picture of his girlfriend.

"Like them?" he grins.

"I love them. I can only afford the little ones."

"Yeah, but when you've got a job and that you can buy big ones, can't you?"

I tell him I don't want to go in the army, but Nan wants me to.

"I didn't either," he says, "but Nan wanted me to an' all. I had to do National Service anyway and after that, I couldn't think of nothing else to do."

"Yeah, but Terry, what did you wanna do before you done your National Service?"

"I dunno," he sighs. "That age, you don't know what you want to do, do ya? You just want to have a laugh. Only that's the time they make you make up your mind."

He shows me the photo of his girlfriend.

"What do you think of that?" he says.

"She's nice."

He puts the photo back carefully.

"Yeah. She is. Nan hates her," he says.

"Why?"

"I dunno, do I? Probably because she doesn't go to the same church."

"Probably because she's not in the army."

He laughs. "Yeah! She don't like anyone who ain't got a uniform on."

He tells me he's going to marry her anyway. She's called Delia. He's going to run away with her to a place called Gretna Green.

"What, near Palmer's Green?"

"No . . . Scotland. You can get married there and no one can stop you. Not even Nan."

I'll remember that, in case I meet a girl Nan don't like. I'm bound to, aren't I?

"Why don't you get out the army if you don't like it?" I ask him.

"I've got used to it," he says. "It's too late now, anyway. I can't do nothing else."

He sits up. "And anyway, it means you don't have to think. You just obey orders. After a while, thinking becomes too much like hard work and I've got to like having it done for me."

I'd never thought of it that way before. He makes it sound like they work for him, not the other way round.

"And it keeps you fit," he says. "The birds like that, Mick. Feel my belly."

He pulls his shirt up and braces himself. His belly is a mass of hard, square knots.

"Punch me," he says. "Go on. It won't hurt."

I give him a little tap.

"Harder than that," he snorts.

So I belt him one. He doesn't even flinch. My fist just bounces off.

"Again!" he says. "And again."

So, with his permission, I lay into him. I whack him over and over, but he's invincible. He takes his shirt off.

"Sit-ups," he says, "that's what does it. I'll show you."

He gets on the floor and shows me how to do them. He does eighty and he's not even sweating. I'm on my twelfth staring up at the aeroplanes.

"Pretend you've got an orange under your chin," he says, "or you'll hurt your neck."

I collapse backwards.

I'm going to have a belly like his. He's not good-looking, I don't think, but he looks dead hard in his uniform. I wouldn't fancy being his enemy.

"Push-ups," he says. And he's down on the floor, going up and down, up and down, making it look really easy. Then he does it on one hand. I try and copy him and he counts me along. My face is shaking with the effort.

"Come on," he says. "One . . . two . . . three . . . don't stick your bum up in the air . . . come on . . . four . . . five . . . six . . ."

My head's pounding with the effort. My arms buckle under my weight and I collapse onto my nose.

"Seven . . . oh, what are you like?" He helps me up.

"I've got a bad knee," I tell him. I've still got a bandage on it from the bike accident.

"How did you do that?"

It wasn't that I didn't trust him, but I'd got to like the idea of me being a rescuer of cats rather than a stupid idiot who rode straight in front of cars.

"Rescuing a cat."

"Don't believe you," he says, "nor does Nan."

Funny she never said nothing if she didn't believe me. Mind you, I suppose if I'd still got a bike, she wouldn't have let me get away with the cat story. She'd have had the bike off me, no question.

"I got hit by a car," I said, "but it didn't hurt much."

"You must be a very hard little man," says Terry.

After that, I go round to see Andy Harris to see if he's seen any decent bikes up Finsbury Park. I need to replace my old knackered one. It's no good having no transport. We walk most places, but it's a long way, Spaniard's Wood, even for a hard man.

Andy's mum opens the door. She's been washing her hair and it's dripping all over her bare shoulders. She's wearing one of those flesh-coloured girdles and a pair of mules.

"Oh, it's you," she says. "Andy ain't in. He's gone up Hampstead Heath with his uncle."

His uncle's a film director.

"Oh . . . When will he be back?"

"I don't know. They're filming," she says. "Go along. You could be in it, I expect. They need extras."

I quite fancy being in a film. Better than just sitting around, isn't it? It's a long way though. I clap eyes on Andy's bike leaning against the fence.

"I would go," I tell her, "only I haven't got a bike no more. Mine was stolen."

She wraps a towel round her head and looks at me from under it.

"Oh? I thought it got wrecked when you hit that car."

"That was a different bike," I tell her.

I never used to lie, did I? I'm doing it all the time now. I must have learnt it off the grown-ups.

Mrs. Harris raises her eyebrows and puts her head to one side. The towel slides off.

"I wasn't born yesterday," she says, wrapping her head up again. "You can borrow Andy's if you want. He don't need it. He went up there in a van."

"Thanks, Mrs. Harris. Mind how you go."

"You're a cheeky little devil, aren't you?" she says, but she's quite friendly.

Most of Andy's mates fancy her, actually, even though she is at least thirty-five. I think Jean's about as old as I'd go. Joyce is a bit over the hill as far as I'm concerned.

You learn a lot about women, sharing a bedroom with them, like I do. When Jean and Joyce think I'm asleep, they natter about all sorts . . . who did what to who and how, women's things. All sorts. Just as well I listen, because I'd never find out otherwise. Nan's not likely to tell me, is she? Probably doesn't know anyway. I can't see Grandad Charlie giving her one, please God, if there is a God.

When I arrive at the Heath, there's stuff everywhere . . . great big lights on legs, men holding lumps of cardboard, a woman putting make-up on an old geezer. A bloke with a microphone comes over to me.

"Do you mind? You've driven onto the set," he says.

"What?"

"We're filming here. We're about to turn over."

I tell him to carry on then, I don't mind, but he says I've got to shift my bike because it's in the shot. Just then, Andy sees me.

"Mick! Wotcha! Over here!"

I walk my bike over to him.

"That's my bike," he says.

"Your mum said I could borrow it."

He's not that bothered. I ask him what the film's about. He tells me it's called *Mr. Perriwinkle's Day Out*. He points to a man in glasses and a trilby.

"That's him."

"Who?"

"Mr. Perriwinkle. Well, he's the actor who plays Mr. Perriwinkle. What happens is, he goes and sits on that bench and then an old girl sits down next to him to have a read, and then he's supposed to drop his glasses. Watch."

Andy's uncle shouts, "Roll camera," and this kid with a wooden thing comes in and holds it in front of the camera.

"*Mr. Perriwinkle's Day Out*, Take One," he says.

"That's the clapperboard," says Andy.

"Action!" roars Andy's Uncle Stan.

The actor walks over to the bench and sits down. Then an old actress in a huge hat goes over to him, sits down and takes a book out of her bag.

"Cut," yells Uncle Stan. "Why didn't you drop your glasses, Raymond?"

The actor looks baffled.

"Oh, you want me to drop them in the grass?" he says, sounding surprised. He pulls a script out of his pocket and peers at it.

"If you don't mind," Uncle Stan snaps. "Are we ready?"

Just then, Tommy turns up.

"Has it started?" he wants to know.

"Just re-shooting the first bit," says Andy. "Shut up and watch."

They do the scene again, and this time, Mr. Perriwinkle drops his glasses and starts rooting around on the floor for them. Then he accidentally touches the old lady's leg and she screams.

"She thinks he's a nonce," Andy explains.

Next thing, the old trout's chasing Mr. Perriwinkle with her umbrella, trying to hit him with it.

"And cut!" shouts the director.

"We need to go again, guv," says the cameraman. "She went off her marks."

Andy's uncle goes over to the old lady and has a word. She looks a bit upset. He grabs hold of her and marches her up and down a line of tape someone's put on the grass.

"*This* way," he says, "not over there! Can we hurry up because I don't want to lose this light."

A bloke with an eyeglass looks up at the sky.

"It's gone behind a cloud, guv," he says.

Uncle Stan decides to set up the next shot and go back to this one, which means he's ready for the extras. He spots us and comes over.

"You three." He clicks his fingers. "Andy, over here."

"Told ya," whispers Andy. "We're going to be in it!"

We sit there sensibly while Andy's uncle explains what we've got to do.

"The old lady is going to chase Perriwinkle into the pond," he says.

"Can we chase him and all?"

"Yes, and then after that, I want two of you to lie at the bottom of the bank, so when Perriwinkle jumps over it, he gets a soft landing. You're sort of human padding." Tommy's a bit confused.

"Doesn't he really fall in the pond then?"

"No."

"Well, how will it look like he falls in the pond on the film then?"

"It just will," Uncle Stan says. "Believe me. It's all down to camera angles and special effects . . . anyway, can we get on?"

The special effects turn out to be Andy chucking a bucket of water up in the air to make it look like Mr. Perriwinkle has really fallen in the pond, whereas in reality he'd just rolled down a bank and landed on top of my head. I yell out.

"Ow! Fuckin 'ell, Mr. Perriwinkle, that hurt!"

"Cut!" booms Uncle Stan.

There's a horrid silence. Mr. Perriwinkle is apologising like anything to me. He's really sorry, he says, he didn't realise he'd have to do his own stunts. He normally acts on the stage, not on location. This is quite a different kettle of fish. Suddenly I cop the director glaring at us, over the top of the bank.

"Don't talk while we're filming. We are shooting for sound. Do you understand?"

We nod sheepishly, but none of us do.

"Oh dear," whispers Mr. Perriwinkle, "someone got out of bed the wrong side this morning."

The filming carries on all day. By the end of it, we're all knackered and we've had so many cups of free tea, we keep having to run off into the bushes.

Finally, it's all over. Andy's uncle looks very relieved and shakes us by the hand.

"Thank you, lads," he says. "I think it's in the can."

"What is?" asks Tommy.

"The film. When it's all cut together, it will be very funny, I think."

"What?"

Uncle Stan clearly can't be bothered to explain so Andy tries, but Tommy gets bored halfway through, so he gives up.

"You'll see," he says. "They're going to show it at school when it's finished at the end of term. Anyway, are you coming to the party or what?"

I never knew there was a party attached. Andy says there's always one when the film's finished, to say thanks to the crew and the actors, because a lot of them are doing it for nothing.

We all pile into Uncle Stan's van and we go to this flash place somewhere in Hampstead and stuff our faces silly.

"I can't wait to see us in it," says Tommy. "It will be a right laugh at school."

For a minute, I agree with him. Then I catch sight of myself in one of the huge mirrors. I'm wearing National Health specs, I've got a filthy bandage round my knee, I'm wearing a pair of short trousers covered in mud so it looks like I've pooped myself and worst of all, I'm wearing a jumper with a bumble-bee on the front.

I want to die.

twenty

Mr. Perriwinkle has the whole school rolling in the aisles. Whether it's the acting or the sight of me in my bumble-bee pullover, I don't know.

"Ha, ha! Look at the state of Stokes! His trowsies have had a row with his ankles."

"I wish my mum could knit!"

And those were just the polite kids.

I go home and beg my dad for hard cash.

"What's it for?"

"A pair of jeans. Please. I'm top juniors. It's embarrassing."

He says he's sure Glen's got an old pair I could have.

"Take your shorts off," he says. "I'll go and get them."

He comes down after a while with this massive pair. He holds them up to my waist. They need about a foot cut off the bottom unless I'm going to do them up under my chin.

"Oh, Dad! They'll drown me. Anyway, Nan won't have time to sew them up."

"Get Jean to do it. Or Joyce. I'm a bit skint at the moment."

I'm trying to cover myself up when Glen comes in with his mate, Paddy. They're all booted and suited, ready to go up

West. Glen's hair looks amazing. His quiff is the highest I've ever seen. He's Brylcreemed it until it looks like glass.

I feel such a berk standing there in my underwear. Just as well Nan makes me wear clean stuff. She's got a thing about clean underwear. She says it's next to godliness. Glen looks at me, then he turns on Dad. He's really angry for some reason.

"He can't wear them jeans!" he snaps. "He looks a right prat. How much do you need, Mick?"

I've never bought a pair before, so how would I know?

"I dunno. Ten bob?"

Glen digs in his pocket, peels off some notes and stuffs them in my hand.

"That should do it," he says. "Get drainpipes, yeah?"

That's really good of him, I reckon. I wish I was as old as him.

"Cheers, Glen."

"Yeah, alright. Put something on, will ya?"

I step back into my shorts.

"Can't have my brother going round like that," he says.

It sounds nice when he says that. "My brother."

Nobody's ever called me that. Terry would have, but he wasn't old enough. Shirley won't ever call me that because she can't bear the fact that Dad gives me the attention and not her.

I have to wait two days before I can buy the jeans. I get them off the market in the end. Brilliant, they are. I rush home, sneak up into the bedroom and try them on. They're lovely. OK, they look a bit daft with my sandals Nan cut the toes out of, but at least it's a start. They actually fit round the bum. I've never had a pair of anything what done that before. Janice bursts in and wolf-whistles.

"I like those," she says. "Take them off."

"No!"

"Go on. I want to try them on. They'd fit me."

She starts trying to pull them down and I end up slinging her on the bed and hitting her with a pillow. She's giggling like mad and kicking her legs in the air, so I have to sit on her.

"Get off! Mick, get off! I can't breathe!"

"Stop pulling my trousers down then." At which point, Nan walks in behind us.

"Pack it in, you two. I'm trying to watch *Popeye*." She gives me a clip round the ear and pulls Janice off the bed.

"You!" she says. "Pull your dress down, young lady. We don't all want to see your drawers, thank you."

Then she cops my jeans.

"Dear God!" she says. "Where'd you get those horrible things?"

"Glen. Don't you like them?"

She calls Grandad. "Char-lie! Charlie. Come and look at this, will you? We've got a spiv in the house."

He doesn't come up, so I have to go down.

"Go on," she says, "show him what a banana you look. Charlie!"

Grandad's got his head under the sink, unblocking something.

"What?" He's not pleased at being disturbed.

"Him!" she says, pushing me forward.

"What am I supposed to be looking at?" Grandad snaps. "He's wearing long trousers. So what?"

"He looks like a Ted. He's not wearing them outside the house, tell him."

Grandad let a spurt of filthy water out into a bucket, by way of a reply.

"He's not a baby!" he says. "He needs long trousers. Have you been pouring dripping down this sink again?"

"No, it's Fred's plumbing." She gives him a look and pushes me down the hall.

"If you think I'm washing those, you've got another think coming," she says. "I don't approve."

My cousin Jean liked them though. She thought they were really smart. She told me they made me look much older. We sat and read a bit of my aeroplane book on her bed.

"I reckon you're going to pass your eleven-plus easy next year," she says.

"Really?"

"Your reading's ever so much better. And your writing."

She's been helping me with my spelling. When I get ready for bed she calls out words and I have to tell her what all the letters are. She makes it fun though. She shouts out the names of rock and rollers and sometimes we even let Janice join in.

"Spell 'brassière'! Spell 'stockings.'"

It was never like this at school. One day, I ask Jean to help me write a letter. I've been thinking about it for ages, but I want it to be perfect.

"OK," she says, "who's it to?"

"Mum."

She's so sweet. She fetches me some really classy paper and a matching envelope she got for her birthday and a loan of the pen they gave her at work for when she's on the tills. I keep smelling the paper. It smells like roses and talcum powder.

"It's scented," she says. "Don't sniff it all off!"

I lean on my aeroplane book and suck the end of the pen. I can't think of a single thing to write.

"Go on," says Jean. "Dear Mum . . ."

"Shall I put my address at the top or what? Only she knows where I am, don't she?"

"Put it on anyway. Top right-hand corner."

She shows me how to line it all up and where to put the date. I'm worn out by the time I've done all that. My hand's shaking from trying to make the letters neat.

"Dear Mum . . ." I'm stuck again. Jean's watching me.

"What's the matter?"

"What shall I say?"

She shrugs. "What do you want to say?"

"I dunno, do I?"

There's too much to fit on a pretty piece of paper. There's too much to fit in a great big book. It's all too much. I scribble a horrid black rage, scribble all over the paper, harder and harder until the pen makes a hole. She puts her arm round me.

"Don't cry, Mick."

"I'm sorry . . . about the paper. It's a waste. I'll buy you some more, it's just . . ."

"I know it's just," she says. "Shall I tell you what I'm going to do?"

"What?"

"I'm going to take you to see your mum. After work tomorrow, OK?" She dries my eyes.

"OK."

"You go to bed now. By the way . . ."

"What?"

"Your new jeans." She picks them up and folds them for me. "You could wear them to go and see her, couldn't you? They look really smart."

I can't sleep for excitement. I feel ill with it. I wake her in the middle of the night and tell her I'm going to be sick.

"It's just nerves," she says. She gives me a barley sugar to suck, out of her handbag.

"Where will I meet you?"

"Corner of Marlborough Road and Sussex Way, about five o'clock. Don't tell Nan though, whatever you do. She'll kill me."

"And me."

"Yes, most likely. Now try and go to sleep."

I can't of course. I keep going through what I'm going to say when Mum opens the door. Perhaps I'll just play it really cool and say, "Wotcha!" like nothing's happened. Like I've just walked round the block and I've always lived there.

No, I can't do that. What about, "Hello, Mum? How'ya doing?" That don't sound right, either. What if she don't know who I am? I'm a lot taller since we last saw each other and what with new jeans and arm muscles, she might not even recognise me.

"Hi, Mum. Remember me? It's Mick."

She'll throw her arms around me, won't she? She'll tell me how much she's missed me and welcome me back home. On the other hand, she probably won't. She'll probably say, "Alright?" and I'll say, "Yeah. You alright?" and she'll nod and we'll both leave it at that. We'll both be lying, but if we both tell each other what we're really thinking, we'll probably end up never speaking again.

"Jean?"

"Shush and go to sleep."

Next morning, I can't eat a thing, which is unusual for me. Most of the time I'm starving. It's not like Nan underfeeds us or anything. It's just that five minutes after I've eaten, I get this aching gap in the pit of my stomach. Nan's wormed me and everything, but I'm still permanently hungry. Must be all these exercises I'm doing. The push-ups and the sit-ups.

Nan don't even notice my lack of appetite. She's in a stinking mood. She's just got a letter from Terry, all the way from Scotland. He did run off to Gretna Green with Delia after all. He's gone and married her behind Nan's back.

"He could have had anyone! Why that little slut? What's worse, she's a Catholic!"

I've never seen Nan cry before, but she did then. Grandad tries to calm her down, but she keeps saying, "That's it. I haven't got a son. I do not have a son."

Then she screws his letter up, throws it in the bin and starts peeling a pan of carrots.

"Leave them," say my grandad.

"No! I'm doing them," she says.

We all creep out of the kitchen. I should have gone to school but I never. I'm too on edge. I go to Finsbury Park and row round and round the lake. There's no one else there, except for a wino eating someone else's old piece of cod and a couple of women with prams. Every time the boat man calls "Come in number three," I just give him some more money and row round again.

"Here . . . ain't you got no home to go to?" he laughs, third time round.

"Yeah. I have as it happens," I tell him. "I'm going round my mum's. What's the time?"

"Three o'clock."

I've got two hours to kill. I get a light off the wino and have a fag on the grass. Between puffs, I keep chanting the words like a magic spell.

"I'm going round *my* mum's." I try saying it all different ways. "*I'm* going round my mum's. I'm going round my *mum's*." Over and over, until the words stop making any sense. The wino gives me a look, spits out a bit of cod and backs away from me.

"You're mad, pal," he says. "You're scaring me."

Clearly, I've upset him. But I'm not mad. I'm happy! Maybe it's the same thing. I get up and start to head back, really slowly, looking at everything. I like to look up when I'm walking. A lot of people don't do that in case they fall over, but it you look up, there are all sorts of things you've never noticed before. Little monsters on the church roof. Old shops signs, painted high on walls, but all worn out. Upstairs windows with canaries in. Swirly bits of plaster with faces.

"I'm *going* round my mum's. I'm going *round* my mum's."

I sit on benches I've never sat on before, outside shops I never go to. I look at things in shop windows I've never been interested in before. Material shops with yards of stuff in great long rolls, all different patterns and colours. Three different pinks, like sherbet. Plain stuff with a kind of watermark in, draped and shimmering over a chair.

I want to buy Mum something, but what? Flowers are for dead people. If I get her sweets, she'll think I bought them for myself. Fags? They're not much of a present. Then I think, why should I? I'm the present, surely? It will be enough to see me after all this time. Or will it?

In the end, I buy her a magazine and some rubber gloves, because then she won't get her hands all red when she does the cleaning. I can't go empty-handed. It would be rude.

At ten to five, I'm waiting on the corner of Marlborough Road for Jean. It's a dreadful thing, waiting. It would be alright if there was nobody about, but there always is. Everyone's wondering what I'm doing there. Several cars slow down and wave me over the road, thinking I want to cross it, but I don't, which really annoys them. One older kid looks me up and down and says, "Stood you up, has she?"

"No, I'm waiting for my cousin."

"Yeah, yeah."

What's it got to do with him anyway? I wouldn't go up to someone who was just standing there and ask him what he was up to. I decide to have a look at the rubber gloves to pass the time. I try them on. They're nice and powdery inside and they smell warm and interesting.

"'Ere! You can come and do my smalls, darling."

There's two tarts hanging out of a window over the road, wearing nighties. Must be my mum's age or more. They look a bit rough.

"I can't. I'm going round my mum's."

"Oh, bless," says one of them. "Come on. Come and give us a scrub. We're filthy, aren't we, Beryl?"

Just then, Jean turns up. They're still leaning out the window.

"Is that your date, darlin'? How much does she charge?"

Jean tells me to take no notice of them. They're drunk, she says. They're just a pair of poor old scrubbers. I tell her what they wanted me to do and she throws her head back and laughs.

"What are you doing with those gloves anyway?"

"They're for Mum."

"I don't think so," she says. "Women don't really like presents like that. They like chocolates and perfume."

I stick them back in my pocket. My face has gone red, I can feel it.

"Oh, don't be daft," she says. "Give them to me. Nan can use them. Anyway, the magazine's a lovely idea."

"Is it?" I've got something right, then. "Do you think that's enough on its own?"

Jean nods. "I think she's lucky to get anything," she says. "It's you that deserves a present, Mick."

She takes me to a house in Sussex Way in front of some warehouses.

"I won't stop," she says. "It will be better if I'm not there."

I stand there, staring at the front door. I just don't know what I'm going to find on the other side of it. Jean's walking away. I feel lost. So small, even in my new drainpipes.

"Go on," Jean mouths.

But I can't. I seem to have lost all use of my door-knocking hand. She comes back up the path and does it for me. Then she pinches my arse to lighten me up a bit.

"Get on with it. She won't bite you. She's your mum for goodness sake."

I don't watch Jean leave. I can hear her heels clicking off into the distance, then they're gone. Suddenly I think, what if

Mum's not in? I stare at the door, willing it to open, listening for footsteps. Then I hear them, but they're not hers. The door opens. For the moment, there's silence, then . . .

"Mick!"

"Terry?"

He's all over me, jumping up and down. He's so big. Last time I seen him he was only that high.

"Mick! I never knew you was coming! Mum! It's Mick." He drags me into the hall and up the stairs.

"Come and see my new bike. Dad bought it for my birthday."

Coming down the stairs is a woman with a baby on her hip. I have to look twice to make sure it's Mum. It is her though. Same eyes.

"Hello," she says. "I wondered what all the fuss was about."

She tries to tidy her hair. All the chestnut colour has gone and she's skinny as anything. The baby peers at me from behind its fingers.

"Is that Gary?"

"Yeh. That's Gary. He's a bit clingy at the moment, aren't ya!"

She tickles his belly and he curls his toes up. He looks like Harry Spicer when he smiles. He pulls his dummy out with a pop and gives it to me.

"You're honoured," she says. "How did you get here, by the way?"

I tell her Jean brought me.

"Does Nan know?"

"No."

"Didn't think she would."

We go upstairs into my mum's place. She's only got two rooms. A kitchen and one bedroom.

"If you need the toilet, it's in the back yard," she says. "How are you? You look alright."

"So do you."

She laughs and says to leave off, she looks awful. I give her the magazine.

"What's that for?"

"It's a present."

"You didn't have to do that," she says.

Terry wants to know why I never got him a present. I tell him I'll get him one later. I never got him nothing, because I didn't know what he was into.

"Are you staying?" he says.

"Terry," says Mum, "leave him alone."

"Yeah, but is he staying?"

Mum ignores him.

"How's school? Did you get your eleven-plus?"

"No."

"Join the club," she says. "I was never any good at school. Have you had your tea?" She starts opening cupboards and closing them again.

"No. It doesn't matter."

I'm starving as it happens. I feel alright now. The worst bit's over. She taps half a loaf of bread. It's rock-hard.

"I haven't got a lot in. I never knew you were coming. Will Nan do you something?"

"I'll probably have it round Dad's."

She pulls a face. "Oh, him," she says.

He's not very popular, my dad. Nan hates him. Mum hates him. Shirley hates him and Glen don't think much of him either. I'm the only one who's trying to love him at all. I don't like him much, but I'm still trying to love him because he's my dad. Talking of which, where's Harry Spicer?

"He's working," she says.

"When's he coming home?"

"Anybody's guess," she says.

She's so thin. She's much shorter than I remember too, but then she's wearing slippers, not heels, which isn't like her. She's still got her orange lipstick on though. She looks tired.

"Come and see my bike," says Terry. "It's in the yard. Come on, Mick."

"Take Gary with you," she says. "Go on, Gary." She puts Gary on the floor. He crawls over to Terry and puts his arms up for a carry.

"Bike," he says. "Bike-bike."

"Oh, Mum! Does he have to come?" Terry moans. "He'll ruin it."

Gary shuffles towards the stairs. I'm terrified he's going to fall down them.

"Bike-bike."

I pick him up. My baby brother, eh? He kicks his legs. He don't want to be picked up. He wants to go downstairs by himself. Terry's got a right sulky face on him.

"It's alright," says Mum, "put him down. He can do stairs now."

Gary goes all the way down on his bum. It looks like we're stuck with him. I don't mind, but Terry does.

"I'm always looking after him," he says. "She's so lazy. All she does is sleep."

Terry's got a little tin of lavender polish from the Betterware man, so we both have to get a rag and polish his bike. Every time Gary reaches for the polish, Terry snatches it away.

"He ruins everything I do," he says. "When are you coming back?"

I wish I knew.

"I dunno."

I've got a feeling Mum don't want me back. She's pleased to see me, but maybe she just can't afford me.

"I'll ask Mum if you can live with us again," he says.

"Where would I sleep, Tel?"

"In my bed, with me. Gary, don't. He's putting polish on my brakes, Mick."

By six o'clock, the bike is gleaming.

"You're lucky," I tell him. "I never had a bike when I was your age." I'm starting to talk like an old man. It's living with Nan what does it.

"What . . . you never had a bike?"

"Not off Mum and Dad."

I don't know how much they've told him about whose dad is whose. I've always had this feeling Harry Spicer wasn't Terry's dad either. I expect they're saving that one up for him for when he's older, like they done with me. We go back indoors. Mum's reading the magazine I've got her.

"It's good," she says. "Thanks for it."

"Mum. Can Mick stay?" asks Terry.

"How can he?" she says. "Where am I going to put him?"

She turns to me. "You can see how pushed I am, can't you?" she says.

She's begging me to understand.

"He can have my bed, I'll sleep on the floor," says Terry.

Mum picks Gary up. "Oh yeah? And where's he supposed to sleep? In a drawer?"

"He can stay with Nan and Mick can stay with us."

"Nice try," she says.

There's no chance then. I knew there wouldn't be, or she'd have come and got me, wouldn't she? I stay for another hour or so, talking about nothing in particular. She never mentions prison, so I don't either. That way, it never happened. I'm beginning to think it never did. It seems so unlikely. Nan's probably lying about her stealing the money and all. She would do that, the old cow.

There comes a point where we both run out of things to say.

Also, if I don't go back to Nan's, she'll start asking questions and she can spot a lie a mile off. I'm already a bit late as it is.

"See you then," says Mum. "Look after yourself."

"I will."

I suppose at this point, she should put her arms round me and give me a kiss goodbye, but she never done it before, so why should she do it now? There's a look in her eyes though. Sad and sorry, like she wanted to do it, but just couldn't.

I pat Terry on the head. He's about to cry.

"Love you, Tel. See you."

He nods. He can't talk in case it sets him off. I know that.

"See you, Mick."

I don't look back up at the window and wave goodbye to him, even though I can feel him watching me. Poor little sod. He's growing up angry. He wasn't like that before.

I'm just walking away. It's best. I've seen Mum and that's lovely, but I can't stay. I can't change that, so I'm walking away. Maybe if I'd seen Harry Spicer, he'd have let me stay. I wouldn't have minded sleeping on the floor. But that never happened, so walk on, walk on.

By the time I get home, I've gone on the missing list. Nan's got herself in a right state.

"Where the hell have you been?"

"Out with my mates."

She whacks me round the earhole. "No, you haven't. Don't you lie to me. They called round for you earlier, so where were you?"

I forgot to tell Andy and Tommy not to call!

"I went round my mum's."

There was a pause.

"You what?"

I thought she was going to hit me again, but she yelled for my grandad.

"Char-lie! Charlie! Guess where he's been, will you?"

It's quite clear Charlie ain't bothered.

"How should I know?"

"He's only been to her house! He's been up Sussex Way!"
She shakes me by the shoulders.

"Who took you? Was it Jean?"

"No one."

I'm not dropping Jean in it, even if Nan gouges my eyes out
with her new potato peeler.

"Liar," she says. "Who took you?"

Suddenly, Grandad springs into action. He pushes her
down into a chair. Not to hurt her, just to show her who's boss.

"If he wants to see his mum," he says, "it's up to him. Not
you, woman."

He nods his head at me. "Alright?" he says. Then he goes
outside.

Nan can't look at me. She just gets up and walks out. A few
minutes later, she brings my tea in.

"It's liver," she says. "I've taken the little tubes out." She
can't look me in the face.

"You don't have to have it if you've already eaten . . . somewhere else."

I tell her I'm so hungry, I could eat a squashed rat. She manages a thin smile.

"I wish I'd known. I'd have done you one," she says.

twenty-one

My guitar plays really well. I didn't think it would, but it really sounds quite good. Even Glen's impressed. It sounds better when he plays it though, because he knows how. I just twang it.

"Stop twanging that thing and eat your breakfast."

Nan's signed me up to go on a Wayfarer's course during the summer holidays, with the Boys' Brigade. When I go down, she's polishing loads of little badges with a cloth.

"She's got polishingitis," says Grandad. "Don't sit down or she'll polish you an' all."

"They're Terry's," she says.

It's the first time she's mentioned his name since he got married without her permission.

"Nan . . . I thought you said you hadn't got a son."

"You . . . don't be so cheeky," she says. "I have got a son. I just haven't got a daughter-in-law. Do you get me?"

I nod.

"Right. Eat your egg."

It's my last day at juniors today. Would have been my last day for ever if I'd passed that eleven-plus. I could kick myself now. I'm going to be held back with a load of younger kids. I reckon I could walk it now, what with all the help Jean's given me.

Nan takes another badge out of the box, huffs on it and rubs it on her apron.

"Terry got five badges . . . that's his Wayfarer's badge," she says. "He got that when he went camping, like you're going to."

"What did he have to do?"

"Learn all the points of a compass. Go on missions. Go on a hike."

She's dead proud of him for it, even now he's a grown man. I think she still thinks of him as her little lad.

"How far did he have to walk, Nan?"

"Fifty miles."

I've never walked that far in my life I don't think. I'd like to have a go, though. I've never been on holiday before. Never. Tommy's coming, but Andy ain't. He got thrown out of the Boys' Brigade 145 Unit the first week he was in it, for pissing in the equipment cupboards. I don't know to this day why he done it. Something to do with religion, I think.

Andy's always hated going to church. He says he would rather swing from the gallows by his dick. I told him how the army tortured my grandad when he was a soldier. They tied him to a gun wheel by his hands and feet and made him stay like that all night. Tommy wanted to know what he'd done wrong.

"He didn't piss in the equipment cupboard an' all, did he?"

"No, he fell asleep on duty. He said the axle dug into his back all night."

Andy said he'd rather boil his head than go to church. His mum gives him money for the collection every Sunday, but he always throws his sixpence over the wall. He don't want God to have it. I told him I'd have it, but he said no, the devil can have it.

I told him about our ballcock being held up by a mysterious force. That shook him up a bit, but then he said he didn't care. He said if beer had come out of the taps, then that would have been different. We could have had a party for a start.

I think what really got Andy's goat was that his mum and dad never went with him to church. In fact, they didn't seem to be religious in the slightest and he reckoned they only sent him to Sunday school so they could get shot of him for a couple of hours.

I'm not keen on the church either, but I reckon it's worth putting up with for the things that come with it.

Mondays, we have band practice. They started me off on the bugle. I was good at blowing it, only I kept doing it at the wrong time because I was having trouble reading the music. I told them it was my glasses. Anyway, they put me on drums, which is even better because that means I get to stand at the front when we march from our building to and from the church.

Tuesdays is physical training night, which suits me, because we do gymnastics. Vaulting over the horse and such like. I haven't been doing it long, but because I've been doing my press-ups, I'm pretty fit compared to the others.

Thursday night is drill night. That's my favourite bit. I like the feeling of a whole load of us moving along like a machine. After a while, I forget I'm me, I'm part of something much bigger. Sometimes I close my eyes and I seem to float along, just above the ground.

I've even taken a shine to the uniform. I couldn't see the point at first. All that polishing seemed like hard work for no good reason, but after a while, I began to understand what Nan was going on about.

When your trousers are pressed and your shoes and your drum are gleaming and your hair is clean and neat, you feel like a million dollars. Even I respect me. When I'm in my uniform, all done out, I could pass for a rich kid. No one would ever know unless I opened my gob.

Nan puts all Terry's medals back in the drawer. "Go on," she says. "Go to school. See you teatime."

Since Terry's been gone, she's been paying me a lot of attention. She hardly bothers with Janice or Brenda. I think she puts up with Jean because she helps her a lot with the cleaning and that. Min does bugger all. Just sits and watches telly, far as I can tell.

I think Nan prefers boys. Jean told me Nan and Charlie had a little boy before she had Mum, but he died at birth. He's buried round the back of a hospital somewhere with all the other little babies that didn't make it. There's no headstone or nothing. He was called Charlie.

Must have been hard for her, having one girl baby after another, after losing him.

There's a completely different mood at school on the last day. At playtime, a load of kids who were leaving for the tech set fire to their books behind the bins. I'm coming back next term, so I couldn't afford to risk it, but I did give them my matches.

There's a kind of party atmosphere. Nobody's done any work. Even the teachers look happy for once. We're allowed to bring games in if we want. The swots brung Monopoly, but the rest of us brung weapons, mostly. There was a great waterbomb fight in the quadrangle, which would have gone on for ages if the caretaker hadn't got one on the back of his head. He wasn't half cross. I think Cramphorn threw it, but I'm not sure.

"It's alright, sir. You can borrow my mum's hairdryer."

We fell about, because the caretaker's got about as much hair as a ping-pong ball. Cramphorn can be quite a laugh at times. We're almost mates since we sorted out our differences. I don't call him Fatty no more and he don't call me Stupid and he don't pick on the first years. He knows what'll happen if he does.

I haven't had a fight for ages and I'm having such a good day, it's the last thing I want. Then what do you know? Andy comes round the corner, crying. It's not like Andy to cry. Only time I've seen him do it is when his dog was run over, which is fair enough.

"What's up, Andy?" He's clutching his guts, all crumpled up.

"Some big kid hit him," Tommy says. "You wanna see the size of him."

"What? Is he from our school or enemy?"

"He just jumped over the school gates. Andy never got a proper look at him, did ya?"

"No."

He must have got Andy from behind. Andy's not soft. If he'd seen him coming, he'd have had a go at least. Apparently it all happened in the other playground.

"Right." I roll my sleeves up. "Where is he, anybody know?"

I wade across the pile of smouldering books. Everyone's watching me. I can feel them gathering to my left, to my right. Following me. Mick is the leader. The kids in my path part like the seas in the Bible. The Red Sea, I think it was. Doesn't matter.

I've got Tommy on one side, Andy on the other. Andy's rallying now.

"Over there!" He points. "There he is!"

I stand still. Let the mountain come to Mick. I'm not walking all the fucking way across the playground. Let him come to me. He's got a real swagger on him, this geezer. He really fancies himself. I lean against the wall and pretend to ignore him.

It's only when he gets nearer that I realise just how big he is. He's got to be fifteen, at least. Years old, and stone. The kids behind me start to step back a bit. They're scared. They don't want to see him beat me, because then who's going to look after them?

"Kill him, Mick," whispers Tommy.

"Give us a chance, Tom. Here, take my glasses."

He's about six foot away, then he stops. Suddenly, Andy digs me in the ribs.

"Jesus, Mick," he hisses. "It's him."

"Who?"

"It's the Hard Man of the Swings."

"Oh, you're joking, aren't you?"

I snatch my bins back off Tommy and put them back on.

"Oh . . . shit."

It's him. The one who splattered me against the wall down the Holloway Flats and kicked my head in. He's come back for more. The last time I was this scared was when I last saw him.

I'm praying my feelings don't show. If my legs go, I've had it. I brace them, flex them, brace them. I think about what Jean said. Beat or be beaten. I don't take my eyes off his. Brown eyes, they are, dead as a shark's. Nothing behind them. I can't back out, because there's a circle of kids round me. The chant starts.

"Bundle . . . bundle . . . bundle."

"Oh," he says, "it's you, you four-eyed little twat." Then he smiles.

That done it. Without thinking, I walk straight up to him, grab him by the throat, put my right leg behind him and sling him right on his arse.

"And if you don't leave my mate alone, I'll give you a bigger hiding, so clear off and don't come round this way again."

I think he must have hit his head. He stays down and doesn't move. From where I'm standing, I can see my fingermarks on his throat. The circle surges forward to get a good look, then starts to widen, a bit like a country dance. They're cheering and calling my name and jeering at the bloke on the floor.

In a way, I wish they wouldn't. There's something revolting about it.

I never asked for that fight, did I? Something in me feels sorry for him now. That's why I'd be no good in the army, except as a drummer.

I'm scared I've killed him. Andy leans over.

"He ain't breathing, Mick."

Everyone goes quiet. There's a sense of excitement and shame. Tommy kneels down and listens for a heartbeat. Suddenly, the Hard Man sighs deeply and moves his arm. Tommy screams and jumps back.

I'm so relieved he ain't dead. I never meant to kill him. I just wanted him put in his place. He gets to his knees and crawls off. Andy can't stand it. He runs up to him and kicks him so hard up the backside his shoe almost gets stuck. It's so funny, I can't help laughing, but I still tell him off. It's bad form hitting them when they're down.

"Leave it out, Andy! It's over."

"No!" he grins. "I've been dreaming of this for ages."

I have to pull him off in the end. Two of the bigger top-year lads join hands and make a human chair and lift me up in the air, above the crowd.

"Micky Stokes! Micky Stokes! Micky Stokes!"

From up high, I can see the Deputy Head running across the school field with a fire extinguisher towards the smouldering books. He looks up and spots me.

"Stokes! Come here!"

The top years let go of each other's hands and I fall through my throne onto the tarmac. The crowd scatters. Three first-year girls trample me in their hurry to run away from the dinner ladies. Nan's right. How the mighty fall.

I never got caned or expelled or nothing. The Deputy took me and Andy to the Head but when he heard our story, he was pretty good about it.

"He jumped Andy from behind, sir," I tell him, "and Andy's my mate. I only tripped him up and told him to leave Andy alone. I could have given him a right pasting, but I never."

"Really?"

He keeps a selection of canes in a brass umbrella stand. I've got all the way through school and never been caned yet. He doesn't cane people very often and when he does, he hardly puts much effort in. Cramphorn's had it twice and he said it was quite nice.

"Anything else to say in your defence, Stokes?" he says.

"He was trespassing, sir. He came over the gate into our playground and being as he's not at our school . . ."

"Thank you, I do know what trespassing means." He flapped his jacket like a tired, dusty, old bat.

"We take a very dim view of violence in this school," he says.

"So do I, sir."

"You're interrupting. Given the circumstances . . ." He trails off and looks out the window and leans back in his chair with his thumbs in his eyes. ". . . I suggest you go home because I am rather tired."

"Thank you, sir!"

"Have either of you got any cigarettes?"

I think the least I can do is give him a fag, being as he's so reasonable. As it happens, I've got two Weights in my pocket. I open the packet and offer him one. He shakes his head slowly, in despair.

"No, no," he says, crumpling up the packet. "We do not smoke in my school, not now. Not next term. Not ever."

"Yes, sir."

He lobs them in the bin. What a waste. He stinks of whisky, does Cleggy. I don't think he's at all well.

After he lets us go, we have a look through his study window and sure enough, he's fishing my fags out of the bin and lighting one up.

Andy dares me to tap on the window, but in the end we both agree to leave the poor sod alone.

It's great to wake up knowing you haven't got to go to school. Even though it can be quite a laugh sometimes, I do find it a strain having to get up early. Funny thing is, I always wake up with the larks on Saturday and Sunday, raring to go.

I can't wait for this camping trip. Trouble is, I need some money to take, spending money, like. I keep dropping the hint to all my family but they keep ignoring me. I know Tommy's got a pound note already.

In the end, Nan gives me five bob.

"Don't ask for more," she says, "because you're not getting it. You're going on this trip to learn how to survive. If you can't survive on five bob, there's no hope for you."

So that's that. My bag is packed. I'm wondering about taking the guitar, but I can't fit it in. Anyway, the bits that hold the strings keep falling off. I go through my checklist:

- Money
- Fags
- Lighter
- Knife
- Mars bar
- Mars bar
- Mars bar
- Wagon Wheel
- Copy of the *Dandy*
- Pair of pants

Nan comes up the stairs with some ironing. She hands me more pairs of pants than a bag can hold.

"Put them in," she says. "You can't have too many."

It looks like I'm taking pants for the whole of 145 Unit.

"Don't be silly," she says. "It's two weeks' worth, that's all. Now, have you got your pencil case?"

"Yeah." When we go on our mission, we've got to write everything down.

"Flannel?"

"Yeah."

"Soap?"

"Er . . ."

She goes and fetches me a half-used bar of soap from the scullery wrapped in a bit of cardboard and grabs my bag.

"I'll do it," I insist, but she taps my hand.

"I'll do it."

Only she puts the soap right next to my Mars bars, so when I get to camp, they taste of coal tar. I spit a mouthful out onto the grass. We're in Somerset, by all accounts, in the middle of a field.

"Tents up, lads," bellows our leader. We're allowed to call him by his Christian name, which is Trevor.

"Those who have done it before please help the new ones."

He hands me and Tommy our tent. He showed us how to put it up in the church hall, but only using a diagram. I'm quite good at this sort of thing though, so I try to organise Tommy.

"Grab hold of that end and pull it tight, Tom."

"No, it's this end, isn't it? This is the front, Mick."

"No, it ain't."

Two older lads come over. They've done it all before. They stand there, shaking their heads at our tent.

"Where's your pole straightener?" says the blonde one.

"You can't get it up without a pole straightener," says his mate.

I ask him where they're kept, but he just shrugs his shoulders.

"You're on a survival course," he says. "Go and look for it."

Me and Tommy go round asking everyone.

"Ask the older ones," Tommy says. "The new boys aren't going to know, are they?"

Everyone we ask says they don't know, but to ask the geezer over there. So we do. On our travels, we even very helpfully suggest to the other new boys struggling with their tents that they need a pole straightener an' all.

Eventually, we go and ask Trevor.

"It's with the elbow grease," he says.

"Where's that then? . . . Oh!"

It suddenly dawns on us that they've been winding us up something chronic. At first I feel really annoyed, but the blonde guy comes over and says, "No hard feelings. We do that to all the new boys. It's all part of it."

Oh, ha, ha, ha. Still, he helps us put our tent up, which is good of him. It's lovely inside. It's quite a warm evening and the groundsheet and the canvas have trapped the smell of the grass and the mud. I lay back and breathe it in.

There's a canteen nearby. We both have a big plate of sausages which we balance on our knees while Trevor goes through the plans for tomorrow.

We've got to get up at six-thirty, fold our blankets up, roll our sleeping bags and get all our kit together, with our knives and forks packed in a special way.

"And if you don't do it properly, you will be put on jankers," he says. All the experienced ones groan. I know what jankers is, because Nan told me. Tommy don't know though.

"What's jankers, Mick?"

"It means having to peel all the spuds."

"They can stick that."

After that, we sing a few songs round the camp fire and then Trevor makes us all go to bed. I'm quite grateful, actually. What with the journey and all the sudden fresh air, I'm knackered.

We sort out who's going to sleep which side of the tent and get into our sleeping bags. I've got Glen's old one. Nan's washed it, but it still smells of him. We look like a couple of caterpillars, all zipped up.

"Listen," Tommy says.

"What?"

"I can't hear nothing."

It's so quiet, it's scary at first. It's much darker outside than it is in London, because there's no street lights, no cars, no houses. Tommy's panicking.

"Mick! I can't see my hand."

"So? You know where it is, don't you? Anyway, what do you want it for?"

"Nothing, I'd just like to be able to see it and it's too dark. Got any matches?"

He makes me light a match. I'm dying for a fag, but I daren't have one, in case one of the team captains catches us. They throw you out if you're caught smoking.

The match light makes strange shadows in the tent. Tommy's trying to figure out what they are.

"What the hell's that, Mick? It looks like a wolf."

I move my head and hands to make the shadow move.

"It's me, you idiot."

"Oh . . . that bit looks like its ears."

He keeps this up for ages. I must have fallen asleep before him, because when I wake up, he's still sound asleep. Probably awake most of the night, poor thing.

I go outside and have a leak in the bushes in my bare feet. It's so fresh and clean out here. A squirrel climbs down a tree and watches me. I keep very still, so as not to frighten it. You get squirrels in the parks near us, but this is a proper country one. I bet it's happier than the ones in Finsbury Park. I stand there watching it for ages. I can almost hear the leaves breathe.

Suddenly, Trevor starts banging his gong and the squirrel shoots back up the tree. Everybody starts getting their kit together for inspection. Tommy hates doing it, but Nan's trained me, you see. I've come to enjoy the sight of everything in the right place, looking immaculate. It clears my head somehow. The team captain nods at me and says, "Good."

Tommy's got his knife and fork round the wrong way, but they let him off being as it's the first day.

"I don't think it matters which way round they go," he moans to me. "Stupid, if you ask me."

"It's one of those things," I explain. "It has to be right. If you get the little things out of order, everything gets out of order and it all ends up in a big mess."

"Oh."

He's not convinced. He doesn't like this side of things at all, I can tell. He reckons it's worse than being at school. But it ain't. To me, it's heaven. After breakfast, we're allowed to go and do what we want. Tommy goes off fishing with a lad called Malcolm Dean, but I'm not really into fishing. Tommy's dad takes him so he knows what to do, but I don't. Instead, I latch onto this big lad called Eric. He's six-foot-four at least. He says a load of them are going for a bike ride and do I want to come?

I don't need asking twice. He's a great bloke, Eric. Much older than me, but he's a right giggle. Quite posh, but not a bit snobbish. We get to the bike shop and most of the good bikes have gone, so he says, "What about a tandem? It's only a shilling."

I offer to pay half, but he gives me my sixpence back.

"My treat," he says. "I'm loaded, actually."

I've never seen a tandem in my life. It's got two seats and four pedals. It's like something out of a circus.

"How am I supposed to ride that?" I laugh.

"Easy peasy," he says. "I'll sit on the front and you sit on the back and we both pedal, OK?"

We both get on. I can hardly touch the pedals and his knees are hitting the handlebars.

"OK," he says, "when I say three, start pedalling. One two three!"

What I didn't realise is that he couldn't steer to save his life. We career into a gate and fall off.

"Whoops," he shrieks. "Are you alright?"

"Yeah!"

"Shall we get on again?" he says. "I'll hold it up and I'll pedal and you just sit there until we get down the hill."

We head off towards the sand dunes and for a whole hour, he tells me all the names of the birds he sees: "Yellow busty warbler . . . nargshank . . . tippleboffin."

I ask him how come he knows so much about birds.

"I don't!" he roars. "I'm making it all up!"

He's completely daft. He tells me his old man is an optician in Islington so I tell him mine is a doctor in Hornsey.

"Is he really?" he says.

"No! I'm making it up!"

He throws his head back and chuckles. I've never met such a happy person in all my life. I think if they told him he was dying, he'd see the funny side of it.

"Oh, frig!" he says after what seems like no more than ten minutes. "Our time's up."

A whole hour has passed. It seems impossible.

"Let's just not go back," he says.

I'm a bit worried we might get into trouble if we don't. I'm not being feeble or nothing, I just couldn't bear it if I got sent home.

"Oh, you're right," he says, "we can always do it again later. I know, we'll take the bike back and then we can go to the café."

The café is only a little walk from camp. It's got a jukebox playing. Every time it stops, Eric bungs more money in it. It plays "Living Doll" over and over again.

There are lots of girls there. The older boys are pulling them, but there are no youngsters for me.

Eric didn't seem bothered about us having no girls. He bought me a coffee in exchange for a fag and he smoked it like he was in the movies. I could see him in a dinner jacket.

Trevor never came into the café. I think he knew what went on in there, but he was good enough to give us some privacy. He wouldn't have us pratting about on the camp site, but what we did in our own time didn't seem to bother him. Maybe he had his own things to do in private, I dunno. Whatever, it was the perfect set-up.

Then, a few days later, one of the team captains was caught rolling about with the café-owner's daughter. After that, no one was allowed to go there and the team captain disappeared. No one was quite sure what happened to him. Some of the lads said Trevor had him shot and it's true, we had heard a gun going off.

"Someone hunting rabbits, I expect," Eric reckoned. "They're not allowed to shoot you just for kissing a girl. Or we'd all be dead, ha! ha! ha!"

"I wouldn't," says Tommy.

Tommy's not into girls. I've tried to get him interested but he's got four older sisters and that's really put him off.

"They're boring," he says. "I'd rather kiss a fish anyday." He goes on to tell us how he caught a roach with a piece of cheese.

"Works every time," he says.

"Doesn't work with girls," Eric tells him. "Chocolate does though."

He says he's got a girlfriend called Katy. She's very good at tennis and have I got a girlfriend?

I don't want to tell him about Janice. For a start, she's my cousin, and also I'm a bit fed up with her. It was fun playing with her at first, but she hasn't got all the right bits yet and apart from that, she's got a screw loose, I swear.

I caught her nicking money out of Jean's purse before I came away. When I grabbed it off her, she said she was going to give it to me because she knew I needed it for camp. She's a lying little cow, she really is. I made her put it back before Jean found out.

"Yeah, I have got a girlfriend," I tell Eric. "She's called Rosie Diamond."

"Great name," he says.

She isn't my girlfriend yet, but I've seen her in church a lot recently. Her dad's just taken over the butcher's shop in Hornsey Road. She's about twelve, very pretty with long, dark hair in a ponytail. I've been thinking about her a lot recently. She's in the Girl Guides.

Next day, Trevor prepares us to go for our Wayfarer's badge. We have to walk fifty miles over rough terrain. He gives us all a map and our instructions. I can't wait to get started and almost break into a run, I'm so keen.

"Nice and steady," says Trevor. "Stay together, and if you get lost, release your flares."

We've each got a flare and a whistle in case of emergency. Just as well, as it turns out. I do really well for the first fifteen miles, then my socks give out. I never put my thick ones on because I thought I'd be too hot. Every time I walk, it's like someone's cutting my ankle with a knife.

It's boiling hot too. No breeze or nothing. I'm just getting to the top of a hill when I start feeling sick and giddy.

"You alright, Mick?"

Tommy's really worried. He's doing alright, because he's still got some wool left in his socks and he's wearing a hat. I never wore my hat.

"I think I'm going to puke. What are those little stars?" Next thing, it all goes black.

I wake up having water poured over my face. It's the blonde lad and his mate. I can hear them talking.

"He's got heatstroke, I reckon."

"Where's his hat? Fancy not wearing a hat."

"Take his shoes off . . . oh . . . pwhoar! . . . Look at the state of his feet."

My feet are in ribbons. I can't put them on the floor, it just hurts too much. I can't focus my eyes properly either. One of them gives me a drink of water and then they pick me up and carry me all the way back. My head's reeling.

Tommy asks them if I'm dying. I'm not, but it feels like I might. They put me in the MO's tent, on a camp bed. I throw up, then I start shivering. The MO bathes me with a cold sponge and puts a dressing on my blisters. By morning, my lips have swollen up like a pig's.

"It's the change of air," the MO tells me. "Your system's gone into shock."

For the next two days, I just lie there and drift in and out of sleep. I'm not too bothered. They're nice dreams. Dreams of Rosie Diamond. Sausages. Mr. Perriwinkle. Every now and again, Tommy and Eric come to see me and tell me what's going on.

Tommy's caught a rudd with a piece of spam. Eric found a pine marten cub. "Not really, Mick! Ha, ha, just making it up." The café's open again. Eric even bought me a packet of custard creams. I've lost quite a lot of weight because I didn't feel like eating with my head swimming.

I take it easy the next day. I can just about walk now, with sticks. The MO tells me to stay in my tent and read, or write up my experience as part of the course.

I've already read my *Dandy* twice and I'm starting to get bored, so I carve a little bird out of a piece of wood I found outside the tent. Eric comes into the tent to see how I'm doing. He's very impressed with the carving.

"Cor . . . What species is it?" he says. "Is it a Rosie Diamond tit?"

He keeps a very straight face for a second, then he beams from ear to ear. He's got a smile like a banana. Cracks me up, he does.

"Eric, don't make me laugh! It makes me feet hurt."

Next morning, my feet are a lot better. It's pouring with rain. I'm fed up, because I don't think I'm going to pass my Wayfarer's badge now, what with passing out on top of that hill.

I go and speak to Trevor to see if there's any chance. For once, my luck's in. He tells me that if I pass on my boating skills, I'll have enough marks to make up for flunking the hike.

I've had a lot of practice in Finsbury Park, rowing, so it's a doddle.

On the last day, he gives out the badges. I look at mine all the way home on the coach. OK, Nan's not always my favourite person, but I want her to be proud of me. I want a tin next to Terry's with all my badges in.

I struggle down the front path with my kit on my back. I've got my Rosie Diamond tit in one hand and my badge in the other. Nan will be so proud of me. I haven't got any hands free, so I bend forward and use my teeth to knock the door knocker.

"Nan! I'm home!"

Brenda answers the door.

"Nan's not in," she says. "She's up the hospital. Glen's committed suicide."

twenty-two

Glen never managed to kill himself, but he had a very good try.

He'd taken an overdose of aspirins washed down with a bottle of Warnink's Advocaat. If Nan hadn't gone round to do Harry Stokes's ironing on Sunday, rather than Monday, like she was supposed to, Glen would have died. He wasn't expecting her. He obviously meant to go through with it.

She done a pile of ironing before she even realised he was in the house, dying. The only reason she found him was because she had to go upstairs to put my dad's shirts in the airing cupboard and she heard him puking up.

He'd been sick in his sleep and he was choking. I heard Joyce and Jean talking about it later in bed. Nan had cleared his throat out and made him keep walking up and down, so he wouldn't go unconscious. She called out of the window to the woman next door to go and ring an ambulance because she daren't leave him for a second.

He was in the hospital for two days. Nobody knew why he'd done it. He seemed to have everything going for him. He'd got the birds, the suit, a job. What had he got to be so down about?

Nan never actually said nothing to Glen's face I don't think, but she was ashamed of him, she told us. Religion again, see? Nan reckons it's a sin to take your own life. It goes against the Bible.

I don't know if it ever crossed her mind to ask him what was wrong. I wondered if it might be something to do with Mum having left him when he was little, but then he'd have got over it by now, wouldn't he? He seemed happy enough. He showed no signs of being upset ever.

I tried to ask him what was up, but he just said, "Forget it, alright?"

I asked him when he was going back to Dad's and he said, "I ain't."

Now Glen's moved in with Nan, Dad's got a spare bed at his place. Two, in fact. Nan has arranged for Shirley to live with a school friend. She was having trouble with her insides and Nan reckoned she needed a mother figure.

Next time I go round to Dad's, he asks me if I want to live with him instead of Nan.

I'm not sure at first. I've got used to sharing with Jean and Joyce and although Nan's a cow and a half sometimes, at least she cares for me in her own funny way.

Then, one night I have the Eileen dream. I haven't had one of them in ages and, of course, the usual happens. Instead of ignoring it and just washing the sheets, Nan calls my mates in and shows them the wet mattress.

They didn't give a toss. In fact, they thought it was quite funny, but I thought it was a wicked thing to do. A quiet word would have done. I'd have even washed the sheets if she'd asked. Maybe she thought it was the best way to teach me not to do it again, but if that was the case, she must have thought I done it on purpose.

What with that and her banging on about me going in the army, I packed a few things and told her I was moving out. When Glen got wind of it, he went nuts.

"You don't have to move out just because I'm here," he says. "Suicide ain't catching, you know."

It's the first time he's admitted that's what he did.

"Nan's getting on my wick," I tell him.

"Well, don't say it was me that pushed you out," he says. "Right?"

He's never spoken to me like that before. We always got on really well. Maybe it's because he's been ill.

"Alright, Glen. Don't get the hump. I'm going because I want to. Nothing wrong with living with my dad, is there?"

He ignored me, so I left that evening.

Dad seems really pleased to see me. It's just me and him there. He gives me a cup of tea and a fag and makes Glen's old bed up for me.

"Our chance to get to know each other better," he says.

There isn't a bath in his house, so we have to use a bowl of water for a wash. He puts the bowl out on a chair.

"Want to go to a party?" he says.

I quite fancy going out. I've never been out with him before, except to visit relatives, and a party would be good.

"Come on then, Mick."

He fills the bowl with water, strips off and starts having a wash-down. I'm watching telly, minding my own business. He empties the bowl and puts fresh water in.

"Your turn," he says.

I feel a bit embarrassed getting undressed in front of him, but then I think, no, he's my dad. Don't be so daft. He has a way of giggling, but when I ask him what he's laughing at, he just says, "Oh, I was just thinking."

I rub a bit of soap over me and rinse it off, quick as I can.

"That's no use," he says.

He soaps his hand up and starts to wash me. It feels a bit strange, because I'm not a kid any more, but then Nan still checks the back of my ears and my head for nits, so I suppose he thinks he's just being a good father, given that Mum isn't around. At one point he sticks his finger up my backside. I don't half yell.

"Yeah, well you've got to keep that clean," he says, "or you'll get a disease."

"Nan never said."

"No?"

I'm as clean as a whistle, inside and out now. I'll have to remember to do that thing with my arsehole. Fancy not cleaning it properly all these years. Someone might have told me. I get dried and dressed.

It turns out the party is round at Keith's. The room's heaving with people. Most of them are men, but there are a few women. Dad introduces me to some of his friends. One of them, Max, takes a real shine to me.

"Is this your son?" he says. "I always wanted a son. Anybody's son."

A woman next to him starts cackling. She's spilling beer out of her glass all down her frock.

"Don't you take any notice of him, dear. He's a nasty one . . . oops!" She slips backwards down the sofa.

"God save the Queer."

I ask my dad what she's on about.

"She's just a drunken old slapper," he says. "Don't take no notice. Go and talk to Auntie Bunny."

He leads me over to a woman wearing a dress like they do in the westerns, in the saloon bars. I never even knew I had an Auntie Bunny.

"Are you my real auntie?" I ask her.

"I'm everybody's auntie. Want to dance?"

She must be at least fifty, probably more, but she's all dolled up and her dress is slit so high, you can see her knicker elastic.

"Come on, don't be shy," she says. "Don't you like me?"

"I can't dance very well."

She hands me a glass of gin. I've never had gin before. Whisky, yes, and a sip of my grandad's beer sometimes. The gin smells like perfume, not something you ought to drink.

"Put some tonic in it," she says, "it's nicer like that."

"No, it's alright." I've never had tonic either.

She puts her arms round my neck, still holding onto her glass. She moves her hips, swaying. She's leaning on me quite hard. I drink my drink back in one and try to hold her up. She empties her glass and holds it out for some more.

Someone changes the record for a slow one and she starts leading me round in a circle.

"Why haven't I met you before?"

"I was living with my nan."

"Oh. How old are you? Fifteen?"

She's having me on, isn't she?

"No."

She looks into my eyes, holds me at arm's length.

"You look old enough to me."

There aren't many women about. Dad's having a dance with Keith. Mind you, Keith's like an old woman anyway. Suddenly, I feel something wet in my ear. It's Auntie Bunny's tongue. It's very difficult to know what to do, so I just put up with it.

"Shall we got upstairs?" she whispers. "I want to show you something."

I'm hoping she's going to show me her Airfix collection, but I have my doubts. She starts to drag me up the stairs. I manage to catch Dad's eye and he stops her.

"Back off, Bunny," he says. "Get back in your kennel, there's a good girl."

"Oh," she says, "whose party is it? Yours?"

He pulls me back down the stairs. "No. But he's my kid."

He's had a few too many as well. I pull away from both of them and make my way into the garden. Keith has strung coloured fairylights between the trees. There are couples dancing in the shadows. I don't know who they are. Nobody's interested in the bowls of nuts, so I eat them all.

Now, of course, I'm thirsty. I don't want to go back indoors in case Auntie Bunny grabs hold of me again. Never mind, there are plenty of half-finished drinks lying around. I knock them back, trying out all the different tastes. I wish Andy could be here. He'd have enjoyed this.

I sit on the cold step and think about Rosie Diamond. In a few days' time, we've got our Boys' Brigade tournament and she's going to be there. We've trained for it for over six weeks. Gymnastics, pyramids, all in formation.

All the parents will be coming too. Dad won't want to come, but I suppose I'll have to ask Nan. Wish I could ask Mum, but that's out of the question. She's never seen me play my drum. I'm going to strip down and polish all the brass on it and I'm going to bang it so hard, Rosie Diamond will hear me coming a mile off. Then I'm going to go over to her and say . . . what the hell am I going to say?

"Alright, Rosie? Fancy going up the Nag's Head?"

That's where Glen goes. To the Tower. That will impress her. I wish I had the money to buy her a steak dinner after, but that's way beyond my means. Perhaps she'd put up with a packet of chips and a walk.

Everything looks a bit blurred. I stand up to go and look for my dad, but I lose my balance and fall over on the terrace. It don't hurt. In fact, it's very, very funny. I'm laughing like a crow. Soon, quite a crowd gathers. I'm staring up at all these faces and I don't recognise any of them. They all seem to be moving round in a circle. Or is that me? Then the ground starts spinning.

"Come on, drink this." It's Dad.

"Hee . . . hee hee."

"Drink this. It's black coffee, you silly little sod. Fancy drinking all that." He props me up against a plant pot.

"I'll have to take you home," he says. "Are you going to be sick?"

"No. Are you?"

Somehow, I'm aware of Keith. Probably his aftershave.

"I want a balloon. Give me a balloon." I can see a big bunch of them tied in the doorway.

"Oh, give him a bloody balloon!" snaps Keith. "Sorry there wasn't any Punch and Judy."

I don't remember how we got home. All I know is I woke up on the settee with a pounding headache. Dad must have undressed me. All my clothes were in a pile on the floor. I ached all over and there was a huge bruise on one of my legs. It must have been a crackin' party.

Come Sunday, I'm feeling well enough to go and get my drum from Nan's. She's a bit offhand with me at first.

"Who's this? The prodigal son? Excuse me while I put the fatted calf in the oven."

"Alright, Nan?"

I think she misses me really. I remind her about the tournament and ask her to come.

"You do want me there then? Only I thought perhaps we weren't good enough for you these days." She doesn't like my dad one bit.

"I don't know why you can't stop here," she says. "What about your reading? What about your eleven-plus or doesn't that matter any more?"

"I can still come round, can't I? See Jean and that?"

I do miss Jean, but I've got my dad now. I know she understands. I go upstairs to Auntie Min's and get my drum. She's watching telly, as usual.

"Alright if I get my drum?"

"Glad to get rid of it, cluttering up the place." Not, "Hello, Mick, how are you?"

"See you then, Min."

"Ta-ta."

I go back down. Nan's in her Everything Room. Grandad's gone down the offy. I expect he misses me fetching his stingoes for him.

"He does," Nan says. "Glen won't go, Brenda's never in and he daren't give Janice any money. We'd never see it again."

She spreads a sheet of newspaper out in front of her, on the table. "You can strip the drum down on there if you want," she says. "Did you bring polish?"

"No."

"Thought not." She puts a tin of Brasso on the table. "Wear these gloves or you'll get yourself filthy."

They're the rubber ones I was going to give to Mum.

"What are you grinning at?"

"Nothing. They're just funny things, aren't they? Rubber gloves?"

"You are, you mean," she says. "Have you had your dinner?"

I haven't of course. I timed it specially so I could have dinner at Nan's. I knew once I'd asked her to the Boys' Brigade do, she'd warm up a bit. She wants to know how I'm getting on at Dad's.

"Great. We went to a party." I never told her I got pissed.

"Oh yes?" Her eyes narrow into little snake-like slits. "Many there?"

"Quite a few. Keith and Max. Auntie Bunny."

"Never heard of her," Nan snorts. "Did you take your uniform round Harry Stokes's?"

She gets her ironing board out.

"No, I left it here."

"Yes, I know you did," she says. "I expect you want me to iron it for you an' all."

"Would you?"

"Yes. But this is the last time, got it?"

She spits on the iron. It hisses and the little ball of spit rolls around on the metal plate.

"Thanks, Nan."

The room fills with steam and the smell of starch. She whisks over the uniform and leaves it on a hanger, over the door.

"The buttons need a polish," she says. "I'm just going to strain the cabbage."

I think she thinks I'm doing all this for her. I'm not though. It's all for Rosie Diamond. I rub the brass with a soft cloth until it's so bright, it could take your eye out. It takes ages to put it back together properly, but I don't mind. This is more than a drum. It's a Diamond trap.

The day of the tournament arrives. Nan's sitting in the audience in her fur coat. It's late summer, but she reckons it's her Sunday best. I should be flattered. Rosie Diamond has been busy baton-twirling and hasn't noticed me yet.

I run on in my shorts and take part in the PE routine. It all goes like a dream. Then we do the formation drill without command and apart from one kid who decides to go in the opposite direction to the rest of us, that goes quite well too. The audience clap loudly.

Offstage, I change into my uniform and strap my drum on. Tommy huffs on my brass, just to get my dander up, so I slap his head.

"Don't! Took me ages to polish that!"

Trevor tells us to shut up and get in line. This is my chance to impress Rosie Diamond. It cannot fail. I'd have crossed my fingers but that's no way to hold a drumstick. We're just about to lead off, when the solo drummer leans over and taps my drum skin.

Doof.

It's a completely dead sound.

"That's not right," he says. "You haven't tuned it, have you?"

"Yes, I have!"

Then I realise I've forgot. I'd put it all back together round at Nan's, had my stew and cabbage followed by rhubarb crumble and then gone home. I've forgotten to tune the bastard!

It's too late to do anything. I march on, pretending to play. The others all have to hit their drums really hard to play me out. I can't wait to get it over with. I can't even see if Rosie is watching me or not. I hope she ain't. I'm so thrown by the whole business, I don't even bother to look for her afterwards. What's the point? She's better off without me.

"I thought it was very good," Nan says, when we get back to her place. "Why don't you join the army? They need good drummers."

There's no answer to that. I reckon she could see I wasn't really hitting the drumskin, because she's got eyes like a hawk. She's just trying to butter me up to turn me into a soldier.

"Cheer up," she says. "What's the matter with you? Don't you go all Glen on me."

I couldn't explain to her about Rosie. She'd only have laughed or said she wasn't good enough for me, like she did to Terry. I go upstairs, throw my uniform in the back of Minnie's wardrobe, dump the drum and go home.

September comes and it's back to the old routine at school. Dad leaves me a couple of fags. One to have after breakfast and one for after school. Then, when I get back, it's my job to peel the spuds and get dinner ready. I put chops or sausages in the oven about five-thirty so we can have dinner straight away when my dad gets in at six.

Shirley used to do all that, but she ain't here. It's my job now.

Nan does the washing and cleaning and sometimes leaves food in the larder, but mostly I do it all. I don't mind. It feels more like sharing a house with a mate than living with a dad.

Not that I like his company that much. He's OK, but a grown man's no company for someone my age, I don't think. Not like Andy or Tom.

Come winter, I light the coal fire and bank it up when I come home. One thing I'll say about this place, it's like an icebox. I just can't get warm sometimes. Dad's put a little paraffin heater in my room, but I still have to sleep with my clothes on.

One afternoon late November, I'm coming home later after school through Bovey Place when I see a man standing on the corner. As I approach him, he steps out towards the pavement and blocks my way.

"Is your name Mick?" he says.

"Yeah."

I look at his face, but I'm not sure who he is. He's got his hat pulled down hard over his head and he's wearing glasses. Must be about fifty, I reckon.

"I know you," he says. "Are you going home to see your dad?"

"Yeah."

I'm starting to feel pretty bad about this bloke. There's something not right about him. I try to walk past, but he grabs me in his arms.

"You're coming with me."

He doesn't look that strong, but I'm having a real job getting him off. There's no one around, so I start swearing and kicking at him.

"Get off me, you bastard . . ."

He starts laughing and walking along the pavement with me, trying to drag me into an alley. Suddenly, he loosens his grip just enough for me to lean forward. I nut him in the face with the back of my head, which knocks his glasses off. He lets go for a second, just long enough for me to get away.

I leg it down the road so fast, I can hardly feel the pavement. I don't know where I'm going, I'm just running like a rabbit. I daren't look behind me in case he's following. For all I know, he's got a car. As I'm running along, it suddenly clicks where I've seen him. It was Keith's party.

I run until I haven't got any breath left, then I jump over someone's front wall and hide while I try to get my head together. Should I go to the police? No, what are they going to do? Should I run to Nan's? What if she don't believe me? I can't run to Mum's because she might not even be in and if she was and I stayed there, I'd get into trouble with my dad.

I decide the best thing to do is go back home to Harry Stokes. He might even remember who the man is. I wonder why he come after me like that. Must be a nonce or something.

My legs are shaking all the way home. I try to walk normally, but every little noise makes me break into a trot. Then when I see someone, I feel a prat for running. It's only half-past five. Dad won't even be in yet.

I let myself into the house. It's pitch dark. I'm scared to cross the hall in my own home. I feel for the light switch . . . click . . . That's a bit better. Then suddenly every room in the house has got the madman in it. He knows where my dad lives. He could have got here before me and let himself in with the key.

I start seeing him everywhere now. There are his feet, sticking out from under the curtains. Now he's under the bed. He's going to jump out of the larder. I can't rest until I've checked every room. I'm flinging open doors, banging them against the walls in case he's behind them, and I'm shouting, "I know you're in there, I can see you!"

I'm sweating cobs. In the end, I can't take it any more. I back into a corner, turn the light back off so he can't find me and crouch there, shivering. I try to take deep breaths, but I can't get any air in. I've got pins and needles in my arms and I think I'm going to choke. Then I hear footsteps. The light goes on and I scream. My dad screams.

"What the hell are you playing at, Mick?" He's clutching his chest. "You scared the shit out of me."

I burst into tears. I tell him what's happened. He holds me. Strokes my head.

"It's alright," he says. "Probably just some nutter. Walk home with Tommy in the future."

"I saw him at Keith's party. He was with Max."

"No . . . can't have been. What did he look like?"

I tell him. I describe everything I possibly can about this man. His yellow teeth. His fat, puffy hands. Dad shakes his head.

"Doesn't ring a bell," he says.

He puts the kettle on and moves the paraffin heater out of my room into his.

"You can sleep with me tonight," he says. "It will be warmer that way too."

I'm so glad. I really can't sleep on my own tonight. My hands are still shaking so hard I spill tea on my trousers.

"Take them off and go to bed," he says. "I'll be in after the film. I'll leave the light on and the door open, yeah?"

"OK."

I feel about five years old again. It's like I've climbed up this big mountain and then, someone's pushed me off. I've fallen. I feel all smashed up inside. It's like I never had a great left hook. And the Hard Man of the Swings? Did I ever beat him and if I did, what was the point? There'll always be a bigger bastard, just around the corner. How long do I have to keep my guard up?

I can hear the telly in the background but I can't make any sense of the words. I'm so tired I can feel myself slipping away. I'm hardly aware of my dad sliding into bed with me.

When I wake up in the morning, he's got his hand on my dick.

twenty-three

He's moving his hand backwards and forwards. I've got my back to him, facing the wall. All I do is open my eyes. I daren't move. For a moment, I think I must still be dreaming. I wait a bit longer to see if it stops, but it doesn't.

I'm begging him silently to let go. Let go. Let go. It feels disgusting. It's nothing like when Janice does it. That just tickles. This makes me want to throw up.

I daren't tell him to stop, he might get cross. If he gets cross, I'll have to go back to Nan's. If I go back to Nan's, I'll end up in the army. Please stop, Dad. Please stop.

Maybe this is what happens between fathers and sons and nobody talks about it. I don't know. Only Harry Spicer never done it and it just feels so wrong.

I can't stand it any more. I pretend to be waking up, pretend I never realise what he's up to and roll onto my back. He lets go. I lie there for a while, pretending I've gone back to sleep. He gets up and goes to the toilet.

He never says nothing over breakfast and I'm still pretending I never knew what he'd been up to. If anything, I'm over-friendly. Then that worries me. What if he knows I knew what he was doing and thinks I like it?

When I get to school, I still can't get it out of my mind. We've got PE today. When it's my turn to go over the vault, the PE master guides me over with his hand. I feel like decking him. He put his hand under my bum. Maybe he done it on purpose or maybe, if you think about it, there was nowhere else to put his hand. I'm so confused.

Andy knows something is up, but I can't talk to him about it. What could I say? I've boasted so much about having my own dad I can't start slagging him off, can I? Also, what if it is the normal thing and everybody does it? I'll look a right prat then.

I try hanging around after school so I don't have to go home, but Tommy has to leave early, which means I'll have to walk through Bovey Place on my own. That nutter might be there. This time he might manage to kidnap me.

I ask Andy if he wants to come round my dad's to watch telly. He says he can't because it's his sister's birthday and his mum wants him there.

I've got no choice but to go home and get on with it. It crosses my mind to tell Dad I'd rather sleep in my own bed because . . . then I can't think of a good enough reason. He'd know why straight away.

I bank the fire, do the spuds, open a tin of ham that Nan's left and go and watch telly. Dad's quite chatty when he comes home. We have our tea and he asks me about my day.

"It was alright. We did PE."

"Got any homework?"

"No."

He turns the telly over and plumps himself down next to me. There's no need, because there's another chair. I glue my eyes to the screen. I don't know what the film's about. Nothing's going in. I'm in a trance.

I'm praying he doesn't put his arm round me. He used to do that, but there was nothing funny in it. It was just a hug, like I'd give to Auntie Joyce. Or was it? I can feel how warm he is through my trouser leg.

Then he gets up, fetches himself a beer and sits in the other chair. I feel my whole body relax. I'm being stupid! He's my dad and he can sit next to me if he likes. What's my problem?

He goes out for a bit, after the film. Round to Keith's. While he's gone, I get the bowl and have a wash. I take the bowl into the other room though, just in case he comes back too soon. I don't want him to see me with no clothes on. Not any more. I'm thinking ahead all the time. If he comes back and tells me to have a wash, I can tell him I've already done it.

He doesn't come back until quite late. I'm still watching the telly. He sits down and has one last fag, then he stands up again and stretches.

"Coming to bed?"

"In a minute. I just want to watch the rest of this."

"Night, then."

I'm too scared to go to bed. I sit there until the epilogue comes on and the little dot disappears. I know I can't stay on the settee. I know he don't like me sleeping with all my clothes on, so I take them off except for my pants, get into bed and roll onto my stomach. If I sleep like that, he can't grab hold of it.

He's asleep anyway. His mouth's hanging open. I watch him, thinking, maybe I could poison him or put a pillow over his head and sit on it until he suffocates. Then I feel evil for thinking it. He's not so bad and he probably loves me a little bit. He asked me to stay. No one else did. Glen said I didn't have to go, but no one actually asked me to stay. Not Mum, not Nan. Only Harry Stokes.

I stay awake most of the night, on guard, but nothing happens. It's such a relief, I think I must have made the whole thing up. I reckon my mind was playing tricks on me after that nonce tried to drag me off. It makes sense. It's the kind of dream you would have, isn't it? I was in shock, after all. I calm down. Everything's back to normal.

Two weeks later, it happens again. Only this time, I've got my hand on him. He must have put it there. I know I never would have done that by myself. Every now and then, he moves backwards and forwards, trying to make out he's shuffling in his sleep. I try to loosen my grip. Very, very slowly, so he won't notice I'm moving, won't know I've sussed his little game.

I've managed to do it. I let my hand go all floppy onto his thigh and then I turn over, sighing, like I'm waking up. He lies there and doesn't move. I don't know if his eyes are open or not. I get dressed, go downstairs and get out of the house.

If he asks why I got up so early, I'll tell him I went fishing with Tommy. I walk the Cally Road for hours. There's nobody about except a roadsweeper. I'm trying to decide where to go. I need to live somewhere else. There is no way I can stay at my dad's house. If I tell Nan what he's done, she'll get the police involved. She does that at the drop of a hat, remember. She's already landed my mum in it and I'm sure she'd love to have a go at Harry Stokes.

I wait until the shops start opening and then I go round to Mum's. She's still in bed when I get there. Terry answers the door. He offers to make me some breakfast. He's trying to get Gary to eat his too, but he won't. I ask him if Harry Spicer is in.

"No. He's gone away for a bit." He looks sad.

"What, working?"

"No."

The sparkle's gone out of Terry. He wasn't too bad the last time I saw him. A bit fed up maybe, but not like he is now.

"What's up, Tel?"

"I'm fed up with him," he says, pointing at Gary. "Can I come and live with you?" I tell him there's no room. What else could I say?

"Same here," he says, then, "Hey . . . if Dad don't come back . . ." He trails off, because Mum has come in the room. She looks a bit of a state.

"Hello, Mick. What are you doing here?"

"Come to say hello, that's all."

"Oh . . . that's nice."

She sits down. Doesn't help Terry or nothing. She looks done in. I ask her if she's alright.

"Yeah," she says. "You?"

"Yeah, fine. Listen, I was thinking. If I came back here, I could get a job and pay my way."

She sighs. "Oh, please don't start that again," she says. "Count the bedrooms. Go on."

"I'll sleep on the floor."

"I know you would," she says, "but it's silly when your dad's got all that space."

I can see Terry's face fall. "Please," he whispers.

"You know I would if I could," she says.

She never asked me if there was a problem with my dad. I catch myself staring at her, thinking, I bet she knows. I bet that's why she left him for Harry Spicer. She knows what he's like.

"Don't look at me like that," she says. "You don't know the half of it."

Nor do you, I think. You don't know anything about me and you don't want to, because half of me is Harry Stokes and every time you look at my face, it reminds you of him and you hate me for it.

It's all so clear now. No wonder it's easy for her to love Terry. Even if he's not Harry Spicer's, he's nothing to do with Harry Stokes. Same goes for Gary. I have my breakfast and leave. Terry clings to me on the step.

"Don't go," he says.

"I'll see you, Terry."

"You won't though, will you!" he's shouting at me. "I know you won't."

He slams the door. Normally, it would break my heart, but I'm feeling cold today. I don't give a toss any more.

I'm going round to Nan's. I want to speak to Glen. I know why he wanted to kill himself now. It's because he wanted to kill Dad, but he couldn't find it in him, in case his mind·was playing tricks too.

Nan's up the Co-op. Jean's gone for a bike ride with Joyce. Janice opens the door.

"Alright, Janice? Glen in?"

"Yes. Look what I've got!"

She lifts up her blouse and shows me a little white bra. There's not much in it, but she's so proud. It makes me want to cry for a second. I tell her the bra's very pretty. She pulls her blouse back down and seems happy with that for the moment and runs out into the garden. She seems like a little kid, even though she's the same age as me.

Glen's in his room, cleaning his gun. I'm surprised Nan lets him keep one.

"She doesn't know," he says. "I'm not stupid."

"Can I have a look?"

He hands the gun over. "It's alright, it won't go off," he says. "There's no bullets in it. I left them round Dad's."

"What does it take?"

".22s."

I turn the gun over and over in my hand. It's a lovely thing. I ask him what he uses it for.

"Shooting squirrels," he says.

I think about the squirrel I saw at camp. I couldn't shoot a squirrel. What kind of kick would you get, shooting something harmless like that? None, surely. I'm trying to find the right moment to talk to Glen about Harry Stokes.

"Did you like living with Dad?" I ask.

"Why?"

"Just wondered, that's all."

He lies back on the bed and looks up the barrel of the gun. He's being cagey with me, like he don't trust me any more. Funny, because we used to be quite close and I never done nothing to upset him to my knowledge. I had to go for it. It was hard finding the words. They all sounded so comical. Dick. Willy. Bollocks.

"Glen . . . did Dad ever touch you up, like?"

He looks at me for a moment then he roars with laughter. Never said nothing, just laughed, like it was the most stupid thing he'd ever heard anybody say. That's when I knew for sure.

"Can I borrow the gun, Glen?"

"What for?"

"To shoot tin cans."

He thinks about it quite carefully for a minute, then he says no.

"You're not old enough," he says. "I'd let you, but if anything silly happened, it would be my fault, wouldn't it?"

He says maybe one day he'll take me over the woods and we can bang off a few. He wraps the gun up in an old jumper and puts it in his lap.

"I'm not hiding it until you've gone," he smiles. "And don't tell Janice about it."

I tell him she showed me her bra.

"That's nothing," he says. "You should have seen what she showed the breadman. She's sick in the head. Nan took her to see a shrink. He's given her tablets but she won't take them."

My poor little Janice.

I know exactly what I'm going to do when I get home. I don't know if it's going to work, but it's worth a try.

Dad works Saturday mornings, so he won't be back till half past one at the earliest. I go into my bedroom, which used to be

Glen's bedroom, and search through the jacket he's left behind, then every drawer, every cupboard. Nothing.

I'm not sure if I'm looking for a little bag or a tin or what. I know they're in here somewhere. I can smell them.

I've got ages yet, so I make myself a cup of tea and have a think. Maybe they're under the floorboards. I get a torch and shine it down the gaps. Nothing. I feel under the window sill. He could have taped them there. I think back to all the films I've seen, when the police are looking for something. I think of stories in comics. Where would Dennis the Menace hide something from his dad?

I go out into the garden, climb up and have a look in the toilet cistern. Nothing. False panels in the wardrobe? I go back in and have a look. Still no joy.

I roll myself a fag and have a think. I bet they're in a tobacco tin. So, I'm looking for something about this high and about that long, green and gold.

I stand on the bed and jump to get some height. I can see the lip of a tin just poking out from behind the moulding on top of the wardrobe. Bingo!

I can't reach it from the bed, so I get a ladder from the shed, calm as you please, and climb up it. It's very dusty up there. I pick up the tin and shake it. Something's rolling about inside. I can't open the tin with my thumbs, it's been pressed down too hard. Possibly with a hammer, because I can see some dents. I know they're in there though.

I blow the dust off the tin and carry it into the kitchen. I get a spoon and wedge the handle under the little lip on the edge. I lever it up, and there they are. There must be twenty squirrels'-worth of bullets.

I put the lid back on the tin and press it gently. I put the tin in my pocket and start packing my bags. My drainpipes are getting a bit small, but they'll do. They're still the best thing I've got. I remember Nan's pants advice and shove several pairs of the better ones in with a jumper and one of Glen's old shirts. It'll go quite well with the jeans.

I have a quick look through my dad's wardrobe to see if there's anything I fancy. He's got a little leather pot on his table, where he keeps his loose change. I better not take that. Too obvious.

I go through his jackets. I take a hanky, a pen and a few notes. It's enough to get me to Southend. I don't need a return ticket, after all. There's an old shoebox in the bottom of the wardrobe. I decide it's worth having a quick ruffle through it. There's a square green box under a load of papers.

His wedding ring's inside it. I stick it in my pocket. I can flog that. It will keep me going until I get a job. I'll try the deckchair man first. It's out of season, but I can always stay in his hut a bit until the weather improves. I'll mend the deckchairs or something.

I don't want nothing else of Dad's. I put my bag in the cupboard under the stairs, ready. Then I make a sandwich, bank up the fire and wait for him to come home.

I watch for him through the window. It's starting to snow. I put the kettle on, so when I see him, it will only take seconds to boil. I keep the gas very low once it's steaming and put his cup out. I fill the teapot with tea leaves and go back to the window.

The snow's starting to settle. Suddenly, I see him coming down the road with his head down. I pour the boiling water in the pot and wait until he's come in.

"Cor, it's freezing out there," he calls.

I can hear him stamping the snow off his shoes on the mat. The front door slams.

"I've made you a cup of tea. It's by your chair, Dad."

"Cheers. I'll just take my shoes off. Had a good day?"

While he's doing that in the hall, I loosen the lid off the tobacco tin and put the bullets in my hand. I'm still not sure what's going to happen, but something has to. Just before he comes in, I grab the poker. Only, I'm not really poking the fire, I'm arranging the bullets on the coals.

Dad flops down in his chair. I go into the hall and get my bag. Nothing's happening. I can hear him stirring his tea. I can see Eileen's face looking at me through the gap in the door. It's madness to go back into the room, but if anything happens, if the bullets do what they're supposed to, I'll just slam the door and go. I take a deep breath and walk over to the dresser.

The second I've grabbed her photo, the flames catch. A bullet whistles past my ear.

"Come on, Eileen."

I hold my baby sister to my chest, slam the door shut and run out into the snow. I can hear the bullets flying, I can hear my dad screaming, and it feels so good.

glossary

blag	*obtain by lying or other scam*
bog	*lavatory*
brothel creepers	*thick crepe-soled shoes*
doing a runner	*running away (in the sense of dodging payment)*
dummy	*pacifier*
eleven-plus	*an exam taken between the ages of eleven and twelve before leaving primary school*
fag	*cigarette*
git	*a silly or contemptible person*
interval	*intermission*
jumper	*sweater*
kip	*sleep or nap*
MO	*medical officer*
nappy	*diaper*
nonce	*pervert; specifically, one who abuses children*
offy	*short for "off license," an establishment with a license to sell liquor for consumption off the premises*

on tickover	*idling*
one-and-nines	*cheap front seats that cost one shilling nine pence*
pants	*underpants*
pull someone	*pick someone up; seduce*
quiff	*a hairstyle in which a tuft of hair is brushed upward off the forehead*
skint	*broke*
spivvy (also spiv)	*flashy; a spiv is a con artist, a flashy dresser who lives by his wits*
taking the micky (or mick) out of someone	*teasing; making fun of somebody*
Teddy boys (or Teds)	*British youth culture movement of the 1950s, characterized by a manner of dress—usually an Edwardian-style jacket with velvet collar and cuffs and tight "drainpipe" trousers—and, sometimes, a reputation for violence*
tipper	*a truck constructed to empty out its load by tipping the carrier; a dump truck*